Ruin Me Softly

A.L. Wilder

Paperback ISBN: 979-8-9995874-1-1

Published by A.L. Wilder Publishing

Printed in the United States of America

Other Works by A.L. Wilder

No More: A Story of Survival and Strength

The Girl in Smoke

Forged in Her Fire

The Body Trail

Dedication

For the women who stayed too long — and for the ones still finding the door.

Trigger Warnings

This book contains mature and potentially distressing material. Reader discretion is advised.

Themes and content include, but are not limited to:

- Domestic violence and intimate partner abuse

- Emotional, psychological, and physical abuse

- Coercive control and manipulation

- Abduction / kidnapping

- Sexual exploitation and human trafficking

- Imprisonment and confinement

- Depictions of sexual assault (non-graphic)

- Threats of violence and gun violence

- Murder / death of a major character

- PTSD, trauma responses, and dissociation

- Gaslighting and media manipulation

- Power imbalance in relationships

- Political corruption

- Misuse of authority and privilege

- Public humiliation and loss of autonomy

- Discussions of mental health and institutional abuse

- Fear, captivity, and survival situations

While this story ultimately centers on survival, reclamation, justice, and healing, it does not shy away from the realities of abuse or the lasting impact it leaves behind.

Please prioritize your well-being while reading.

Authors Note

This book is not a love story.

It is a survival story.

It is about what happens *after* the wrong man.
And after the next one.
And after the one everyone else believes is perfect.

This story exists because too many women are taught that endurance is the same thing as love — that if we are patient enough, quiet enough, accommodating enough, a man will eventually stop hurting us. That if he provides, protects, or performs goodness in public, then what happens behind closed doors must somehow be our fault.

Eden's story is not meant to shock for shock's sake.
It is meant to tell the truth.

About emotional manipulation that looks like devotion.
About control disguised as protection.
About how power makes predators invisible — and victims unbelievable.

This book contains abuse. It contains violence. It contains moments that are difficult to read. They are included intentionally, not gratuitously. Because pretending these things happen quietly, gently, or rarely only serves the people who benefit from silence.

But this is not a book about staying.

It is a book about leaving.

About reclaiming the self after being erased.
About desire without apology.
About choosing pleasure, curiosity, and autonomy after being
told your body exists for someone else's use.
About women who survive — and then decide survival is not
enough.

Eden will not be saved by a man.
She will not be redeemed by love alone.
And she will not be punished for wanting more than safety.

There are people in this story who help others disappear.
There are systems built to protect monsters.
And there are women — watching, waiting, gathering
evidence — who are far more dangerous than the men who
underestimate them.

If you are reading this and recognize yourself — in Eden, in
her doubt, in her fear, in her rage, in her hunger to become
someone new — know this:

You are not weak for staying.
You are not stupid for believing.
And you are not broken for wanting love again.

This book is for the women who left.
For the women who are planning to.
And for the women who aren't ready yet — but need to know
they're not alone.

Take care of yourself as you read.

And remember:
Survival is only the beginning.

— A.L. Wilder

Table of Contents

Prologue

The door closed behind him with a soft, ordinary click.

It was the kind of sound Eden would've missed on any other day. The kind that blended into the background of shared living—the refrigerator humming, the pipes knocking, the distant city traffic slipping through the walls.

But this time, it landed.

Ryan, the man she'd been with since high school, had left her.

Eden stood alone in the kitchen, arms slack at her sides, staring at the spot where he'd been seconds before. The keys he'd left behind sat on the table, metal catching the light. Not forgotten. Abandoned. An afterthought. Proof that he'd already decided she wasn't worth the inconvenience of circling back.

She waited for something to happen.

For anger to rise sharp and sudden. For hysteria. For tears that bent her in half and made the whole thing feel real.

Nothing came.

Her body stayed stubbornly still, like it hadn't gotten the message yet. Like it was conserving energy for something worse.

Instead, her mind drifted backward—because it always did—to the last fight they'd had. The one that had started as a joke.

"You really think you're a New York person?" Ryan had laughed, stretched out on their couch, thumb flicking lazily across his phone. "You'd hate it. Too loud. Too fast. Too many people who don't care about your feelings. You wouldn't last a day there."

"I could make it work," she'd said. Too quickly. Too earnestly. "I want more than this."

He'd smirked, eyes never leaving the screen. "You always want more. That's kind of your thing."

She'd laughed then. Shrugged it off. Told herself he didn't mean it the way it sounded. Apologized for pushing. For wanting. For being too much in a life that had taught her to stay manageable.

Now she stood in the wreckage of that moment, understanding too late that he hadn't been teasing.

He'd been telling her who he was.

In the bathroom, she turned on the sink and splashed cold water on her face, gripping the porcelain edge as she lifted her head. The girl staring back at her looked older than she felt. Quieter. Her mouth was set in a line she didn't remember practicing, her eyes dulled by something like resignation.

She looked like someone who'd learned how to take up as little space as possible.

Eden reached for her phone.

Her mother answered on the second ring.

"Hey, baby," her mom said, voice soft with instinct. "What's wrong?"

The question cracked something open.

"Ryan's leaving me," Eden said. Her voice sounded steadier than she felt, held together by will alone. "He met someone else. She's younger."

There was a sharp intake of breath on the other end of the line. "Oh, honey…"

"I'm okay," Eden rushed to say, the words tumbling out before the truth could catch up to her. "I mean… I will be. I just wanted you to hear it from me."

A pause. "Where is he now?"

"Gone."

Another pause—longer this time. Weighted.

"And what are you going to do?" her mom asked gently.

Eden looked around the apartment. The walls felt closer than they had an hour ago, as if the space itself were shrinking now that he'd left it behind. Like the room had only ever existed to hold the version of her he'd approved of.

"I'm moving," she said.

"Moving where?"

She swallowed. Her throat burned.

"New York."

Silence.

Then, softly, "New York?"

"He always said I wouldn't last there," Eden continued, the words gaining strength as she spoke them. Anger threaded through now, thin but present. "Said it wasn't for me. That I was too sensitive. Too much. But I can't stay here, Mom. I'll disappear if I do."

Her mother didn't interrupt. Didn't rush her. Let the truth settle between them.

"I need a fresh start," Eden said. "Somewhere no one knows me. Somewhere I don't have to explain why I want more."

Another breath on the line—steadier now.

"Okay," her mom said. "Then we'll make a plan."

Eden closed her eyes, relief flooding her chest so fast it made her dizzy.

"I'm proud of you," her mother added. "For choosing yourself."

After the call ended, Eden packed a single suitcase.

She didn't take much. Clothes. A few books Ryan had never bothered to open. Her laptop. A journal she hadn't written in for months, its pages still blank with all the things she'd been too careful to say out loud.

New York wasn't a dream.

It was a refusal.

A promise she made to herself in the quiet aftermath of being left.

She didn't know yet that Ryan was only the first man who would teach her how easily love could become something sharp.

She only knew this:

She was done letting anyone laugh at her wanting more.

So she left.

Chapter One

New York was loud in a way Eden hadn't expected.

Not just noise—movement. Constant, unyielding motion. Even standing still felt like being swept along by something larger than herself, like the city had a pulse and she was trying to learn its rhythm without getting knocked over. The subway breathed her out onto the platform, and the crowd surged forward—a living thing made of elbows, impatience, and purpose.

She adjusted her grip on the coffee cup, the cardboard sleeve already warm and soft beneath her fingers. The lid rattled faintly as someone bumped her shoulder. No apology. No pause.

She didn't look back.

This was her life now. Not because it was perfect, but because it was new. Because it didn't belong to anyone else yet.

She'd been in New York for six weeks. Long enough to learn which subway entrance smelled the least like urine. Long enough to stop flinching every time someone brushed past her. Not long enough to feel settled.

The thought lodged unevenly in her chest as she walked. She focused on the rhythm of her steps, on the way the city smelled—exhaust, damp concrete, something metallic that stung the back of her throat. It was nothing like home.

That was the point.

She hadn't come with a safety net. Just two suitcases, a half-finished goodbye, and a job offer she'd accepted over the phone before she could talk herself out of it. Bright Horizons Youth Shelter hadn't asked many questions. They'd needed help. She'd needed a reason not to turn back.

Her apartment still smelled like fresh paint and cheap cleaner. The mattress sat directly on the floor. She hadn't unpacked the box labeled miscellaneous because she was afraid of what she'd find inside it—things she'd kept without meaning to, proof that she hadn't left everything behind as cleanly as she pretended.

Her phone buzzed in her pocket.

She knew without checking what it wasn't.

No messages asking if she'd arrived safely. No follow-up apologies. No sudden change of heart.

She let the vibration fade on its own, another small ending she didn't have to witness. Another door closing without ceremony.

Bright Horizons came into view, the brick façade weathered and unassuming. The sign above the door hung slightly crooked. Someone had tried to fix it once and given up halfway through.

Recognizing the feeling, Eden took a breath and stepped inside.

She reached for her lanyard, fingers brushing the laminated badge resting against her chest. *Administrative Assistant.* A strange title for how the job actually felt—answering phones, filling out forms, listening when no one else had time to.

The door stuck when she pushed it open. She had to lean her weight into it, shoulder braced, a small, private effort no one saw. Inside, the city noise dulled, replaced by the low hum of voices and the clatter of dishes.

The smell hit her next. Old books. Cinnamon oatmeal. Industrial cleaner. It wasn't comforting, exactly—but it was consistent. Predictable.

"Morning, Edie."

Tonya's voice came from behind the front desk. Warm. Unrushed.

Eden exhaled without realizing she'd been holding her breath.

"Hey," she said, and this time the smile came easier.

She passed the community room on her way to her desk. A boy with a shaved head pretended to sleep on the couch, one sneaker dangling from his foot. A girl with purple braids watched Eden carefully over the rim of her mug, eyes sharp and assessing.

Trust took time. Eden knew that better than most.

Her desk was small, tucked into a corner that didn't quite belong to anyone. She set her bag down carefully, lining it up with the edge, as if order might transfer if she was precise enough.

She was just pulling up her computer when the director appeared in the doorway. His tie was crooked, his expression tight, like he was already bracing for impact.

"Change of plans," he said.

Eden looked up. "Okay?"

"Mayor Whitmore's team is here early. Like—today early."

Her stomach dipped. "Today?"

He nodded, eyes flicking briefly to her outfit. Not judgmental. Practical. "No offense, Eden, but do you have something… a little more formal? He's touring youth programs for that initiative he's pushing. Cameras, aides, the whole thing."

Heat crept up her neck. She glanced down at herself—soft cardigan, flats scuffed from the rain. An outfit meant to blend in. To disappear.

"This is what I've got," she admitted.

He sighed, already halfway back into problem-solving mode. "See what you can do. And—" His voice dropped. "—don't mention funding while he's here."

Eden nodded, even though politics made her uneasy. Too many men who spoke confidently and left nothing behind. Too many promises that evaporated under scrutiny.

"You okay?"

Tonya appeared beside her like she always did—quiet, observant.

"Do I look like I belong in a photo op?" Eden asked, attempting humor and missing.

Tonya scanned her once, then snorted. "Girl. No. But that's fixable."

"I keep a blazer in my locker," Tonya continued. "Black. Boring. Makes everyone look like they know what they're doing."

Relief hit Eden so hard her knees went weak.

By noon, the shelter was scrubbed within an inch of its life. The kids were ushered into the gym with pizza and reassurances. Eden changed blouses in the bathroom, splashed water on her face, studied her reflection longer than necessary.

She looked… fine. Tired. A little thinner than she remembered being. Still herself.

Then the doors opened.

Daniel Whitmore entered like he belonged everywhere.

The room adjusted around him—people standing straighter, voices lowering. He was taller than she'd imagined, broader through the shoulders. His suit fit like it had been chosen with intention. His hair was streaked with gray in a way that looked earned, not aged.

His eyes moved quickly, cataloging.

When they landed on Eden, they didn't slide past.

They stopped.

He smiled.

Not wide. Not forced. Measured.

"You must be the assistant," he said.

The way he said it wasn't dismissive. It was curious.

"Eden," she replied—and hated how soft it sounded.

"Eden," he repeated, testing it, as if deciding where it fit. "Beautiful. Biblical."

Heat crept up her neck.

"My mom liked symbolism," she said.

"Don't we all?" he replied, and something about the answer felt practiced.

The moment stretched a beat too long before someone cleared their throat. He turned away—but not before glancing back.

Smiling again.

That night, Eden lay awake in her studio, the city leaking through the walls in low, restless sounds. She replayed the moment the mayor's gaze had caught hers—not passing, not polite, but deliberate.

She told herself it was nothing.

The lie settled in her chest, warm and insistent.

Sleep came slowly. And when it did, it brought no dreams—
only the sense that something had shifted, whether she was
ready for it or not.

Chapter Two

The shelter was quieter today, but quiet at Bright Horizons was never peaceful.

It was the kind of quiet that came from exhaustion—kids curled into themselves like they were trying to take up less space in the world, staff moving with softened voices so they didn't set something off. The rain helped. It tapped against the windows in thin gray ribbons, blurring the street outside into a watercolor smear of umbrellas and brake lights. Even the city sounded muffled, as if New York were holding its breath with them.

Eden sat behind the front desk, staring at an intake form she'd already filled out twice.

Her fingers hovered over the keyboard, then landed lightly. Click. Click. The keys were sticky from years of coffee spills and hurried hands. The office smelled like wet wool and stale coffee—someone's cardigan steaming in the corner, an abandoned mug going cold on the shelf beside the phone. The heater beneath the desk kicked on and off with a tired rattle, the air swinging between clammy and too warm.

Her blouse clung damp under her arms. Her flats squished faintly every time she shifted her feet.

She should've brought boots. She had boots. She just…
hadn't thought about it this morning.

She hadn't been thinking about much lately, not in a way that
felt organized. Her days came in pieces—tasks, calls, faces—
and her mind scattered itself between them, as if staying too
present might make something else rise up. If she kept
moving, kept typing, kept making herself useful, she didn't
have to look directly at the parts of herself that still felt raw.

A teen drifted by the desk, hood up, eyes down. Eden watched
the hem of his sweatshirt, the way his hands disappeared
inside it like he was trying to hide his own existence. He
paused near the bowl of granola bars, hesitated, then took two
and stuffed them into his pocket with the speed of someone
who'd been punished for needing things.

Eden pretended not to see.

Not because she didn't care—because she did. Because the
first rule here was dignity. The second was survival. You let
people keep what little they could without making them pay
for it with shame.

He slipped away without a sound.

Eden's gaze returned to her screen, but the words swam. She
blinked hard and forced her hands to move, to type the
information into neat little boxes. Name. Age. Emergency
contact.

Some boxes were empty more often than not.

The phone rang once. Eden answered it on the second ring, voice steady. "Bright Horizons Youth Shelter, this is Eden speaking."

A caseworker wanted to confirm an appointment. Eden flipped through the calendar, scribbled a note, repeated the time twice to make sure it was understood. When she hung up, her reflection caught in the black monitor screen—eyes a little too wide, lips pressed together, a faint crease between her brows she didn't remember earning.

She smoothed her hair behind her ear as if that could smooth everything else.

Then, as if her brain had been waiting for the moment her hands stopped moving, he slipped back into her thoughts.

Daniel Whitmore.

Mayor Whitmore.

Yesterday he'd walked into this place like he'd never once been unsure of himself. Like every doorway he'd ever stepped through had been meant for him. He'd looked at Eden— actually looked—and in the second it took her heart to skip, her whole body had reacted like she'd been starving without realizing it.

The stupid part was that she didn't even know him.

She knew the shape of him in a suit. The cold blue of his eyes. The way his smile had felt measured, like it had weight behind it.

Eden stared at the blinking cursor on the intake form. Her hands went still.

She told herself it had been nothing. A charming man doing his job. A public figure making staff at a youth shelter feel seen for five seconds before moving on to the next photo op.

But something about the way he'd said her name—slow, deliberate—had lodged under her skin.

Like a splinter she couldn't stop touching.

Her fingers tapped the desk twice. A nervous habit she'd been trying to break since—since before New York. She pressed her thumbnail into the side of her index finger until the sting gave her something real to focus on.

The rain deepened. Streetlights outside glowed hazy through wet glass. A bus sighed to a stop, doors folding open like an exhale.

Eden exhaled too.

She opened a new tab.

Just a peek, she told herself. Just curiosity. Like checking the weather. Like looking up a restaurant menu she wouldn't go to.

Like scrolling someone's social media even though she'd promised herself she wouldn't.

Her throat tightened at that thought, and she didn't follow it. She didn't. She wasn't going to fall into that spiral again. She wasn't going to—

Her fingers typed before she could talk herself out of it.

Daniel Whitmore, Mayor of New York.

Search.

His face filled the screen almost instantly. Clean, controlled images. Press conferences. Smiling beside schoolchildren. Standing in front of microphones with flags behind him, mouth mid-word, eyes focused somewhere beyond the camera as if he were addressing something larger than the room.

There was a photo gallery. Eden clicked without meaning to.

One of the first images was black-and-white—Daniel and a woman beside him, both dressed formally, her hand tucked into the crook of his arm like it belonged there. His smile in that photo was softer. Less measured. More… human. The woman was striking—dark hair, elegant cheekbones, eyes that looked like they knew how to be confident without trying.

The caption mentioned his late wife.

Eden's stomach dipped, and she was surprised by the sharpness of it. Not jealousy. Something closer to awe. Like looking at a life that had been complete, tidy, finished—while Eden's felt like it was made of loose ends and half-healed seams.

She studied the woman's face longer than she meant to, tracing the curve of her smile, the poise in her posture. Eden tried to imagine what it felt like to be chosen so fully that the world put your picture beside a powerful man and labeled you an era of his life.

She clicked away, then clicked back, then away again, as if moving quickly would keep the feeling from settling.

An article from *The Times* loaded.

She read the headline twice before the words sank in. **"Whitmore's Reform Agenda: A Mayor's Quiet Crusade."**

Eden scrolled.

Whitmore had risen quickly through the ranks, praised for his calm demeanor and firm moral stance. A moderate with bipartisan charm. Quietly philanthropic. Focused on juvenile reform and education. Known for avoiding scandal…

Avoiding scandal.

Eden almost snorted. The idea of any powerful man being scandal-free felt like a fairytale. But as she read, the article didn't feel like fluff. It was detailed. Names. Dates. Programs. The kind of thoroughness that made a person sound real.

A video link sat halfway down the page. Eden hesitated, then clicked.

He appeared on screen mid-sentence, the sound crisp through her cheap desktop speakers. His voice was lower than she'd expected. A slight rasp to it, like he'd learned how to speak through exhaustion and still sound steady.

He was talking about youth poverty. About housing insecurity. About how the foster system failed kids the moment they turned eighteen. His hands moved rarely, but when they did it was purposeful. His gaze didn't flit. It held.

Then he told a story about a seventeen-year-old boy who'd aged out of care early—paperwork, bureaucracy, a missed signature—and ended up on the street.

Daniel's jaw tightened, almost imperceptibly.

"No one should become invisible the day they legally become an adult," he said. "No one should have to prove their worthiness to survive."

Something shifted in Eden's chest.

It wasn't even the words. It was that he sounded like he meant them. Like he was furious in a controlled way—anger channeled into sentences instead of fists. Like grief turned into policy instead of silence.

Eden swallowed hard.

She'd heard men speak confidently before. Men who could sound convincing while lying through their teeth. Men who could make promises in the same voice they used to break you down. Men who knew exactly how to say *right* so it sounded like *safe*.

But this—this felt like conviction.

The video ended. Eden's cursor hovered over another clip.

She clicked again.

This one was a town hall. Someone asked about education funding. Someone else asked about gun violence. Daniel answered in that same steady voice—no dodging, no posturing. He even admitted uncertainty once: "I don't have the perfect solution, but I know we can do better than this."

Eden sat back in her chair, surprised by the ache behind her ribs.

Because the truth was, she hadn't trusted anyone's certainty in a long time.

The office door to the file room squeaked open.

"Googling your boyfriend already?"

Tonya's voice broke the quiet like a match striking. Eden jumped so hard her knee slammed the underside of the desk and pain shot up her leg. She snapped the laptop shut as if it were caught fire.

"I—what? No!" The words came out too fast. Too defensive. "He's not—he's the mayor."

Tonya grinned, leaning against the doorway with a folder tucked under her arm. Her hair was pulled into a loose bun, rain-speckled at the edges, mascara smudged like she'd been running around all morning. She looked amused in a way that felt affectionate, not cruel.

"Sure," Tonya said. "And I'm the Queen of England."

Eden's cheeks burned. She reached for her coffee as if having something in her hands would make her look less suspicious—then realized the cup was empty. Great. Perfect. Wonderful.

"I was just—" Eden started.

"Just curious," Tonya finished for her, voice softer now. "I get it."

Eden laughed awkwardly, the sound too thin. "He smiled at me. People smile all the time."

Tonya's eyebrow lifted. "Not like that, they don't."

Eden opened her mouth to deny it, then closed it again. Because she wasn't sure she could, not honestly.

Tonya stepped closer, lowering her voice like they were sharing a secret. "Girl, I've been working here long enough to recognize the difference between a man being polite and a man noticing."

Eden's throat tightened. Not because she wanted to believe it—because part of her already did.

"A man like that doesn't notice women like me," Eden said before she could stop herself.

Tonya's expression shifted, something sharp and knowing passing through her eyes. "Women like you?"

Eden's fingers curled around the edge of the desk. She didn't know how to explain it without making it sound pathetic. She wasn't tragic. She wasn't some sob story. She was just… she was just not the kind of woman people wrote articles about.

"I'm not—" Eden started, then stopped. "I'm not from here. I'm not… important."

Tonya made a sound that could've been a laugh or could've been anger. "Honey, you don't have to be important to be chosen."

The word landed heavy.

Chosen.

Eden felt her stomach twist in a way she didn't entirely understand. Because that word was a comfort, wasn't it? It was supposed to be. It was supposed to sound like safety.

But it also sounded like something that could be taken away.

Tonya's voice gentled again. "Look, I'm not saying he's going to ride in here on a white horse and ask for your hand in marriage. I'm just saying… he saw you."

Eden looked down at her hands, at the faint red mark on her thumb where she'd been pressing too hard. "Maybe he was just… doing his job."

"Maybe," Tonya agreed. Then she tilted her head. "Or maybe you're not as invisible as you've been feeling."

Eden's heart stuttered at that—because it was too close to the truth.

Tonya pushed off the doorway, the folder tucked under her arm again. "Anyway. I'm going to make more coffee before I die. You want some?"

Eden managed a real smile. "Yes. Please. Before I start chewing on this desk."

Tonya laughed and disappeared, leaving the air a little lighter behind her.

Eden stared at her closed laptop for a long moment.

Then she opened it again.

Not to watch another video. Not yet. She scrolled back up to the black-and-white photo of Daniel and his wife. Her chest tightened, and she hated that she couldn't tell if it was sadness or envy or some strange, hollow hunger.

She clicked a different article this time, one less polished. Local paper. Smaller quotes. More human.

A reporter asked him something about his personal life, about how he kept going.

Eden read the question twice before she noticed she was holding her breath.

"What keeps you going, Mayor?"

Daniel's answer was simple.

"Hope," he said. "Even in the dark, I believe there's always someone worth saving."

Eden's eyes stung unexpectedly. She blinked quickly, annoyed with herself. It was just a quote. Just a politician saying something that played well in print.

But the words didn't feel like performance.

They felt like a hand offered, palm up.

Someone worth saving.

Eden closed the tab.

She didn't want to sit in that feeling in the middle of the office. She didn't want the teens to see her staring too long at nothing. She didn't want Tonya to come back with coffee and find Eden looking like she might cry over a stranger's sentence.

So she went back to work.

She took calls. She filed forms. She printed a list of supplies and circled things they couldn't afford. She smiled at the teens who glanced her way and looked away when their eyes held too long. She made herself useful the way she always had, because usefulness was a kind of armor.

But even as her hands moved, her mind kept slipping—back to Daniel's voice, back to his eyes, back to the way his attention had felt like warmth on cold skin.

By the time her shift ended, the rain had eased into a steady drizzle. Eden stepped outside and the air was damp and sharp, threading into her lungs. She pulled her coat tight and walked home with her head down, dodging puddles, listening to the city's wet hiss.

Her apartment was still too small. Still too quiet.

She kicked off her shoes by the door and stood there for a moment, staring at the blankness of her walls—the cheap paint, the single framed print she'd bought because she thought it would make the place feel less temporary.

Temporary was a lie she told herself. A comforting one.

She heated up microwave soup and ate it straight from the bowl, perched on the edge of her couch. The spoon clinked faintly. The TV stayed off. Silence pressed in around her—not peaceful, just present.

Her phone sat beside her on the cushion, face down.

She flipped it over.

No new messages.

Of course not.

Eden swallowed another mouthful of soup, tasting salt and something bland and safe. The kind of food you ate when you didn't want to feel much.

After a few minutes, she set the bowl on the coffee table and reached for her phone again.

She opened her browser before she could talk herself out of it.

She wasn't obsessed.

She was just… curious.

She watched one clip of Daniel speaking at a fundraiser. Then another of him at a school. Then a short interview where he laughed at something off-camera, and the sound was startlingly normal—like he could be someone's neighbor, someone's friend.

Like he could be a man you could trust.

Eden set the phone down and leaned her head back against the couch, staring at the ceiling.

She wasn't broken. She told herself that. She was just bruised. Just recently reminded how quickly people could move on, how easily you could be replaced by something shinier, newer, easier.

She hadn't said it out loud to anyone in New York. Not Tonya. Not the director. Not the friendly barista downstairs who called her sweetheart and handed her an extra sugar packet like it was kindness.

She hadn't said it because saying it made it real.

But the ache was real anyway.

A man like Daniel Whitmore had looked at her like she mattered.

Not like she was convenient. Not like she was a placeholder. Not like she was the person you kept until someone else came along.

Like she mattered.

Eden closed her eyes, letting the thought settle into her chest where loneliness usually lived.

She wondered what it would feel like to be chosen—without having to earn it. Without having to perform for it. Without waiting for the moment it disappeared.

And she hated herself a little for how badly she wanted to believe it could happen again.

Chapter Three

Three days passed, and Eden told herself she was done thinking about him.

She filled the days with motion. Inventory spreadsheets. Scheduling changes. Phone calls that never quite resolved anything. She sat with a teenage girl who cried for nearly an hour without saying a word, the sobs coming sharp and quiet, like she was afraid of being heard even now. Eden didn't interrupt. She handed over tissues. She kept her voice low and steady and let the silence do the work.

She picked up extra shifts. Came in early. Left late. Skipped lunch because it was easier than explaining why she didn't feel hungry.

She avoided Tonya's smirks, the raised eyebrows from the other staff, the gentle curiosity that felt too close to exposure. She didn't want to talk about it because talking would make it real.

It had been one moment. One look.

That was all.

She wasn't the kind of girl who believed in fairytales. She learned early how those stories ended—messy, painful, soaked in regret. She'd seen what happened when women confused attention for safety.

So when the shelter doors opened that Friday afternoon, she didn't look up.

Not at first.

"Ms. Blake."

Her heart stuttered—one solid, unmistakable thud, like a knock from inside her chest.

She knew that voice.

Eden lifted her eyes slowly, like she was afraid the movement might shatter something.

Daniel Whitmore stood just inside the doorway, rain darkening the shoulders of his charcoal suit. The cut was immaculate, the fabric expensive in a way that didn't beg for attention. A pale blue pocket square softened the severity, made him look almost approachable. His hair was damp, though not a single strand seemed out of place, and in one hand he held a black umbrella.

In the other—

A check.

For a second her brain lagged behind her body. As if her mind was watching from a distance while her nerves did the reacting.

She stood too fast, chair scraping loudly against the floor as it tipped backward. "Mayor—sir—I—"

"Daniel," he said easily, like it had already been decided. "Please."

Her mouth opened. Closed. She pushed the chair upright with a clumsy hand and smoothed her cardigan like that could restore composure. "We weren't expecting—"

"I enjoy surprises, don't you?" he said, smiling, and there was something conspiratorial about it. Like they were sharing a moment no one else was allowed into.

He extended the check across the counter. "I wanted to follow up on my visit. A small donation. I know it's not enough, but…" He shrugged, casual, practiced. "I couldn't stop thinking about this place."

His gaze flicked to her.

"About you."

The words landed carefully. Deliberately. Eden felt them settle between them, heavy and electric, like something set on a table that shouldn't be there.

"That's… very kind of you," she managed, eyes dropping to the check as if numbers could anchor her.

He leaned closer, forearms resting lightly on the counter. His voice lowered, warm without being intimate. It was the kind of warmth that could be mistaken for care if you weren't careful.

"Are you free for lunch?"

She blinked. "I—I'm sorry?"

"You've been working yourself into the ground," he said gently. "I called ahead. Tonya mentioned you haven't taken a break in days."

Of course she did.

"I admire dedication," he continued. "But even the most committed people need to eat."

The word *need* brushed something raw.

Eden opened her mouth to say no. She felt the refusal forming—polite, automatic, safe.

But she hesitated.

And that was all it took.

Fifteen minutes later, they were seated in a quiet café two blocks from the shelter, tucked into a corner booth away from the windows. The rain blurred the outside world into streaks of gray. The lights were low, the tables half-empty. It felt like a pocket carved out of the afternoon, separate from everything else.

Daniel ordered soup. Eden asked for tea.

Neither of them touched what they ordered.

Instead, Daniel asked questions.

About the shelter. About the kids. About why she chose this work. His tone wasn't interrogative—it was curious, attentive. He didn't interrupt. He didn't rush her. When she trailed off, he waited, like he knew silence would do more than prompting.

It disarmed her.

Eden talked—more than she meant to. She told him about growing up somewhere small. About wanting more without knowing exactly what that meant. About going to school because it had felt like the only way out—community college first, then transferring when she could afford it. She talked about the classes that mattered, the ones that stuck with her long after graduation. Social work electives. Child psychology. How she'd always gravitated toward the systems that failed quietly, the ones no one noticed until it was too late.

She didn't call herself ambitious. She didn't say she wanted to help people. She just said it made sense.

She skirted around the breakup, kept the details vague, but his eyes didn't move away when she dodged. He seemed to hear what she didn't say.

"You came here for a fresh start," he said eventually, folding his hands together on the table. "Did you find it?"

She hesitated. "Sort of."

A corner of his mouth lifted. "That usually means no."

Eden looked down at her hands. Her nails were short, unpainted. Practical. "It's complicated."

He studied her for a long moment, and she felt exposed in a way that wasn't quite uncomfortable.

Not yet.

"Let me guess," he said quietly. "You gave everything to someone who didn't deserve it. And now you're pretending it didn't change you."

The air left her lungs in a rush.

He was too close.

Too perceptive.

She didn't answer because she couldn't—because acknowledging it felt like reopening something she'd sealed shut just to survive.

Daniel reached across the table.

His fingers grazed hers, barely there. A whisper of contact, easy to dismiss. So slight she could tell herself it had been accidental.

But his hand didn't retreat right away.

"I would never hurt you, Eden," he said.

His voice was steady. Certain.

Something inside her fractured.

And something else slipped quietly into place—soft as a lock turning, final as a door closing.

Chapter Four

The car ride back was silent.

Rain tapped against the tinted windows in delicate, rhythmic streaks. The driver kept his eyes forward, posture rigid and professional, hands steady on the wheel like the city could not touch him if he refused to acknowledge it. Eden sat with her hands folded in her lap, the streetlights sliding past outside in softened blurs of light and shadow.

The inside of the car smelled faintly of leather and something clean she couldn't name. Not air freshener. Not cologne. Something like money disguised as simplicity.

She felt suspended. Not quite in her body. Not quite out of it.

Like the afternoon had tilted her just a degree off-center and she hadn't found her balance again.

Daniel watched the city through the opposite window, profile sharp in the passing light. He hadn't spoken since they'd left the café. He didn't fill silence the way other men did, with jokes or explanations or little reassurances meant more for themselves than for her. He simply existed in it—comfortable, unbothered.

That should've felt calming.

Instead, Eden found herself listening for what wasn't being said.

Her pulse flickered at her throat. She pressed her thumb into the side of her index finger, a small anchor, a quiet reminder that she was here. She was in her own skin. She could still decide what to do with it.

When the car pulled up in front of the shelter, the driver eased to the curb with practiced smoothness. The wipers hissed, back and forth, back and forth.

Daniel turned toward her.

"May I see you again?"

The question was gentle. Not demanding. Not rushed. Not the kind of invitation that could be framed as pressure.

It would've been easier if it *had* been demanding. Easier to name. Easier to refuse.

Eden's breath caught on the inhale.

A thousand answers crowded behind her teeth. *Yes. No. I don't know. I shouldn't. I want to.*

Her mind tried to find the safe response first. The polite one. The one that didn't change anything.

She didn't speak quickly enough.

"I don't want to pressure you," he added, and the fact that he anticipated it—anticipated her pause—made her skin prickle. "But I'm hosting a dinner this Saturday. A small gathering at the mayor's house. Technically a fundraiser." His mouth curved slightly, like he knew how ridiculous it sounded to call anything at the Whitmore house *small*. "I'd like you there. As my guest."

As my guest.

The words felt too big, too polished for her life. Like they belonged on an engraved invitation, not in the mouth of a man sitting across from her in a car that smelled like control.

"I don't really have anything to wear to something like that," Eden heard herself say.

It wasn't an excuse. It was the truth. Her closet in New York was still half survival—work clothes, sensible coats, things meant to blend in and not ask for attention. She didn't own anything that said *I belong in a room full of donors and cameras and power.*

Daniel didn't hesitate.

"I'll send something," he said smoothly, like this was the most normal solution in the world.

Eden's stomach tightened—not with disgust, exactly. With the sudden awareness of how quickly he took things over. How naturally the problem became his to solve.

She shook her head. "You don't have to—"

"I insist."

Two simple words. Calm. Controlled. Not raised. Not harsh.

Still, they left no space.

Daniel reached into his jacket and pulled out a sleek black card. The movement was economical, practiced. Like he carried certainty the way other people carried keys.

He offered it to her.

Their fingers brushed—brief, light contact.

It should've been nothing.

But Eden's body registered it as a signal, a flare. Heat bloomed at her wrist where his skin had grazed. Something in her tightened, as if preparing for impact, and she hated that she couldn't tell if it was anticipation or warning.

"My assistant will be in touch," he said.

The driver opened her door.

Rain kissed her shoulder as she stepped out, cold and immediate. The city's damp breath rushed in around her, washing away the car's warmth like it had never been there.

"Thank you for lunch," Eden said. Her voice came out smaller than she meant it to.

Daniel smiled, slow and assured. "Thank you for your time."

Time.

Like it was currency. Like it belonged to him now that he'd asked for it.

The door closed.

The car pulled away, taillights sliding into the rain.

Eden stood for a moment on the sidewalk, watching until it disappeared, feeling the quiet space it left behind like a vacuum in her ribs. Then she turned and went inside.

Inside, the shelter buzzed with end-of-day noise. Phones rang. Someone laughed down the hall. The smell of coffee and cleaning solution clung to the air. A staff member called a teen's name, gentle but firm. A chair scraped. A microwave beeped.

Life continued the way it always did here—messy, loud, held together by routine and people who didn't have the luxury of falling apart.

Tonya was waiting in the office, arms crossed, eyebrows arched like she'd been practicing the look.

"You didn't even text me."

"I was with the Mayor," Eden said, shrugging out of her damp coat. Water droplets fell onto the linoleum, darkening it in little circles. "Kind of hard to be subtle."

Tonya whistled. "Damn. How was it?"

Eden hesitated—not because she didn't know, but because naming it felt like making it real.

Then she shrugged, a smile tugging at her mouth despite herself. "It was… nice."

"Nice?" Tonya blinked, scandalized. "Girl. That's Daniel Whitmore. Mayor of New York. Widower. Walking PR dream.

Owns three houses and got a bill passed expanding women's shelters."

"I know," Eden said, laughing softly. "Remember I googled him."

"Of course you did." Tonya leaned against the counter, gaze sharp. "Was he charming?"

"He was…" Eden searched for the word, feeling it catch in her throat. "Attentive. He listened. Like—really listened."

Something in Tonya's expression softened.

"That's new for you," she said gently.

Eden's smile flickered.

She sank onto the breakroom couch, shoulders slumping as if her body had been holding itself upright all day out of sheer stubbornness. For a second she stared at her hands, folded in her lap like a child told to behave.

"Yeah," she breathed.

And then the name slipped out before she could stop it.

"Ryan never really listened," Eden said. "Not unless there was something in it for him."

She hadn't said his name in months. Not in New York. Not out loud. Like the syllables could call him back, could invite the past into her new life.

But once she started, it spilled.

The criticism disguised as jokes. The disappearances that somehow became *her* fault. The gaslighting dressed up as concern. The way love had turned into something she had to earn by shrinking. The final cruelty of being replaced like she'd been interchangeable.

Tonya didn't interrupt. She didn't offer easy comfort. She just listened, eyes steady, face open—like Eden wasn't too much. Like Eden didn't have to apologize for taking up space in her own pain.

When Eden finished, silence stretched between them. The kind that had weight, not emptiness.

Then Tonya said, very calmly, "Well. Fuck Ryan."

Eden laughed, and the sound broke in her throat, half laugh, half sob she refused to name. She covered it with a hand, as if she could press the feeling back down.

"I'm serious," Tonya said. "Fuck him. And good for you for having lunch with someone who sees you."

Eden didn't answer.

Because she was thinking about Daniel.

The way his attention had felt like clarity. Like cleanliness. Like the possibility of starting over without dragging the past behind her.

Like maybe—just maybe—he could offer the life she almost forgot she was allowed to want.

And even as that hope warmed her chest, something else whispered underneath it, quieter but persistent:

No one offers you something that expensive without wanting something in return.

Chapter Five

Friday morning arrived sharp and clean, autumn threading itself into the city overnight.

The air smelled like damp leaves and cold metal, clinging to Eden's coat as she walked the few blocks from the subway to the shelter. Her heels clicked against the cracked sidewalk—a sound that usually steadied her, proof that she was upright, moving forward, not lost.

Today, it did nothing.

Her thoughts kept circling back to the car ride. To the way Daniel's voice had softened when he asked to see her again. To the smooth certainty of *my assistant will be in touch.*

The memory tightened her chest in a way that felt equal parts thrilling and unsettling, like stepping onto a glass floor and realizing you could see straight down.

She told herself it was ridiculous. One lunch. One invitation. A man doing what powerful men did—collecting good optics, building alliances, choosing what made him look generous.

Her body disagreed.

It carried the moment like a bruise you couldn't stop pressing to see if it still hurt.

She was barely out of her coat when Tonya poked her head around the office door, eyes bright with poorly concealed excitement.

"You've got a delivery," Tonya said. "And before you ask— yes. It's definitely for you."

Eden blinked. "For me?"

Tonya stepped aside.

A slim black box sat on the corner of Eden's desk, tied with a deep crimson ribbon. It looked deliberate. Heavy with intention. Completely out of place among intake forms, chipped mugs, and stacks of paper that smelled faintly of toner.

Eden approached it slowly, as if sudden movement might make it vanish.

A small envelope was tucked beneath the ribbon.

Her name was written in elegant, slanted script.

Eden's throat went dry.

She slid her finger under the flap and pulled the card free, careful, like it was fragile—or like it could cut her if she moved wrong.

Eden,
I'm looking forward to tomorrow evening.
Everything has been taken care of.
— D

Her pulse stuttered, hard enough she felt it in her wrists.

Everything has been taken care of.

The sentence read like comfort.

It also read like a door closing quietly behind her.

She untied the ribbon carefully, fingertips trembling despite herself. Inside, wrapped in soft tissue paper, was a dress—sapphire silk that caught the light like water. The fabric was cool and impossibly smooth, lace tracing the neckline and sleeves with quiet precision.

It was stunning.

It was also unmistakably not something she would have chosen for herself.

It wasn't loud. It wasn't flashy.

It was restrained in the way expensive things were restrained—designed to look effortless, designed to make other people assume you belonged.

Tonya let out a low whistle from the doorway. "Girl… that's not a dress. That's a decision."

Eden laughed, breathless, and her laugh didn't sound like her. "Is it too much?"

Tonya stepped closer, studying the fabric, the cut, the careful restraint of it all. "It's… intentional. Which is kind of his whole thing, don't you think?"

The comment landed softly.

But it landed.

Eden lifted the dress and held it against herself in the mirror by the supply cabinet. The color made her skin glow, her posture straighten without her meaning to. For a moment she didn't look like someone starting over.

She looked like someone already placed into a frame she didn't build.

"He didn't have to do this," Eden said quietly.

Tonya shrugged. "No. He wanted to."

That distinction settled deep in Eden's chest—warm, steady, and unsettling all at once.

Wanting meant choice.

Wanting also meant intention.

And intention meant expectation.

Eden folded the tissue paper back over the dress like she was closing a lid on something she wasn't ready to name.

They ate lunch together later, squeezed into the breakroom with vending machine snacks and lukewarm coffee. Eden barely tasted hers. Her tongue registered heat, salt, nothing else. Food had become a background task lately—something you did so your body didn't betray you mid-shift.

Tonya kept glancing at the box like it might start speaking.

Chapter Seven

The car slowed as it turned onto a long, curving drive, gravel whispering beneath the tires.

Eden sat very still in the backseat, hands folded tightly in her lap, staring through tinted glass as the Whitmore house came into view. Stone columns rose from manicured grounds, pale and imposing, framed by pink peony hedges trimmed within an inch of perfection. Light spilled from tall windows, warm and golden, giving the illusion of welcome. Voices drifted faintly from somewhere inside, layered with music and laughter.

The place looked untouched by time.

Or consequence.

The car stopped.

"Ms. Blake?" the driver asked gently as he stepped out and opened her door.

Cool air brushed her bare shoulders. The scent of peonies was stronger here—sweet and deliberate, like it had been curated too. Eden stepped onto the smooth stone drive, her heels clicking sharply in the quiet.

Then she saw them.

Not a crowd—nothing chaotic.

"So," she said eventually, nodding toward the desk, "that's not a casual invitation."

Eden exhaled slowly. "No."

"A mayor doesn't send a dress unless he's making a statement," Tonya continued. "And not just to you."

The words settled heavier than Eden expected. The implication was a weight. Cameras. Guests. People who would look at Eden and decide what she was the moment she walked in.

"I didn't ask for it," Eden said, though even to her own ears it sounded defensive.

"I know," Tonya said gently. "That's not what I meant."

Eden wrapped her hands around her coffee cup, letting the warmth ground her. "It just feels surreal," she admitted. "Like I skipped a few steps."

Tonya studied her. "How does it make you feel?"

Eden thought about the assistant's voice on the phone earlier in the week—efficient, polite, already assuming compliance. About the dress being exactly her size. About the note saying everything had been taken care of.

"It makes me feel…" She trailed off, searching. Her chest tightened around the truth. "Seen. And small. At the same time."

Tonya's eyebrows lifted. "That's a hell of a combination."

Eden let out a quiet, humorless laugh. "Ryan used to make me feel small. This doesn't feel like that."

"No," Tonya agreed. "This feels like elevation."

The word sent a shiver through Eden's spine.

Elevation implied distance.

From the ground. From where she'd been standing.

From who she'd been allowed to be.

"He doesn't make me feel like I have to disappear," Eden said softly. Then, because she needed to be honest even if it scared her, she added, "Not yet."

Tonya nodded once. "Intentional is the right word."

She paused, then added carefully, "Just make sure you're still choosing, too."

Eden nodded, though she wasn't entirely sure what that meant anymore.

Because a part of her—the part that had survived Ryan by shrinking—had always believed that being chosen meant you didn't get to be picky about the cost.

That night, Eden laid the dress across her bed like something ceremonial.

Her apartment was quiet, the city muffled by cooling air. The silence wasn't peace; it was absence. It highlighted everything she didn't have—furniture, friends, proof she belonged here beyond a lease and a job.

She touched the silk again, marveling at how something so soft could feel so heavy.

Tomorrow, she would walk into the mayor's house wearing something he had chosen.

The thought sent a shiver through her—not fear, not excitement, but something suspended between the two. Her body didn't know whether to lean in or step back, so it did neither. It held still, waiting.

She told herself it was just dinner.

Just a dress.

Just a man who noticed her.

Still, when she turned off the light, she left the dress uncovered.

As if she was afraid that if she hid it, it might disappear.

Or worse—

As if she was afraid that if she hid it, she'd admit she wasn't ready to be seen.

Chapter Six

Eden stood barefoot on the cool tile of her bathroom floor, a towel wrapped securely around her damp skin. Steam clung to the mirror in faint clouds, softening her reflection. She swiped at it with her palm and watched herself come back into focus in pieces—flushed cheeks, damp lashes, the faint indentation the towel left against her collarbone.

The curling iron hummed quietly on the counter, heat building, patient.

Everything tonight felt patient. Prepared. Like the world had already decided what would happen and she was just catching up.

She twisted her hair into a loose bun, fingers slightly unsteady, and reached for the lotion bottle she'd bought last week because the label had promised hydration and confidence in the same sentence. The scent was clean and subtle, unfamiliar but pleasant. New. Controlled. Like something that belonged to someone else's life.

Her phone buzzed against the counter.

FaceTime.

She glanced at the screen.

Mom.

Eden hesitated for a heartbeat. Not because she didn't want to talk to her mother—because she did. Because her mom's voice always did something to her nervous system, softened it, returned her to herself. And tonight she wasn't sure she wanted to come back fully.

Tonight she wanted to float.

She swiped to answer.

"Hey, honey!" her mother's voice filled the bathroom, warm and immediate. Her face appeared on the screen, glasses perched low on her nose, curls pulled back into a loose braid that Eden recognized instantly. Behind her, the familiar green couch slumped against the wall, cushions worn thin in the places they'd always sat. The chipped coffee table was still there, a stack of mail shoved to one side.

Home.

"Hey, Mom," Eden said, and some of the tightness in her chest eased, like her ribs remembered how to expand.

Her mother studied her for a moment, eyes narrowing slightly. "You look… glowy."

Eden snorted softly. "Glowy?"

"Yes," her mom said. "Like you slept. Or smiled today. Or both."

Eden propped the phone against the vanity mirror. "I might've smiled."

"Mmhmm." Her mom leaned closer to the camera. "Finally met someone?"

Eden laughed under her breath, reaching for her brush. "Not exactly. But maybe… sort of."

"Oh?" Her mom's tone sharpened with interest—careful, but curious. The kind of curiosity that came with motherly radar, the quiet awareness that life could pivot fast if you weren't paying attention.

Eden drew the brush slowly through her hair, bristles tugging gently at a knot. "His name is Daniel Whitmore."

Her mom waited.

"Mayor of New York."

There was a pause.

Her mother blinked once. Then again. "The Daniel Whitmore?"

Eden grimaced. "Yeah."

"Well," her mom exhaled, sitting back. "That's… unexpected."

"I know." Eden shrugged, then immediately regretted it when the towel slipped a fraction and she had to readjust. She held it tighter, like she could secure herself with fabric. "He stopped by the shelter to donate. We had lunch. Now he's invited me to dinner."

Her mom's expression softened, but there was something beneath it—awareness more than alarm. The look of a woman who'd seen men charm, and seen women pay for believing it.

"And how do you feel about that?" she asked.

Eden looked at her reflection instead of the phone. At the way her shoulders weren't curled in tonight. At the fact that she didn't feel braced for impact.

"I feel…" She searched for the right word, and it wasn't a clean one. It came with too much history. "Seen."

Her mom nodded slowly. "And safe?"

Eden didn't answer immediately.

She thought about Daniel's voice—calm, steady. The way he didn't interrupt. The way he seemed to anticipate her hesitations without pushing through them. The way his attention felt like warmth on cold skin.

"I do," she said quietly. "It's early. I know that. But he doesn't make me feel small."

Her mom watched her carefully. "That matters."

"I think he might actually be a good man," Eden added, as if she were testing the words out loud, letting her tongue learn them.

Her mom smiled—hesitant, but sincere. "Then I'm happy for you." She paused, and her voice gentled. "Just… keep your eyes open, okay? I don't want you getting hurt again."

Eden swallowed. Her throat stung like the air had turned too dry.

"I know," she whispered.

She met her mother's gaze through the screen, letting herself be seen by someone who loved her without conditions. "I'm not Ryan's anymore."

Her mother's face shifted at the name—pain, then resolve. "No. You're not."

She straightened slightly, as if saying it made it truer. "You're stronger than before."

Emotion pressed unexpectedly behind Eden's eyes. She blinked it back before it could spill. She refused to cry in front of the mirror with a towel on her body like a child playing dress-up.

"Okay," she said quickly, forcing brightness into her voice. "Enough heavy stuff. He sent a dress to the shelter. Tonya practically lost her mind."

Her mom's eyebrows lifted. "Oh. I definitely need to see that."

Eden laughed and stepped into her bedroom, lifting the black box from the bed like it might be fragile. She opened it carefully, angling the phone so her mom could see.

The sapphire satin caught the light immediately, deep and rich. The neckline was modest, the back dipping low in an elegant curve that felt intentional rather than provocative. The whole thing looked like it had been chosen by someone who understood restraint as power.

Her mom let out a low hum. "Well. He's got taste."

Eden hesitated, then added, "His assistant called earlier in the week. Asked my size."

Her mom waited—still, quiet, letting Eden fill the space.

"She asked if I had any preferences," Eden continued. "And I told her to let him choose."

Her mom's eyebrows lifted slightly. "Why?"

Eden studied the dress again—the careful cut, the quiet confidence of it. "Because I didn't trust myself to pick the right thing," she admitted. And because the truer part had to come too, even if it made her stomach twist. "And because… it felt easier to let someone else decide."

Her mother nodded slowly. "Well," she said gently, "he chose beautifully."

Eden pulled the dress over her head, the fabric sliding coolly over her skin. It settled against her like it already knew her measurements. She smoothed it down, adjusted the straps, then turned slightly so her mom could see.

Her mother's smile grew, soft and proud. "You look like a woman who knows what she wants."

Eden stared at herself in the mirror.

For a moment she didn't see the girl who'd learned how to make herself smaller to please a man. She didn't see the one who waited for affection like it was a reward you earned by behaving.

She saw someone stepping forward instead of bracing.

"I think I'm ready," Eden said.

Her mom's voice softened. "Then go. Enjoy it. Just remember who you are."

"I will," Eden whispered, and she meant it in the way people mean promises when they're scared they might break them.

They hung up a few minutes later.

Eden finished getting ready in silence, slipping on heels, checking her reflection one last time. She dabbed perfume at her wrists—something light and clean—and watched her own hands tremble before they steadied.

When the knock came at the door just before seven, her heart lifted—quick, fluttering—not with fear this time.

With hope.

The hope startled her. She'd learned to live without it. Hope was what got you hurt. Hope was what made you stay too long.

Still, her body held it like something precious.

When Daniel's car waited at the curb, sleek and dark against the evening light, Eden stepped outside and closed the door behind her.

The city hummed. Sirens in the distance. A stranger's laughter. Someone calling out in Spanish, something warm and quick. The street smelled like rain and hot asphalt.

When the car door opened, Eden hesitated for half a second longer than necessary.

Not because she didn't want to get in.

Because once she did, she couldn't pretend this was casual anymore.

Then she stepped inside.

The door closed behind her with a sound that was soft and ordinary—

and still, it felt final in a way she couldn't quite name.

Just presence.

Cameras at a polite distance. Not aggressive. Not hidden. A few people standing with devices in hand like this was routine, like they were waiting for the next arriving donation and the face attached to it.

Her pulse spiked so hard her vision sharpened.

This was far more public than she'd expected.

She smoothed the front of her dress, fingers brushing silk that still felt unreal against her skin, and forced herself up the steps. She felt the familiar urge to shrink, to angle her body away, to become less noticeable.

But there was nowhere to hide here.

Before she reached the door, it swung open.

Daniel stood just inside, framed by warm light.

He'd shed the tie, the top button of his white shirt undone, his charcoal suit relaxed in a way that felt intentional rather than careless. He looked at ease here—not impressive, not performative.

At home.

His gaze moved over her slowly, appreciatively, without making her feel examined. He looked the way a man looked when he'd gotten exactly what he'd wanted.

"Eden," he said, warmth threaded through her name. "You look incredible."

Her breath caught despite herself. "Thank you. And… thank you for the dress. It's definitely the nicest thing I've ever worn."

A flicker of amusement crossed his face. "I'm glad it fits."

Not *I hoped.*

Not *I guessed.*

Fits. Like it had been a certainty.

He stepped aside. "Come in. I want to introduce you."

Introduce you.

The words were simple. Still, they tightened her spine. The same way a hand at your back tightened your direction.

Inside, the foyer hummed with conversation. Guests moved easily through the space—sharp suits, elegant dresses, voices low and confident. Servers drifted by with trays of champagne and small, artfully arranged plates. Somewhere nearby, a string quartet played soft jazz, the music weaving through the air like something ornamental rather than necessary.

Through wide arches, Eden glimpsed the terrace—tables dressed in linen, lanterns glowing overhead, string lights stretched like captured stars.

Daniel offered her a glass of sparkling water instead of champagne.

He didn't ask.

He simply handed it to her—quietly observant, as if he'd already decided what would keep her steady. The gesture could've been read as thoughtful.

Eden read it that way.

She wrapped her fingers around the cold glass and tried not to think about how quickly he noticed things. How quickly he adjusted the world.

He guided her through the crowd with an easy hand at her elbow, greeting donors, old friends, colleagues. Names blurred together. Faces turned toward Eden with polite curiosity, some with thinly veiled appraisal. A few women looked at her longer than necessary, their smiles tight, eyes assessing what kind of girl wandered into a room like this on the mayor's arm.

Eden felt her lungs contract.

Old instincts rose fast: be agreeable. Be grateful. Don't embarrass yourself. Don't take up too much space.

She swallowed them down.

Daniel angled his body just enough to block one woman's stare. Not obviously. Not rudely. Just a small shift that changed Eden's sightline and forced the woman to look away.

It made Eden's stomach flip with gratitude.

It also made something in her go cold—because she understood the message.

I can move people.

I can move you.

"She works at a youth shelter downtown," Daniel told a small group, his hand settling briefly at the small of her back—not possessive, but unmistakably anchoring. "She does incredible work for the people who need it most."

The phrasing was precise. Elevated. He didn't say administrative assistant. He didn't minimize her. He made her sound important, like she belonged in this room.

Heads nodded. Questions followed. Eden answered carefully, measured and practiced, aware of the weight of the space. Daniel drifted away and returned seamlessly, never leaving her adrift for long. A glance. A touch. A quiet check-in that steadied her when the noise threatened to swallow her whole.

It should've felt romantic.

And it did.

It also felt like being monitored in the gentlest way possible— like he was keeping her within reach without making a scene.

Dinner was served outside beneath the lanterns. Eden found herself seated beside a woman who ran a statewide literacy foundation and across from a senator's daughter who was sharp, funny, and refreshingly unimpressed by the setting. Conversation flowed more easily than Eden expected. She laughed at something and startled herself with how natural the sound was.

Across the table, Daniel spoke with an older man in a tailored navy suit. Even while engaged, his eyes flicked to Eden every few minutes—brief, unreadable checks that made her feel simultaneously noticed and contained.

Midway through the meal, Daniel leaned closer.

"May I steal you for a moment?"

She nodded, relieved and nervous all at once.

They slipped away into a quieter corner of the garden, hedges rising around them, music fading to a distant hum. Crickets chirped softly, the night warm and close.

"I didn't want to keep you too long," Daniel said. "I imagine this isn't your usual Saturday night."

She let out a small laugh. "That's one way to put it. I feel like I'm playing dress-up."

He studied her, expression thoughtful. "You don't need to play at anything. You belong here."

The words hit harder than she expected.

She looked away, swallowing against the sudden tightness in her throat. "You don't even really know me."

"I know enough," he said calmly. "Enough to see that you're intelligent, capable, and far too accustomed to being underestimated."

Her gaze snapped back to his. "Did you Google me?"

He smiled, almost amused. "No. You told me just enough." His voice lowered slightly. "And I'm not interested in details unless you want to give them."

The restraint felt generous. Respectful.

It also felt like a promise with conditions: *I won't ask now. But you will tell me later.*

They stood quietly for a moment, the garden enclosing them in a private pocket of night.

"You really want to help the shelter?" she asked. "That wasn't just something you said because it sounded good?"

"I want to help," he replied simply. "And I want to keep seeing you. If you'll let me."

The steadiness of it disarmed her. She'd gotten used to affection that came with confusion, the kind you had to interpret and earn. This was offered like certainty.

She met his gaze. "I'd like that."

His smile was slow. Certain. Not triumphant—assured.

When they returned inside, he didn't touch her again. He didn't stake a visible claim. He let her circulate, speak, exist on her own terms.

But all evening, Eden felt his attention—quiet, constant.

Not demanding.

Not overtly possessive.

Just watching.

As if she were something worth keeping track of.

And when the cameras caught them near the foyer—just one flash, polite and distant—Eden realized, with a sudden cold clarity, that tonight wouldn't stay private.

Tonight would become a story.

And whether she meant to or not—

she'd already stepped into it.

Chapter Eight

The bouquet arrived Monday morning, bright and unmistakable against the gray routine of the shelter.

Wildflowers spilled outward in careful disarray—daisies, lavender, pale blue hydrangeas—wrapped in cream paper and tied with a silk ribbon too smooth for this place. It didn't belong among donation bins and intake forms. It looked like it had wandered in by mistake, like someone had carried a different world through the front door and set it down on Eden's desk.

Tonya spotted it first.

"Well," she said, appearing beside Eden with a slow grin, "someone's setting a tone."

Eden laughed softly, heat rising to her cheeks as she lifted the small card tucked between the stems.

Saturday was only the beginning.
Hope these brighten your week.
— D

Her fingers lingered on the paper longer than necessary. The cardstock was thick. Expensive. The kind of detail you noticed when you were used to people doing the bare minimum and calling it love.

Tonya whistled low. "That man does not ease into anything, does he?"

"He's just… thoughtful," Eden said, though the word felt too small for how this landed in her chest. She brushed her thumb over a petal, surprised by how grounding the simple texture was—velvet-soft, alive.

It had been a long time since anyone had done something for her without dangling it like a hook.

Ryan never got her flowers. Not unless he wanted something. Not unless he'd done something wrong and needed to erase it with a gesture. Those bouquets had come with an invisible invoice.

This—this felt different.

She told herself it did.

Still, her body did what it always did when something good happened: it checked for the catch.

The shelter was unusually quiet—a rare gift. While Tonya sorted donations in the back, Eden slipped into her small office and closed the door. The latch clicked, soft and final, cutting her off from the hallway's low hum.

She opened her laptop.

She didn't pretend she wouldn't do it. Pretending took energy. She was done wasting energy on lies meant only to keep herself from wanting things.

She typed his name.

Mayor Daniel Whitmore.

The results filled the screen: press photos, policy summaries, glowing editorials. Headlines praising reform. Videos of town halls and school visits. In one clip, he knelt beside a teenage boy in a wheelchair, listening so intently that the rest of the room seemed to fade.

Eden watched longer than she meant to.

This was the same man who had held her coat without being asked. Who had remembered she liked peach tea. Who had leaned close at dinner and said, *Tell me what makes you proud. I want to know.*

The man who had made her feel worth listening to.

Her phone buzzed.

A text.

Daniel: Busy week ahead. Would love to steal you for lunch. My treat?

Her pulse jumped—quick, bright, almost embarrassing in its eagerness. She stared at the screen for an extra second, trying to be normal about it, trying to keep the yes from racing out of her fingers like a confession.

She waited a moment before replying, aware of how easily yes came now.

Eden: Only if there's tea.

The response came almost immediately.

Daniel: Peach. I remembered. Noon tomorrow?

The simplicity of it made her chest tighten. Not with fear. With something dangerously close to gratitude.

She set the phone down and stared at the flowers again, their bright chaos making the office feel less fluorescent, less tired.

She shouldn't feel this affected by ribbon and petals.

But she did.

Because the truth was she'd spent years learning to accept crumbs as enough.

And Daniel didn't offer crumbs.

He offered a table.

Lunch was at the Capitol, in a private room tucked just off the mayor's offices.

Eden hesitated outside the door, smoothing her pale pink dress—chosen carefully this time. Not sent. Not curated. Hers. The color steadied her, even as nerves fluttered low in her stomach. It wasn't expensive, but it fit well. It made her feel like herself, not a costume someone else had pinned to her body.

The security guard nodded her through with polite efficiency. Her name was already on a list.

That part gave her a tiny jolt—the quiet realization that someone had anticipated her down to paperwork.

Daniel stood when she entered, a small gesture that shouldn't have mattered as much as it did.

"You look lovely," he said simply.

The room smelled faintly of citrus and polished wood. Framed photos lined the walls—handshakes, ribbon cuttings, children grinning with oversized scissors. Proof of a life that was documented and approved.

"This place is intimidating," Eden admitted as they sat.

He smiled. "It's just walls and people pretending they know everything." Then, more softly, "You have more heart than most of them combined."

She laughed, surprised by how easily it came. Surprised by how her body didn't brace for the joke to turn. For the compliment to become a critique.

Over grilled salmon and lemon risotto, they talked—nothing about politics, nothing about headlines. About the shelter. About the kids Eden worried over long after her shift ended. About choosing service over safety even when it cost more than people realized.

Daniel listened the way he always did. Patient. Focused. As if nothing she said was too small to matter.

He asked about her worst days. Her best ones. What she wanted when she let herself want things. When she answered, he didn't correct her. He didn't laugh. He didn't interrupt to steer the conversation back to himself.

That alone felt like a kind of intimacy she wasn't used to.

When they walked back toward the parking lot, his hand found hers.

The contact was gentle. Warm. Certain.

She didn't pull away.

Outside the Capitol, she slowed, their fingers still intertwined. She could've let go. She could've ended the moment neatly and walked back into her life unchanged.

Instead she held on, because holding on felt easier than letting go.

"This feels… fast," she said quietly.

Daniel's voice softened. "You've spent a long time bracing for disappointment, Eden." He squeezed her hand once, not hard—just enough to make her feel it. "You're allowed to enjoy something good when it comes."

A lump rose in her throat and she hated how accurate it was. Hated how quickly a man she barely knew could name her like he'd been studying her.

She didn't answer.

But she kept holding his hand.

Later that night, Eden and Tonya sat side by side on Eden's narrow fire escape, legs dangling over rusted metal, sharing the last of a bottle of wine while the city hummed below. The air was warm enough to pretend summer wasn't ending.

Somewhere down the block, someone played music too loud. Somewhere else, a couple argued with the kind of fury that sounded familiar.

"He makes me feel…" Eden trailed off, searching. The wine warmed her tongue, loosened something behind her ribs. "Normal. Like I don't have to rehearse every sentence in my head before I say it."

Tonya nodded. "That's how it's supposed to feel."

Eden stared out at the street, watching headlights smear into soft lines through the humid air. "I keep thinking about how long I waited for Ryan to change," she admitted. "How much of myself I shrank trying to make things easier."

Tonya didn't interrupt. Just listened, steady.

"And this feels different," Eden continued. "He listens. That's new."

She took another sip of wine and let the warmth settle.

For the first time in a long while, she didn't feel like she was asking for too much.

She felt like she was finally being met.

And if a tiny voice in the back of her mind whispered, *Be careful—this is how it starts*, she ignored it.

Because for once, she wanted to enjoy something without flinching.

Chapter Nine

Daniel showed up at the shelter on a Thursday afternoon—unannounced, but somehow expected.

Eden spotted him through the front window first, standing near the curb beside his driver, two cardboard trays balanced easily in his hands. He looked out of place and perfectly comfortable all at once, like he could step into any environment and make it adjust around him.

Tonya followed her gaze and arched an eyebrow. "Well," she murmured, "that's new."

Eden wiped her hands on her jeans, heart picking up pace. "Be nice."

"I am being nice," Tonya said. "I just didn't know we were at *Mayor brings lunch* levels already."

Daniel stepped inside like he'd done it a hundred times. No suit today—just dark jeans, sleeves rolled to his forearms, watch glinting softly under fluorescent lights. The casualness should've made him seem smaller.

It didn't.

He smiled when he saw Eden, relaxed and unhurried.

"I figured you wouldn't have time to grab lunch," he said. "Hope I guessed right."

She exhaled a small laugh. "You did."

He handed her a tray first, as if that mattered—like she was the point of the delivery, not the performance of it. The cups were warm in her hands. The smell of broth drifted up, clean and comforting.

They ate in the back room, perched on folding chairs between donation bins and stacks of canned goods. The smell of takeout cut through the usual tang of disinfectant. It felt strangely intimate—like he'd stepped into the most unpolished part of her life and decided to stay anyway.

He asked about the teens, about their favorite foods, the little routines that made the shelter feel less like a holding pen. He didn't speak like someone collecting anecdotes for a speech. He spoke like someone who actually wanted to know.

Tonya drifted in and out under the pretense of reorganizing supplies, making no effort to hide her curiosity. Daniel didn't seem to mind. He included her without making her feel like a third wheel. Cracked a few dry jokes that landed better than Eden expected.

By the end, Tonya was laughing openly, calling him "Mayor Boyfriend" under her breath as she passed.

Eden elbowed her lightly, cheeks warming.

Outside, when Daniel helped carry empty boxes out to the alley, afternoon light slanted low between buildings, turning the air gold.

"You're protective of her," he said casually, nodding back toward the shelter door.

"She's earned it," Eden replied. "One of the good ones."

"So are you."

The words were simple, but they tightened something in her chest.

She didn't answer. Not because she disagreed—but because kindness still caught her off guard, and she hadn't learned how to accept it without bracing for the bill that came after.

Daniel didn't push.

He just watched her a moment longer than necessary, like he was filing the reaction away.

After that, things began to settle into a rhythm.

Good morning texts. Check-ins. *Did you eat? How was your day?* Lunch once. Then twice. Dinner. A spontaneous day trip to the coast when Eden mentioned she hadn't seen the ocean in years.

They walked barefoot through cold foam, shoes abandoned in the sand. Ate fish tacos under a crooked awning while rain tapped the plastic roof. On the drive back, Daniel kept the music low and let her sleep, her head tipped against the window, his hand loosely holding hers like it belonged there.

He never asked for more.

Not out loud.

And that was part of what made it feel safe.

By mid-fall, she kept a toothbrush in his guest bathroom.

By December, her favorite tea sat in his kitchen cabinet, right where she'd reach for it.

She didn't remember deciding on any of it.

That detail should've unsettled her more than it did—the way her life had begun to rearrange itself around his without a single dramatic conversation.

But it didn't.

Because it felt easy.

And easy had become her definition of healthy.

One night, after a long shift at the shelter, Eden propped her phone against the bathroom mirror while curling her hair for another political dinner, this one honoring small business owners.

Her mom's face filled the screen, squinting for a moment before smiling. "Well. Someone's getting fancy again."

Eden smiled, twisting a lock of hair around the iron. "Another dinner. Fundraiser. I promised to make more of an effort."

Her mom raised an eyebrow. "That's… what, the third fancy event this month?"

"Fourth," Eden admitted, a little sheepish. "He keeps inviting me. I keep saying yes."

There was a pause. Not sharp. Not judgmental. Just the quiet before honesty.

"And how is it?" her mom asked. "With him."

Eden considered the question carefully. "It's good," she said. "He's steady. Gentle. He never pushes. He just… shows up."

"And you?" her mom pressed. "You still feel like yourself?"

Eden hesitated—but only for a second. "I think so," she said. "I'm just… softer lately."

Her mom studied her through the screen. "Just promise me you won't disappear into this. Even something good can take up more space than it should."

"I won't," Eden said. "I promise."

Her mom nodded, satisfied enough. "Well. Tell the Mayor thank you. For bringing that light back to your face."

Eden laughed. "I will."

The dinner was crowded—local artists, business owners, young professionals in suits that still smelled faintly of the store.

Daniel never let go of her hand.

He introduced her with care, always by name, always by her work. Always making her sound like more than she felt.

"This is Eden," he told a woman from the small business council. "She works at a youth shelter. She's the kind of person who makes this state stronger."

Pride bloomed warm and unfamiliar in Eden's chest. Not embarrassment. Not disbelief.

Recognition.

She watched him move through the room—confident, composed, effortless. People leaned in when he spoke. Laughter followed him like punctuation. And every few minutes, his gaze found her again—anchoring, reassuring, a quiet check that said *I know where you are.*

Later, in the car outside her apartment, the city quieted by the late hour, he reached across the console and brushed his knuckles along her cheek.

"You're extraordinary," he said.

Eden's breath caught. The words hit like a hand on the back of her neck—gentle, guiding.

Then he added, softer, like it was a truth he'd been holding back on purpose.

"I have fallen in love with you, Eden."

The streetlights smeared across the windshield. The car smelled faintly of his cologne and the leather seats warmed by their bodies. Eden's heart thudded once, hard, as if it was trying to decide whether to run or lean in.

She didn't say it back.

Not yet.

But she leaned into his touch, letting herself be held there, just for a moment longer than necessary.

And Daniel didn't stop her.

He waited.

Like he knew she would.

Chapter Ten

It started with a note tucked beneath her travel mug at the shelter.

The paper was heavy, the ink clean and confident. The mug warmed the corners, as if the message had been waiting for her body heat to make it real.

Weekend plans? You and me. No cell service. Just trees, stars, and maybe a fireplace. I'll drive.
— D

Eden read it twice.

The words were casual—almost playful—but anticipation lifted in her chest anyway, bright and sharp enough to follow her through the day in quiet flashes. She found herself smiling at nothing, catching the expression on her own face in the reflection of the supply closet door and looking away like she'd been caught.

She smiled like a fool all afternoon.

Every time she reached for her mug, her fingers brushed the paper again and her stomach fluttered, as if her body wanted proof it hadn't imagined him. She should've felt cautious. She should've asked questions: *Where? How long? Who knows we're going? Why no cell service?*

Instead, she held the note in her palm until the warmth sank into it and told herself the simplest story.

He wanted her.

And wanting her looked like effort.

On Friday, Daniel pulled up in a dark SUV just as her shift ended. The sun was already sinking behind buildings, the sky bruised with early winter color. Eden stepped out of the shelter and saw the vehicle waiting at the curb like an answer. No security detail. No aides. No crowd.

Just him.

The driver got out, opened the rear door, and Eden froze—not from nerves, exactly, but from the sudden, intimate shock of being anticipated.

The backseat held a small overnight bag already packed for her.

Not *a bag.*

A bag for her.

Neatly folded clothes. Her favorite tea. Extra socks. The granola bars she always kept in her desk drawer.

Her throat tightened.

Daniel leaned back in the driver's seat and watched her reaction like he was reading a result on a screen. When he spoke, his voice carried an easy smile.

"I figured you might forget to pack food," he said. "And I'm deeply invested in you not being grumpy."

Eden laughed as she climbed in. The seat was warm from the car's heater, and the leather smelled expensive, clean. "Thoughtful and self-preserving."

"Exactly."

He pulled away from the curb like he'd been doing it forever—smooth, unhurried. The city thinned behind them, buildings giving way to stretches of highway and darker pockets of sky. There were no calls, no interruptions. He wore sunglasses, one hand relaxed on the wheel, the other resting near the gearshift.

He looked calmer the farther they got from traffic, from people, from anything that could ask him to perform.

Eden watched the city disappear in the side mirror.

She didn't miss it.

The realization startled her—how easily she let the world fall away when he asked. How her body loosened as if the only thing exhausting about New York had been the constant need to be on guard.

Trees closed in. The road narrowed. Fog curled low between pines. The air changed—cooler, cleaner, unfamiliar. Eden cracked the window and inhaled, letting cold slide into her lungs like something medicinal.

Daniel glanced at her and smiled as if he liked the fact she'd done it. As if he liked seeing her respond.

By sunset, they reached a secluded A-frame cabin tucked deep into a hollow of evergreens. Wildflowers climbed the fence posts, stubborn against the season. The porch creaked softly beneath their boots. The quiet out here felt dense, almost physical—like you could press your palm against it and feel it push back.

"Whose cabin is this?" Eden asked, her breath fogging in the chilly air.

"Mine," Daniel said.

Then, after a pause that carried weight, "It was my father's. I come here when I need the world to stop."

Something about that landed heavier than she expected. Not just the confession—the implication. That he'd brought her to a place he used as refuge, as if she belonged in that category now: comfort. Quiet. Safety.

Inside, the cabin smelled like cedar and old paper. A stone fireplace dominated one wall, soot-darkened from years of use. Books lined shelves—some worn, some arranged like they'd been placed carefully and never touched again.

Eden ran her fingers along the mantle, grounding herself in the texture—stone cool and rough, real.

"You weren't kidding about no service," she said, checking her phone out of habit.

"Nope." Daniel's smile was easy. "Out here, it's just us. No noise. No expectations."

The words were meant to soothe.

They did.

They also clipped something away without Eden fully noticing—the invisible tether she kept to the outside world. The ability to text Tonya. To call her mom. To step out if she needed air and still be connected to someone else.

Eden hesitated—just a fraction—then smiled back anyway. "I could live with that."

Daniel watched her a moment longer, then turned toward the fireplace like he'd been given what he wanted.

They cooked dinner together, something simple—one pot, one bottle of wine, the kind of meal that made you feel like you'd earned warmth. Eden padded around the kitchen barefoot, wearing one of Daniel's flannels over her tank top, the sleeves swallowing her hands.

It should've felt odd—his clothes, his cabin, his world.

Instead it felt like belonging. Like slipping into something already shaped for her.

Daniel watched her quietly.

When she noticed and raised an eyebrow, he didn't look away.

"I like seeing you like this," he said. "Unarmed."

The word made her laugh, but it prickled too. "Is that what I usually look like?"

"Guarded," he said—not unkindly. "You don't need that here."

Eden should've asked how he knew. How he could say it so surely. But the truth was, she liked that he'd noticed. She liked that he'd named it without making fun of her for it.

After dinner, they sat on the couch in front of the fire. Her legs tucked beneath her. His arm draped along the back of the cushions, fingers brushing the nape of her neck now and then—never demanding, always present. A touch that said *I'm here* often enough that her body stopped checking for the catch.

The firelight painted the room in gold and shadow. Outside, wind moved through branches with a low, shushing sound, like the forest was conspiring to keep them hidden.

"I haven't felt this safe in years," Eden whispered.

The words slipped out before she could test them, before she could make sure they were true. The moment they left her mouth, her chest tightened—because saying a thing like that felt like handing someone a key.

Daniel didn't answer right away.

He shifted closer, pressed a kiss to her hair. It was quiet, almost tender enough to be unthinking.

"You deserve to feel safe every day," he said. "Not just with me. Always."

Eden turned toward him, their faces inches apart. The fire popped softly, a tiny crack in the quiet.

"What if I don't know how to accept that yet?" she asked.

"Then I'll wait," he said simply. "And I'll keep showing you."

Her throat burned. Not with sadness—with the ache of being treated gently after years of having to bargain for kindness.

She kissed him first—slow, uncertain, full of everything she hadn't said out loud.

He met her with patience, not urgency, hands steady and warm.

Later, when they moved to the bedroom, nothing felt rushed. Nothing felt taken.

There was no hunger in it, no sharp edges. Only care.

He moved as though every touch mattered, as though he was memorizing her rather than claiming her—guiding instead of demanding, pausing whenever her breath changed, waiting until she nodded him closer. It loosened something inside her she hadn't realized she'd been clenching for years. It made her feel chosen, not cornered.

It was gentle. Intentional. Almost cherished.

As if she were something precious rather than fragile.

Eden's body remembered how to soften. How to lean into closeness without flinching. How to trust that a hand at her waist wouldn't tighten without warning. She exhaled slow and deep and let herself be held there—seen, wanted, cherished.

Afterward, he gathered her against him, one arm firm around her waist, his thumb tracing absent circles into her skin. The fire beside them burned low. The room was quiet except for the soft rhythm of his breathing. He pressed a kiss into her hair—unthinking, affectionate, unforced.

For a long while she listened to his heartbeat and let herself believe she'd found something rare.

She fell asleep wrapped in warmth and quiet.

Wrapped in his arms, Eden let herself believe that safety was something you found—

not something you had to keep watch for.

Chapter Eleven

The world still shimmered around her.

Eden floated into the shelter Monday morning with the soft trace of Daniel's cologne clinging to her sweater, like the weekend had soaked into her pores. Three days—just the two of them, sealed away from everything else. The cabin had sat beside a frozen lake, all white pine and stone hearth, the silence broken only by crackling firewood and the sound of her own laughter.

She hadn't realized how long it had been since she'd laughed without checking herself afterward.

Daniel had planned everything.

A picnic laid out by the fire. Poetry books stacked neatly on the nightstand. Silk robes folded at the foot of the bed. Lavender bath salts. Chocolate-covered strawberries arranged like an afterthought that clearly wasn't one.

It had felt like stepping into someone else's idea of love—fully formed, intentional, effortless.

It had also felt like being placed inside a story where there were no messy choices to make. No questions. No awkward "what do you want?" conversations.

All she had to do was accept.

Tonya looked up from the front desk and grinned. "Well, well. Look who got laid and fed compliments."

Eden laughed, heat blooming in her cheeks. "Shut up."

"I won't," Tonya said. "You look like a Hallmark commercial with a trust fund. What did he do—whisk you off to Narnia?"

"A cabin by a lake," Eden said, lowering her voice even though no one else could hear. "Private chef. Fireplace. He even made a playlist. With my favorite songs."

Tonya made a noise somewhere between a purr and a gag. "Mm. Rich-man romance. I see you."

She turned back to her paperwork, but her eyes lingered on Eden a beat too long.

Eden noticed. "What?"

"Nothing," Tonya said lightly.

Then, more carefully, "Just… you talk about him a lot."

Eden blinked. "We just spent three days together."

"I know." Tonya shifted her weight. "I'm just asking—did you get to plan anything? Or was it all his show?"

Eden frowned, caught off guard by the wording. "It was a surprise," she said. "And a good one. He knows I like thoughtful things."

Tonya nodded. "Thoughtful's great."

Then she added, quiet but firm, "Just make sure it doesn't turn into *he always decides things for us.* I've seen that movie."

Eden waved her off, too quickly. "You're overthinking."

"Maybe," Tonya said. "Just don't forget who you are in all that romance."

Eden smiled, but the smile didn't reach all the way. Something in her chest tightened, like the comment had brushed against a bruise she didn't want to admit was there.

Her phone buzzed on the desk.

A message from Daniel.

Daniel: Made us a reservation for Thursday. Hope you kept the night free ☺

Her heart lifted instantly—an automatic, eager response that felt almost physical, like her body had learned his attention was oxygen.

Eden: Wouldn't miss it.

Tonya watched her. "You're glowing again."

"He's taking me to that new wine bar on Fifth."

Tonya's expression shifted. "Thursday?"

"Yeah."

"We were supposed to have dinner with my cousin," Tonya said. "I told you about it last week."

Eden winced. The memory came back in pieces—Tonya's voice in the breakroom, Eden nodding, saying yes, meaning it. "I forgot. I'll ask him to reschedule."

Tonya crossed her arms. "You sure you will?"

Eden looked up. "What's that supposed to mean?"

"It means the last three times I asked you to hang out, you either canceled or disappeared halfway through," Tonya said gently. "Don't pretend I didn't notice."

"I've just been busy."

"You're falling in love," Tonya said. "And that's beautiful. But love shouldn't make your world smaller."

Eden opened her mouth.

Then closed it.

Because the truth tried to rise and she didn't want to look at it:

Her world didn't feel smaller.

It felt quieter.

And quiet had always been Eden's version of safe.

That evening, she curled up on her couch in one of Daniel's hoodies, hair still damp from a bath. The fabric smelled like him—clean, expensive, familiar already. Her phone lit up with her mother's FaceTime call.

"Hey, baby," her mom said. "You look tired."

Eden smiled. "I'm good. Just… full."

"Full?"

"Of him," Eden said, laughing softly. "He took me away for the weekend. It felt like a fairytale."

Her mother's eyes narrowed slightly. "He let you sleep at all?"

"Mom."

"I'm just asking." A pause. "Did he give you space?"

Eden's smile thinned. "He just likes being with me."

"Mm." Her mom tilted her head, studying Eden through the screen the way she had when Eden was a teenager coming home too late, trying to hide the truth behind brightness. "You still writing?"

Eden hesitated. "Not really. I haven't had time."

"And work?"

"I'm still there," Eden said quickly. "Daniel just thinks I'm burning myself out."

"Does he know you," her mom asked gently, "or does he just want more of your time?"

Eden frowned, irritation sparking—sharp and defensive, the way it always did when someone threatened a fragile good thing. "He cares about me."

"I'm happy if you're happy," her mom said, voice careful. "But I've seen you lose yourself before. This time, I want you to stay rooted."

"I am," Eden insisted. "I've never felt more seen."

Her mom said nothing for a moment. Then: "Just make sure you're still seeing yourself."

After they hung up, Eden stared at the blank screen longer than necessary.

The apartment felt too quiet all of a sudden, the kind of quiet that didn't soothe—just exposed. She could hear the building settling. A neighbor's footsteps overhead. The distant siren slicing through night.

Eden set the phone down and pressed her palm to her sternum like she could steady her heart by force.

She didn't want to think.

Thinking made questions.

Questions made choices.

And choices made her feel like she could ruin this if she touched it wrong.

Later, in bed, her phone buzzed again.

Tonya: Don't forget who you are, E. I love you. That's all.

Eden read it once.

Then again.

The words didn't feel like an accusation. They felt like a hand on the back of her neck, gentle but insistent, turning her face toward something she'd been avoiding.

She flipped the phone face-down on the nightstand.

She didn't want to think.

She wanted to stay inside the feeling—warm, certain, effortless.

She closed her eyes and let herself drift toward it.

Toward him.

And somewhere beneath the warmth, the smallest thread of fear pulled tight—not enough to stop her, not enough to name.

Just enough to keep her from fully relaxing.

As if part of her already knew:

If safety depended on one person,

it could be taken away by that person, too.

Chapter Twelve

The restaurant was dimly lit, all golden chandeliers and velvet booths that swallowed sound. The kind of place where even the clink of silverware sounded polite. Candlelight softened faces, turned everyone into a version of themselves that looked calmer, wealthier, easier.

Daniel looked like he'd stepped out of a magazine—crisp dress shirt, sleeves rolled to the elbows, leather watch snug at his wrist. The sleeves made him look approachable. The watch reminded Eden he was still a man who measured time like he owned it.

Eden wore the navy wrap dress he'd said made her look dangerous in the best way.

She hadn't argued.

Not because she didn't have opinions. Because it was easier to let him be right. And because the way he said it— dangerous—made her feel like power could be something gentle and beautiful instead of sharp.

He hadn't stopped touching her since they'd sat down.

His hand rested on her knee beneath the table, warm and steady, thumb occasionally sweeping a slow line along her skin like he was making sure she stayed present. His thigh brushed hers when he leaned in. He pressed a brief kiss to her temple when she laughed at something on the menu, the affection so casual it looked like habit.

Like she belonged.

"You know what I realized this weekend?" he said, lifting his wine glass.

"What?" Eden asked.

"You get quieter when you're truly happy."

She blinked. "I do?"

"You do," he said easily. "Like your soul's resting."

Warmth spread through her chest. The compliment didn't feel like flattery—it felt like being seen through, like he'd noticed a version of her no one bothered to look for.

She reached across the table, fingers tracing the smooth line of his wrist. His pulse beat under her touch—steady. Confident.

"You're poetic," she said.

He smiled. "You bring that out in me."

Dinner arrived—beautifully plated, too pretty to be food. Conversation drifted the way smoke drifted—easy, intimate, dreamlike. They talked about art and music and books that made Eden feel like she was standing in a room that had once been locked. He asked about her childhood, but carefully, like he knew where the tender parts might be and wanted to avoid stepping on them—unless she invited him.

That made her want to invite him.

Then, almost casually, as if it wasn't a trap at all, he asked, "So what's the plan with the shelter? You still working those long hours?"

Eden nodded. "We've had a few new arrivals. A girl with a baby. A woman who won't speak yet. It's… heavy."

Daniel's mouth tightened, just slightly. Not anger. Disapproval disguised as concern.

"You told me you wanted peace," he said. "That doesn't sound like peace."

"It's hard," Eden said. She held his gaze, refusing to shrink just because he frowned. "But it matters."

"I'm not questioning that." His voice softened immediately, as if he'd caught the edge in her. "I just don't want to see you swallowed by other people's pain."

His thumb moved gently against her knee beneath the table, a soothing motion that made her body quiet down even as something in her mind stayed alert.

"You're gentle, Eden," he continued. "Gentle things bruise easily."

She let out a small laugh. "I'm stronger than you think."

"I know," he said, tilting his head. His eyes were warm, attentive. "I just don't want you proving it by hurting yourself."

The words wrapped around her like a blanket.

The blanket also felt heavy.

Because he wasn't telling her to quit. He wasn't ordering her to stay home. He was offering a narrative where leaving the shelter would be *self-care*, and staying would be *self-harm*.

He made it sound like a choice she could be proud of.

Eden nodded slowly, absorbing the care wrapped around the caution.

Something about it unsettled her.

But she didn't pull away.

Later, as they walked toward the car, her phone vibrated in her hand.

Three missed calls.

Mom: Call me when you can. It's important.

A cold ripple ran through Eden's stomach. Her first instinct was to call back immediately—because that was how she'd been wired: *answer, respond, fix.*

Daniel noticed before she could hide it. "Everything okay?"

Eden hesitated. Not long. Just long enough to feel the weight of his attention turn toward the screen.

"My mom's just… intense sometimes," she said, forcing a lightness she didn't feel.

"She doesn't like me," he said—not accusing. Stating, like he'd already organized the problem into a neat box.

Eden stopped walking. "She doesn't even know you."

Daniel took two more steps, then turned back, hands in his pockets. The gesture made him look relaxed. It also made him look untouchable.

"She knows you," he said. "And she knows you're changing."

"That's not a bad thing."

"No," he agreed softly. "But it can feel threatening to people who are used to having access to you."

Access.

The word hit Eden wrong, like biting into something and realizing it wasn't what you expected.

"She's my mom," Eden said, sharper than she intended.

"And you love her," Daniel replied calmly, as if he'd anticipated the defense. "That's part of why she has so much influence."

Eden swallowed. The streetlights reflected in the car's glossy black paint. The night air smelled like exhaust and expensive perfume drifting from the restaurant's doorway.

"You told me you were done letting people hurt you," he continued, voice gentle. "That you wanted something safe." He stepped closer. "Don't let doubt creep in because someone else is uncomfortable with you choosing yourself."

Her chest hummed with the truth of it—because she *had* said those things. Because she *did* want safe. Because she was tired of being pulled in twenty directions by other people's needs.

"We have something good," he said. "Don't we?"

Eden nodded.

He kissed her forehead—lingering just long enough to make it feel like a seal, like he'd stamped the moment into place.

"That's all I need to know," he murmured.

That night, Eden didn't call her mother back.

She saw Tonya's message too—a reminder about dinner with her cousin, a string of question marks after it.

Her thumbs hovered over the screen.

She typed a response.

Deleted it.

Typed again.

Deleted again.

It wasn't that she didn't care. It was that caring felt exhausting. Caring meant explaining. Caring meant arguing her way out of guilt.

Daniel's arm was warm around her waist. His room smelled like clean linen and cedar. The city outside felt distant, irrelevant—noise behind glass.

Eden set her phone down as if it were a weight.

She chose quiet.

The next morning, Tonya cornered her by the coffee machine.

"You okay?"

Eden forced a smile. "Just tired."

"You didn't answer my texts."

"I was with Daniel."

Tonya studied her. "Did you ask him to reschedule?"

Eden paused—just long enough.

"No," she admitted.

Tonya exhaled quietly, not dramatic, just disappointed. "That's what I thought."

"What's that supposed to mean?" Eden's voice sharpened before she could stop it.

"It means you were supposed to be with me and my cousin last night," Tonya said gently. "You used to make space for people. Now it feels like you're asking permission."

Eden bristled. Heat climbed her neck. "That's not fair."

"I'm not saying he's bad," Tonya replied, voice steady. "I'm saying you're disappearing a little. And that scares me."

Eden looked away, jaw tight. Anger flashed—not at Tonya, not really. At the implication that something good could still be dangerous. At the possibility that she was doing it again—shrinking, rearranging, letting someone else become the center.

"Just keep your eyes open, E," Tonya said. "That's all."

But Eden didn't want her eyes open.

Open eyes meant seeing the seams. The little moments. The small choices that stopped feeling like choices.

She wanted the world Daniel gave her—curated, quiet, intentional. A place where decisions were made before she had to struggle with them. Where nothing pulled at her from every direction. Where she didn't have to carry the shelter's grief home in her ribs.

Her mother could wait.

Tonya could wait.

Because when she was with him, the noise stopped.

And right now, that felt like everything.

Chapter Thirteen

Daniel showed up at the shelter with coffee.

Two oat milk lattes, still warm. Croissants folded into a brown paper bag. A bouquet of peonies wrapped loosely in tissue, petals already starting to shed like they'd been cut too early, hurried into devotion.

Eden laughed when she saw him through the glass doors. "You look ridiculous," she said as he stepped inside, flowers brushing his jacket.

"Ridiculously devoted," he replied easily, handing everything over like it was the most natural thing in the world.

The warmth in Eden's chest was immediate. Automatic.

It scared her a little, how quickly her body trusted him.

Tonya watched from the breakroom doorway, her expression unreadable.

Daniel noticed.

"Good morning, Tonya," he said pleasantly.

Not overly warm. Not cold either.

Balanced.

"Morning," Tonya replied after a beat, then disappeared back into the room.

"She's protective," Eden said, feeling the air shift, subtle as a temperature change.

"As she should be," Daniel said smoothly. "People who care about you will always worry when things change." He smiled at Eden. "I don't fault her for that."

The words were generous.

The tone was not.

There was a faint chill beneath the kindness, something controlled and thin, like the surface of a lake you didn't realize had frozen.

Eden felt it.

But she let it pass, because calling it out would make her sound paranoid. Because she wanted this to stay soft. Because she didn't want to be the girl who ruined good things by imagining danger.

That evening, he took her to a private art gallery opening.

Crystal glasses clinked softly. Music drifted through the space like smoke. The walls were lined with bold, intimate pieces— bodies fractured into color and shadow, faces half-erased, mouths open like they were trying to speak and couldn't.

Daniel stayed close. His hand rested at her waist. His thumb traced small, absent circles against her skin.

"You belong in places like this," he murmured near her ear. "You don't belong shrinking yourself to survive."

Warmth flooded Eden's chest, even as something hollow echoed behind it. Like her body loved the words and her mind didn't know what to do with them.

"You're not a tragic charity worker," he continued softly. "You're art."

The word landed strangely.

Flattering.

Reductive.

Still, she held onto it. To him. Because being *art* sounded better than being *tired.* Being *art* sounded like worth. Like value.

Later, in the car, the city sliding past in blurred streaks of light, Daniel spoke without looking at her.

"Your mother called again."

Eden stiffened. "What?"

"I only know because I saw the screen light up," he added quickly. "I wasn't trying to pry."

The sentence was practiced. The kind of thing you said when you wanted to sound respectful while still placing yourself inside someone's private space.

"She's been… persistent," Eden said, already tired.

"That makes sense," Daniel said calmly. "Transitions can feel threatening to people who are used to being needed."

"She's not controlling," Eden said, sharper than she meant to.

"I'm sure she isn't," he replied gently. "I don't know her." A pause. Then, like he couldn't help himself: "But sometimes mothers struggle when their daughters stop orbiting them."

Orbiting.

The word made Eden's skin prickle. It turned love into gravity. It made her mother sound like a planet demanding her.

Daniel smiled, soothing. "I just don't want you absorbing guilt that isn't yours."

Eden looked out the window and didn't respond.

Because if she responded, she might say the wrong thing.

And she didn't want to lose the quiet.

A week later, he brought it up over dinner.

Salmon and risotto. Candles lit low. Billie Holiday humming softly from the turntable. The house felt insulated from the city, warm and enclosed, like the outside world couldn't reach them without permission.

Daniel poured her wine. Watched the candlelight flicker across her face.

"I've been thinking," he said.

"That's never ominous," Eden joked, trying to keep it light.

He smiled, but it didn't soften what came next. "I want you here," he said simply. "With me. All the time."

The words hit harder than she expected.

Not because she didn't want him.

Because the phrase *all the time* had weight.

"Move in," he continued, reaching for her hand before she could pull away. His thumb pressed lightly into her knuckles, steadying her—directing her. "Not to rush you. Not to trap you." He smiled slightly. "But because this feels right."

Eden's breath caught.

He said the word trap like it was absurd, like only a paranoid person would think of it. Like naming it erased it.

"You told me you wanted a fresh start," he said. "A place that felt safe. This could be that." His thumb brushed her knuckles again. "A home without ghosts."

Ghosts.

Eden's mind supplied Ryan's voice. Ryan's smirk. Ryan's dismissive laugh.

Her tiny apartment. The thin walls. The loneliness that settled in when the city went quiet. The constant decisions—what to eat, what to wear, who to answer, who to disappoint.

She searched Daniel's face, trying to find urgency. Trying to find the edge.

All she saw was certainty.

"Think about it," he added gently. "I'll never pressure you. I just… love you. I want to wake up next to you. Take care of you. Build something that doesn't hurt."

Take care of you.

It sounded like tenderness.

It also sounded like ownership, if you listened too closely.

Her heart pounded, loud and unsteady.

She thought of how quiet it was here.

How easy.

How held she felt.

And despite the flicker of unease tightening beneath her ribs—

she said yes.

The relief on Daniel's face was immediate, controlled but unmistakable. His hand tightened once around hers—a small squeeze, like confirmation.

"Good," he murmured, and kissed her knuckles like a vow.

Eden smiled back.

And told herself the tremor in her chest was excitement.

Not warning.

Chapter Fourteen

The boxes were stacked precariously in the corner of Eden's tiny studio apartment.

They leaned into one another like they were conspiring, each one holding fragments of a life she was folding away—worn jeans softened by years of use, dog-eared paperbacks she'd hauled from place to place, a chipped mug she'd bought on a bad day because it made her laugh. Packing felt final in a way she wasn't sure she was ready for.

Terrifying.
Necessary.

She sat cross-legged on the floor, surrounded by cardboard and tape, and let herself look around the space one last time. The faded walls. The scuffed floors. The narrow window that let in more noise than light. Sirens. Voices. The city breathing too close.

It wasn't much.

But it was hers.

Her phone buzzed, and Tonya's face filled the screen.

"You really sure about this?" Tonya asked. Concern pulled her mouth tight, the way it always did when she was trying not to sound like she was begging.

Eden nodded, even though her chest ached. "I have to be. This feels like… my chance."

Tonya exhaled slowly. "Just promise me you'll keep your guard up. I don't want you losing yourself or getting hurt."

"I know," Eden said softly. "Thank you. For always being there."

The call ended, and the quiet pressed in hard and fast.

She reached for the box labeled **PHOTOS** and opened it last.

The stack inside was thin. Birthdays. School pictures. Holidays. Her mother appeared in nearly every frame—sometimes smiling, sometimes tired, always there. Always leaning in.

Her father was harder to place.

Not because he was missing entirely—but because there was never enough of him to miss.

One photo slipped loose and landed face-down in her lap. Eden hesitated before turning it over. She was small in it, maybe four, perched on a man's shoulders at a county fair. Cotton candy stuck to her fingers. Her smile wide and unguarded.

She only knew who it was because her mother had told her once.

He didn't leave in a fight.
He didn't leave in anger.

He just stopped showing up.

Eden stared at the picture for a long moment, then slid it to the bottom of the box and taped it shut. The sound of the tape tearing was loud in the small room.

She didn't cry.

She never really did.

Daniel's world was a universe away.

The Whitmore house rose behind iron gates, marble floors gleaming beneath crystal chandeliers, staircases curving like they were designed for entrances rather than use. Its stone darkened by decades of weather and power. It hadn't been built for one man. It had been built for a family that didn't expect to ever leave. The house had belonged to the Whitmore's for generations. Mayors all of them. That kind of power didn't campaign anymore — it inherited. Eden felt the weight of it the moment the heavy oak doors closed behind her.

She'd spent weekends at his cabin—pine-scented air, crackling fires, quiet that felt earned.

This was different.

This was permanence.

She felt small here. Unfinished. Like she'd stepped into a life already arranged and wasn't quite sure where she fit.

Daniel noticed immediately.

His hand settled at her arm, warm and steady. "Nervous?"

"A little," she admitted.

He smiled, eyes kind but unwavering. "You're safe here. This is home now."

The words settled over her like a blanket she didn't know she'd been reaching for.

That first night, Daniel took over the kitchen.

He moved with the confidence of someone used to command—seared scallops, asparagus arranged just so, a lemon butter sauce that smelled like indulgence. He poured her a glass of chilled Chardonnay before she thought to ask.

Dinner was pleasant. Polite. Almost formal.

He asked about her day. Laughed when she made a joke. Watched her like her presence alone was something to savor. It was the kind of attention she once would have tried harder to earn.

Now it was simply given.

Later, in the vast living room, the space felt too large for the quiet between them. Daniel's hands found her waist, drawing her close—gentle, firm, certain. Their kisses were slow, weighted with promise. His touch was warm, reassuring.

And beneath it, something else.

A subtle tightening.

A guidance rather than a question.

Eden noticed the way he positioned her, how easily she let herself be moved. The comfort of it. The familiarity. The strange relief of not having to decide where to stand or how close to be.

She swallowed, a flicker of unease threading through the warmth.

But when he murmured her name—low, sure—the feeling faded.

Wrapped in silk sheets later, the house silent around them, Eden told herself this was love. This feeling of being held. Of not having to decide what came next.

Still, as she drifted toward sleep, that small voice lingered.

Not loud enough to stop her.

Just enough to remind her that this feeling—of being chosen, of being carried—was one she'd been waiting for a very long time.

Chapter Fifteen

The first morning in the house felt unreal.

Sunlight poured through tall windows, spilling across marble floors in wide, pale bands. Eden stood barefoot at the base of the sweeping staircase, a mug of coffee cooling in her hands, unsure where to settle herself. The house was silent in a way that felt deliberate, like it was holding its breath.

Daniel had already left for the day.

He'd kissed her temple before sunrise, voice still rough with sleep. *Take time,* he'd told her. *Let yourself adjust. You've earned that.*

She'd believed him.

Later that morning, she sat at the small writing desk in the guest wing Daniel had insisted would be hers and opened her laptop.

Your space, he'd said, like he was giving her something rare.

The room was bright and quiet, lined with shelves that were still mostly empty, waiting. A window overlooked the gardens, soft light pooling across the hardwood floor. Everything felt untouched.

Beautiful.

The shelter's email inbox waited on the screen—familiar, steady. After a moment's hesitation, she typed a short message to the director, asking for a week of PTO.

Maybe two.

Just enough to unpack. To breathe. To let the move settle.

The reply came quickly.

Of course. Take care of yourself.

It should have felt grounding.

Instead, the day stretched open in front of her, wide and unstructured.

Eden wandered the house slowly, learning its shape. The drawing room with its untouched velvet furniture. The formal dining room where she'd been a guest at so many of Daniel's dinners and fundraisers. The library—shelves rising higher than she could reach, rows and rows of books she hadn't read yet, leather spines catching the light. The air faintly scented with polish and old paper.

Everything immaculate.
Everything intentional.

At the end of one long hallway, she stopped.

A door she hadn't noticed before stood closed—darker wood than the others, its brass handle dulled with age. A small plaque was mounted beside it, the engraving worn smooth enough that she couldn't quite make out the words.

She tried the handle.

Locked.

The click echoed softly down the corridor.

A ripple of discomfort passed through her. Old houses had locked rooms, she told herself. Offices. Storage. Security.

There was nothing strange about it.

Still, she memorized where it was before moving on.

Back in the guest wing, her boxes sat untouched along the walls. Boxes labeled **BOOKS** and **JOURNALS** sat unopened. She knelt and opened one, lifting out a familiar notebook—the one she'd once carried everywhere.

She flipped it open.

The words felt distant.

Like they belonged to someone else.

She set the notebook aside and told herself she'd come back to it later.

She always did.

She missed the noise of the shelter more than she expected. The interruptions. The hum of people needing something from her. She drafted a text to Tonya, fingers hovering over the screen.

Before she could send it, her phone buzzed.

Daniel: What sounds good for dinner tonight?

Eden stared at the message.

Then she deleted her draft and replied instead.

Eden: Surprise me.

It was easier that way.

That evening, Daniel returned with groceries and stories from his day. He moved through the kitchen with easy confidence, pulling her into a kiss as he passed, asking if she'd rested, if the house was settling in around her.

She nodded. Smiled. Told him it was beautiful.

Later, curled against him beneath silk sheets, Eden stared at the ceiling while the house settled around them—distant creaks, the low hush of something old and vast. She told herself this quiet was temporary.

That soon she'd find her rhythm again.

The shelter would still be there.
Tonya would still be there.

This was just a pause.

A deserved one.

As sleep pulled her under, Eden didn't notice how natural it already felt to let the days be shaped for her.

Chapter Sixteen

The house was beautiful.

That was the problem.

Eden woke each morning surrounded by quiet so complete it felt curated—sunlight filtered through tall windows, hallways polished to a shine, doors that closed softly behind her. The house didn't ask anything of her. It simply waited, patient and still, like it had been built to hold people without ever needing them back.

At first, she told herself this was what rest felt like.

She slept later. She ate when Daniel reminded her to. She stopped keeping time the way she used to—by intake forms and shift changes and the small crises that stitched her days together. In the house, time didn't lurch. It flowed.

Her week of PTO stretched into a second.

Daniel encouraged it gently, never as an order. Always as a gift. He reminded her how long she'd taken care of everyone else, how often she'd gone home with other people's pain caught in her ribs.

"Let yourself land," he told her, brushing his knuckles down her cheek as if he could smooth her nervous system the way he smoothed her hair. "You don't have to be everything all the time."

When she mentioned the shelter, he listened attentively. When she hesitated, he reassured her.

"You'll go back when you're ready," he said. "There's no rush."

It sounded supportive.

It felt supportive.

And so she didn't question how easily the days filled without it.

It wasn't that she stopped thinking about the kids. It was that thinking about them here felt like looking through thick glass—distant, muted, too sad to hold for long. In the house, sadness felt like an intrusion.

Daniel's world didn't make room for intrusion.

When he suggested she help out at his office occasionally, it felt practical rather than permanent.

"Just a few hours here and there," he said, like he was offering her something manageable. "You're already doing similar work. It keeps you close,"—his smile turned soft, intimate— "and I like knowing where you are."

The last part warmed Eden and tightened her at the same time.

Close meant wanted.

Close also meant watched.

She told herself it was romance. She told herself everyone wanted to know where the person they loved was.

She agreed.

At first, it was only a couple of days a week—answering emails, helping coordinate events, organizing schedules. The office was calm, insulated from the chaos she was used to. No emergencies. No sobbing in the hallway. No one needing more than she could give.

It felt… easy.

Eden hated how relieved she was by that.

But even that changed.

One evening, as they sat together in the great room, Daniel's tone shifted—not harsh, just serious. The change was subtle: his shoulders tightening, his jaw setting, his eyes going distant in the way they did when he was thinking in numbers and risks instead of feelings.

"There have been some threats lately," he said. "Political rivals. Nothing concrete, but enough to be careful."

Eden's stomach tightened. A cold little coil, instinctive.

"What kind of threats?" she asked.

Daniel didn't give details. He didn't need to. He spoke like a man who lived with danger as background noise and had learned not to make it dramatic.

"Enough to take seriously," he said. "Enough that I don't want you moving around the city alone. Not right now."

Eden opened her mouth.

To ask questions.

To argue.

To remind him she'd moved around the city alone for months.

But he wasn't asking. He wasn't pleading. He was stating a fact with concern wrapped around it like velvet.

"It's safer if you stay close," he added, and his hand found hers, firm and warm, as if he could anchor her with touch alone.

Eden nodded, telling herself it made sense.

He would know.

This was his world.

Later she called her mother, trying to sound casual, like she was reporting weather.

"He just wants to protect me," Eden said. "It's not safe out there, Mom."

There was a pause on the other end of the line. Eden could hear her mother breathing, slow and controlled, the way she always did when she was choosing her words carefully.

"Eden," her mother said quietly, "I understand concern. But protection shouldn't make your life smaller."

Eden closed her eyes. Irritation sparked, fast and hot. "You're overthinking."

"I'm worried," her mother replied. "You're pulling away. From your work. From your friends. From me."

Guilt bloomed in Eden's chest—familiar, heavy. The kind of guilt that felt like a leash even when no one was pulling it.

"I love him," Eden whispered. "He's different."

She needed it to be true.

Because if he wasn't different, then what was she doing? What was she choosing?

The changes didn't announce themselves.

They arrived in tone first.

Daniel's affection sharpened—still present, still warm, but edged. His touch lingered longer, his grip firmer. His patience shortened when she hesitated, like hesitation itself offended him.

One night, when she paused before agreeing to something small—an event, a schedule change—his voice dropped, low and controlled.

"Don't second-guess me," he said. "I know what I'm doing."

Eden's mouth went dry.

She told herself it was stress. Pressure. The weight of his position. She told herself powerful men carried heavy things and sometimes the weight showed at the seams.

But when he pulled her close after, it was no longer a question. It was expectation. Ownership wrapped in intimacy.

The kind of closeness that left no air between her thoughts and his.

She stopped trying to explain when something felt off.

Love, she told herself, looked different in private.

Still, there were moments—catching her reflection in a mirror, standing alone in the writing room without opening a single notebook—when she barely recognized the woman staring back.

Her shoulders were tighter.

Her smile looked practiced.

One evening, after a silence that stretched too long, Daniel softened again as if he'd felt the distance and decided to close it.

He brushed her hair back and pressed his forehead to hers.

"You're mine," he murmured. "I just want you safe."

Eden nodded, because it was easier than speaking.

Because some part of her still believed that being claimed was the same thing as being loved.

And because admitting the difference would mean admitting how far she'd already drifted.

Chapter Seventeen

Daniel's voice carried down the long hallway, low and even.

"You're not going anywhere tonight."

Eden froze.

The words didn't sound angry. That was what unsettled her most. They were measured, controlled—like a decision already made and filed away. She watched as Daniel reached the door behind her and turned the lock with a soft, decisive click.

The sound echoed.

A small sound. A domestic sound.

And yet it landed in Eden's body like a warning bell.

Her chest tightened as she pressed her palm to the cool wood, the weight of the door suddenly undeniable. The house felt different now—not just large or quiet, but sealed. Every polished surface reflected her back at herself, smaller somehow, contained.

"This is for your safety," Daniel said calmly, as if he could hear the panic blooming beneath her ribs. "I told you there were threats. I won't risk you."

Eden nodded because her throat wouldn't do anything else.

She told herself this wasn't confinement.

It was concern.

Protection.

Daniel brushed a kiss across her hair—gentle, nearly tender—and then he walked away, leaving her standing there with the lock between them like a line drawn on the floor.

Later, alone in the bedroom, Eden sat on the edge of the bed with her knees drawn to her chest. The house was too quiet. The silence thickened until her thoughts began to echo back at her.

She reached for her phone without thinking—then hesitated.

There was no one she could text without inviting questions she didn't have the strength to answer. Her mother would worry immediately. Tonya would hear the pause in her voice and push, gently but relentlessly, until Eden said aloud what she wasn't ready to admit.

And Eden wasn't ready to admit anything that would change the story.

She turned the phone over, screen-down.

It was easier not to explain.

Easier not to choose sides.

Easier to stay still.

The silence settled again, heavy and expectant.

Then the screen lit up anyway.

A message from Daniel.

Pack a bag. We leave at dawn.

Eden stared at the words.

Where?
For how long?
What kind of bag?

Practical questions lined up like soldiers in her mind—
clothes, shoes, documents, weather, medications, chargers,
everything she'd learned to list out when life was
unpredictable.

She glanced toward the closet and felt a strange, hollow jolt.

How little she actually owned here.

How much of her life was still packed into boxes she hadn't
unpacked. How much of herself was still taped shut.

Her thumb hovered over the keyboard.

She could ask.

She should ask.

Instead, she set the phone down beside her.

Questioning him would only start something—a conversation,
an explanation, the subtle shift in his tone she'd learned to
avoid. He didn't like feeling doubted. He'd made that clear
without ever saying it outright.

He wouldn't tell her to pack if he hadn't thought it through.

She told herself that.

She pulled a small suitcase from the closet and began folding—choosing safe things. Neutral things. Dresses he liked. Shoes that wouldn't slow her down. Underwear that didn't make her feel exposed. A cardigan that smelled like his laundry detergent.

She left her notebooks behind.

Her books too.

There wasn't room, she decided.

Or maybe there wasn't permission.

As the bag filled, the questions quieted.

Movement was better than waiting.

Change was better than sitting still.

By the time she zipped the suitcase shut, relief had already taken root in her chest.

She exhaled for the first time all night.

The next morning felt unreal.

Italy bloomed around her in warmth and color—terracotta walls, climbing jasmine, the distant sound of water and bells. The private villa was wrapped in soft light, fairy lights strung across stone archways like something out of a dream.

The contrast was violent.

The night before: cold lock, silent hallway, her own breath too loud.
Now: sunlight and stone and beauty arranged like forgiveness.

Daniel was different here.

Lighter. Attentive. His hand never left hers as if anchoring her to the moment. He ordered for them at cafés, led her through winding streets, pointed out history with quiet enthusiasm.

He laughed more. He touched her more gently. He looked at her like she was a miracle he'd been given.

"This is what life can be," he told her over wine. "When the noise stops."

Eden nodded, because the noise had stopped.

Even the fear quieted in a place this beautiful. In a place where everything was filtered through warmth and romance and the soft illusion that nothing bad could happen in sunlight.

At night, under a sky heavy with stars, he led her into a secluded garden. Classical music drifted through hidden speakers. Roses bloomed thick in the air, sweet enough to make Eden's head feel light.

Daniel's hand trembled when he reached into his pocket.

"My mother's ring," he said softly. "It's been in my family for generations."

He looked at her like she was something rare. Like he was certain she'd fit into the story he was offering.

"It's more than jewelry," he continued. "It's a promise. Stability. Permanence."

Both were things Eden craved so badly she could taste it.

"I don't make promises lightly," he said. "But with you… I know."

He slid the delicate gold band onto her finger. The sapphire caught the light, deep and vivid.

For a moment, the world narrowed.

The fear.

The doubt.

The locked doors.

All of it softened beneath the weight of being chosen.

"Yes," Eden whispered, tears blurring her vision. "Yes."

Daniel pulled her close, holding her like something that might slip away.

And Eden held on like he was the only thing that could keep her from falling back into loneliness.

***

Back home, the reality settled in slowly.

Eden called Tonya first, excitement trembling through her voice as she lifted her hand to the camera.

"We're engaged," she said, holding the ring up. "He asked me in Italy. It was beautiful."

Tonya's smile flickered—then faded.

"Eden," she said carefully, "I'm happy you're happy. I just… are you okay? He's changed, hasn't he?"

The question landed like an accusation.

Eden felt heat rise in her chest, defensive and sudden. "I don't want to hear this," she snapped. "Why does everyone keep looking for something wrong? Can't you just be happy for me?"

Tonya's expression tightened. "I would be, if I didn't feel like I'm losing you."

"You're not."

"You stopped coming to work," Tonya said quietly. "You loved that job. You fought to get it. You said it finally felt like you were doing something that mattered."

Eden's stomach clenched. "I took time off."

"No," Tonya replied. "You took time off, and then you didn't come back."

Eden's throat went tight. "Daniel doesn't want me commuting right now. It's not safe. There have been threats. He just wants me close."

Tonya stared at her. "Close… or contained?"

"That's not fair," Eden snapped. "He loves me. He wants what's best for me. He sees things you don't—the pressure he's under, the risks. He's protecting me."

"And what about what you want?" Tonya asked. "You used to want that work."

"I still do," Eden said quickly. Too quickly. "This is just temporary."

"Everything about this sounds temporary," Tonya said softly. "Except how much you've already given up."

"I didn't give anything up," Eden insisted. "I chose this."

There was a long pause.

Then Tonya said, "You sound like you're trying to convince yourself."

Eden's hands started to shake.

"I'm tired of being questioned," she said sharply. "I'm engaged. I'm happy. I don't need you trying to ruin this."

Tonya's eyes shone, hurt and fear tangled together. "I'm not trying to ruin it. I'm trying to make sure you don't disappear."

"I'm not disappearing," Eden said. "I'm finally happy."

She ended the call before Tonya could respond.

Her hands were shaking.

Her mother answered on the second ring.

"Mom," Eden said, breathless. "We're engaged."

Her mother exhaled slowly. "Honey… that was fast."

"Why does everyone keep saying that?" Eden demanded. "Why can't you just be happy for me?"

"I am happy if you're happy," her mother said gently. "I just don't want you shutting everyone out."

"I'm not a child," Eden snapped. "I don't need you to protect me anymore. I have Daniel."

Silence stretched between them.

"I love you," her mother said quietly.

Eden ended the call before she could say it back.

She sat alone afterward, staring at the ring on her finger as it caught the light. It felt heavy. Important. Real.

A tether.

For a while, she let herself believe in the fairy tale—in the idea that love meant rescue, that permanence meant safety, that choosing him meant she was finally choosing herself.

Because admitting otherwise would mean facing how much she'd already lost.

And she wasn't ready for that yet.

Chapter Eighteen

Morning light spilled through the tall windows of the Whitmore house, gilding the marble floors in soft gold. Eden sat at the breakfast table with both hands wrapped around a mug of coffee, the steam fogging her vision. The warmth seeped slowly into her palms, grounding in a way she'd come to rely on.

Daniel had planned the weekend, of course.

A private retreat in the countryside. His father's cabin. A celebration of their engagement. *A chance to escape the chaos*, he'd said. *To breathe.*

Her heart lifted at the thought. The anticipation carried her, light and buoyant, the way it always did when she let herself lean fully into his certainty.

Daniel entered the room with that familiar, practiced ease—suit jacket slung over one arm, tie already loosened. Power without stiffness. Control without strain. His smile warmed when it found her.

"You look beautiful," he said, leaning down to kiss the crown of her head.

The affection still caught her off guard—how quickly it settled her, how efficiently it quieted the low hum of unease that had started living in her chest. For a moment, the last few days blurred into something soft and distant.

For moments like this, she told herself, everything really *was* perfect.

This was what she had wanted.

Someone steady.
Someone who stayed.
Someone who decided.

Over the next few days, Daniel was attentive in ways that felt almost cinematic.

He brushed her hair back when it fell into her face, fingers lingering just long enough to feel intentional. He kept her hand laced with his as they sat by the fire, the crackle of logs filling the spaces where conversation wasn't needed. At night, he murmured promises into her skin—*forever, us, always*—the words settling deep and heavy, like stones dropped carefully into water.

It felt like being wrapped in something warm and impenetrable.

Safe.

And slowly—so slowly she couldn't pinpoint when it began—the questions started.

"They still don't really understand us," Daniel said one evening, swirling wine in his glass as they sat on the terrace. His tone was casual, observational. As if he were noting the weather. "Your mother. Tonya."

"They're just… worried," Eden replied.

"Of course they are," he said smoothly. "People get uncomfortable when things change." He smiled faintly. "Especially when they lose influence."

The word caught. *Influence.*

Eden paused, something flickering beneath her ribs, but he was already looking at her again—warm, reassuring, unbothered.

When she mentioned wanting them at the wedding, his expression tightened just slightly. A micro-shift she almost missed.

"I don't want anyone there who doesn't support us," he said quietly. "It's our day. We deserve peace."

She nodded, swallowing the ache that rose unexpectedly in her throat.

"They worry," he continued, softer now. "I don't blame them. They don't know what it's like to live under this kind of pressure." A beat. "I just don't want them planting doubt where it doesn't belong."

It sounded reasonable.

Who wanted tension on their wedding day?

Back home, the rhythm continued.

At first, Daniel's questions sounded like anyone else's.

"How was today?"
"Did you get any rest?"
"Did you enjoy yourself?"

Eden answered easily, without thought.

Over time, the questions grew more specific—threaded with concern.

"Who were you with?"
"Did anyone upset you?"
"How long were you gone?"

Not accusatory.
Not sharp.

Protective.

She noticed the shift only once—when she answered out of order and saw his brow crease, just slightly. The tension dissolved the moment she clarified. The moment she reassured him.

Without meaning to, she learned how to keep his expression smooth.

She began answering before he asked. Offering details preemptively. Editing stories mid-sentence so they wouldn't invite questions.

It felt like care.

It felt like consideration.

When wedding planning and the guest list came up again, he was careful—measured.

"I want this day to feel peaceful," he said. "Just people who genuinely support us."

Eden hesitated. "My mom. Tonya."

Daniel didn't argue. He didn't raise his voice. He just met her eyes, steady and calm.

"I don't want anyone there who makes you doubt yourself," he said gently. "You deserve joy without conditions."

She nodded.

The ache in her chest was easy to dismiss when wrapped in that kind of certainty.

At night, curled into his arms, Eden replayed the days and couldn't find the moment where things had changed.

Only that they had.

She answered questions before they were asked now. She avoided topics that led to tension. She leaned into the version of herself that kept everything calm.

Love feels like this, she told herself.

Considerate.
Attentive.
Involved.

And if being loved meant being known this completely—counted, remembered, protected—

Then maybe this was what love had always been meant to look like.

Chapter Nineteen

Daniel was a study in contradictions.

Some days, he was still the man she'd fallen in love with—
brushing a curl from her face with devotion, laughing softly
into her neck, speaking about their future like it was
something sacred. In those moments, Eden could almost
forget the unease humming beneath her skin.

Almost.

With the wedding only weeks away, anticipation should have
filled her days. Instead, everything felt tight. Pressurized.
Conversations that once felt effortless now carried weight,
every word measured before it left her mouth.

She wasn't sure when she'd started holding her breath.

One evening, Eden sat curled into the velvet armchair in the
sitting room, a book open on her lap but unread. Daniel paced
near the windows, his phone buzzing again and again on the
side table.

He ignored it—until the name flashed across the screen.

Her mother.

His jaw tightened instantly.

"She doesn't get it," he snapped after silencing the call. His
voice cut sharply through the room, anger no longer carefully

contained. "Neither does Tonya. They don't want us to be happy."

Eden's stomach clenched.

"That's not fair," she said softly. "They're just worried."

"They're poison," he said flatly. "They plant doubt. They undermine you. They don't understand what we have."

The word *we* hung between them, heavy and immovable.

Eden hugged her arms around herself. "I just don't understand… they should be there. At our wedding. My mom and my best friend."

Daniel turned to her slowly.

"They don't belong there," he said. "Not if they're going to bring that energy into something meant to be pure."

Pure.

The word made her feel small.

"I need them," she whispered. "They love me."

His eyes softened—not in kindness, but in calculation.

"If you want this to work," he said gently, "you have to let go of people who keep pulling you backward."

The room seemed to shrink.

For a moment, Eden felt the urge to fight—to insist, to demand space, to name the fear tightening in her chest.

But something in Daniel's expression stopped her.

Not anger.

Woundedness.

As if *she* were hurting *him*.

"I want them there," Eden said again, her heart pounding. "Please."

Daniel's gaze hardened.

"You're mine now," he said quietly. "This is our life. Our rules."

His hand closed around her arm.

Not violent.
Not sudden.

But firm enough that her breath caught instantly.

"Daniel," she said, trying to pull back. "Please."

His fingers tightened.

"I didn't mean to hurt you," he said quickly, loosening his grip as if startled by his own strength. "You just scared me. I thought I was losing you."

The words rearranged everything.

She nodded, shallow breaths scraping her lungs. "I'm sorry."

The apology tasted wrong.

Later, alone in the bathroom, Eden stared at her reflection under the harsh light. Just beneath her sleeve, a bruise bloomed—faint, but unmistakable.

Her stomach dropped.

Memories surged unbidden—Ryan's voice, sharp with accusation. Doors slammed. Love rationed. Affection earned.

She pressed her fingers to the mark, pulse racing.

This isn't the same, she told herself.
Daniel loves me.
He didn't mean it.

But that night, lying beside him, sleep refused to come.

Every time he shifted, her body tensed.
Every time his arm draped across her waist, she froze—
waiting.

For the first time, the truth surfaced unbidden and terrifying:

Love shouldn't make you afraid.

The thought cracked something open inside her.

And she knew—even as she pressed closer to him, even as she told herself everything was fine—that something precious had already been broken.

Chapter Twenty

Eden stood alone while the house prepared itself around her.

Voices drifted down distant hallways—low, brisk, practiced. Doors opened and closed with soft, obedient clicks. Somewhere, flowers were being arranged and glasses polished and music tuned. The Whitmore house hummed with purpose, every inch of it aware that today mattered.

She barely breathed as she stepped into the dress.

The silk slid over her skin, cool and unforgiving, settling into place like it knew exactly where it belonged. Ivory and lace, pearls stitched so delicately they looked like they might disappear if she moved too fast. The fabric hugged her ribs, the weight unfamiliar—grounding and constricting all at once.

It was a beautiful cage.

She lifted her chin and met her reflection.

The woman staring back was flawless. Composed. Luminous. Unmistakably a bride.

She didn't recognize herself.

The room smelled of gardenias and jasmine, sweet enough to overwhelm. Her hair was pinned back with diamond-studded clips, loose curls framing her face just enough to soften the severity of the look. The makeup was understated—rose-tinted cheeks, soft lips—meant to enhance what was already there, not distract from it.

Everything about her had been chosen carefully.

Including this.

The dress fit her like a promise she didn't remember making. Chantilly lace traced the neckline, dipping just enough to be elegant, not inviting. The long sleeves were sheer, embroidered with fine detail that looked fragile, almost breakable. The skirt fell around her in quiet waves, whispering as she moved.

A hollow ache settled beneath her ribs—sharp and persistent, like her body was trying to tell her something her mind refused to hear.

Daniel appeared in the doorway without knocking.

He looked immaculate in his black tuxedo, every line crisp, every detail deliberate. His dark hair was slicked back, his expression warm and assured—the version of him the world trusted without question.

"You're breathtaking," he said, stepping closer. His voice was low, velvet-soft, threaded with something Eden couldn't quite name.

She managed a faint smile but didn't meet his eyes. "Isn't it considered bad luck to see the bride before the wedding?"

His mouth curved, amused. "Well then I guess it's a good thing I make my own luck, isn't it?"

His hand brushed hers, fingers lingering, not quite a caress and not quite a claim—somewhere in between.

"Smile," he murmured, voice dropping as if the room itself might betray them. "This is supposed to be the happiest day of your life."

Eden's throat tightened.

"And no one is here to ruin it," he added, gentle as a lullaby. His thumb pressed lightly over her knuckles. "You don't need anyone else here."

Her breath caught.

"It's just us," he murmured. "That's all that matters."

The guest list reflected that sentiment perfectly.

No mother.
No Tonya.
No familiar faces from the shelter or her former life.

Just a carefully curated collection of political allies, donors, and socialites—people Daniel trusted to smile at the right moments and ask no personal questions. He'd framed it as simplicity. Elegance. Intimacy.

Standing there, Eden felt the sharp sting of loneliness cut through the silk and lace.

The ceremony unfolded beneath an arch of white orchids and pale pink peonies, petals soft and velvety under the glow of candlelight. Ivy climbed the marble columns, fairy lights woven through it like constellations meant to distract from the enormity of the space.

Each step down the aisle felt heavier than the last.

Not because she didn't love him.

Because love shouldn't feel like walking deeper into a room that had already been locked.

The officiant's voice echoed gently through the hall—words about love and unity and devotion drifting past Eden like something meant for someone else. She kept her smile in place, kept her shoulders back, kept her breathing shallow so the bodice didn't tighten too much around her ribs.

Daniel took her hands.

His grip was steady. Certain. Just tight enough to remind her she was there because he was allowing it.

When he spoke her name, the sound of it was smooth and practiced—perfect for the room, perfect for the cameras, perfect for the story.

"Eden," he said, "today I promise to be your partner, your protector, and your home. Through every season, every storm, I will be yours—and you will be mine."

The phrasing landed heavy in her chest.

Protector. Home. Mine.

When he slid the ring onto her finger—a slender band of platinum crowned with a flawless diamond—the world tilted.

The stone caught the light, brilliant and blinding, anchoring her in place.

"I do," she whispered.

The words felt like both surrender and plea.

Applause erupted. Glasses clinked. The moment sealed itself around her.

At the reception, the grand ballroom glittered beneath crystal chandeliers, light scattering across polished parquet floors. Tables draped in ivory silk overflowed with peonies, hydrangeas, and gardenias in soft shades of blush and cream. A string quartet played, music swelling and receding like a tide Eden couldn't quite keep up with.

Daniel never let go of her hand.

When he led her onto the dance floor, his palm settled firmly at her waist, fingers pressing just a bit too hard. She didn't pull away. She didn't want anyone watching to see even the hint of hesitation.

The waltz carried them in slow circles while eyes watched, approving and envious.

"Now," he whispered into her hair, breath warm against her skin, "we can really start our life."

Her throat tightened.

She caught her reflection in a gilded mirror as they moved— eyes wide, smile carefully practiced. She looked radiant. Adored. Untouchable.

Already bound.

This was supposed to be the happiest day of her life.

But as the music swelled and the room celebrated, something small and cold settled deep inside her—a whisper she didn't yet have the courage to listen to.

She wasn't just married.

She was his.

Chapter Twenty-One

The door closed behind her with a soft click.

The sound echoed anyway.

Eden stood in the center of the honeymoon suite, surrounded by excess so carefully arranged it felt theatrical. Candlelight flickered along the walls. Rose petals scattered the bed in deliberate patterns. Champagne chilled in silver. Beyond the open balcony doors, the ocean breathed—steady, endless, indifferent.

This was supposed to be the beginning.

Instead, her body tightened with instinctive dread.

She could feel it before she could explain it—the way her shoulders rose, the way her hands went cold, the way her breath grew shallow like the room didn't have enough air. She told herself it was nerves. That every bride felt strange in a new place, in a new life, in a dress that still seemed to hold the day inside its seams.

Behind her, Daniel moved without a word.

Fabric shifted. The quiet removal of his jacket. The soft clink of cufflinks placed carefully on a glass table.

When Eden turned, she saw it immediately—something missing in his eyes.

It was subtle. Almost deniable. But she felt it the way she felt storms coming: pressure changing, air tightening, the warmth leaving without warning.

The careful version of him—the one who smiled for crowds, who kissed her forehead, who spoke like tenderness was effortless—was gone.

He didn't look at her like a husband should.

He looked at her like someone inspecting something newly acquired.

"Take off the dress," he said.

No awe. No tenderness. No hesitation.

Just expectation.

Eden's fingers tightened reflexively at her sides, gathering silk like it could shield her. The fabric suddenly felt too heavy, too loud, whispering every time she moved.

"Daniel—" Her voice wavered, thin and unfamiliar.

His gaze didn't soften.

"I won't repeat myself," he said, still calm. That was the most frightening part—how even his cruelty arrived controlled, like it belonged to him the way everything else did. "You're my wife now."

A beat of silence passed, and Eden felt the room tilt.

Not physically.

Internally.

Like something inside her had been holding itself upright with hope, and the hope had been kicked out from underneath it.

She tried again—carefully, gently, the way you spoke to people who had power.

"This isn't… what you said," she managed.

Daniel stepped closer.

Close enough that she could smell his cologne, the faint bite of whiskey, the salt air drifting in through the balcony doors— normal scents in a moment that suddenly wasn't normal at all.

His hand came up—not tender.

Not asking.

Eden flinched before she could stop herself, and she hated the involuntary betrayal of her body. Her breath caught, sharp as a swallow of cold water.

Daniel noticed.

His mouth curved, not quite a smile.

"Don't do that," he said softly. "Don't act like I'm the problem."

The sentence was a trap disguised as reassurance.

Eden's throat tightened.

She stood very still, because stillness had always been safest.

Her hands moved slowly to the zipper, the buttons, the lace—fingers clumsy, trembling. The dress resisted like it was reluctant to leave her, like even the fabric knew what it meant to come off.

When the final clasp gave way, the sound was small.

But the humiliation was enormous.

The dress slid, pooling at her feet like something dead.

Eden stared down at it and felt a strange, floating disconnect—as if she were watching this happen to someone else. As if the part of her that could scream had already fled.

Daniel said something then—her name, maybe.

Or a command.

Or both.

The candles blurred. The room stretched and warped, pulling away from her as if she were sinking underwater. She could feel the mattress. The edge of the bed against the backs of her knees. The cool air on her skin.

She could feel her heart hammering like it was trying to break through her ribs and run.

And then time lost its shape.

Not because it stopped.

Because her mind refused to stay present for it.

There were sounds—the ocean, the rustle of sheets, the low
cadence of Daniel's voice. There was the sick, dissociative
calm that sometimes arrives when terror has nowhere else to
go. There was the unbearable awareness of being *overruled*,
of having her body turned into something she didn't fully
inhabit.

Eden's thoughts fractured into useless fragments:

This can't be real.
This is stress.
He loves me.
He said—
He said—

She couldn't find the end of the sentence.

When it was over, there was no softness.

No apology.

No acknowledgment that anything had happened at all.

Daniel rose and began reassembling himself with meticulous
care—straightening his shirt, adjusting his watch, the same
composed competence he wore in public. He looked cleanly
separated from what he'd just done, as if he could step out of
one version of himself and into another without a seam
showing.

Eden remained where she was, not moving, not breathing
correctly, the room too bright and too dark at once.

She didn't know how long it took before she found her voice.

When it came, it was broken. Barely there.

"Why?" she whispered.

Daniel paused at the doorway and glanced back at her like she
was an afterthought. Like she was something he'd already
finished with.

His expression was almost bored.

"Because I don't have to pretend anymore," he said.

Then he stepped into the adjoining room.

The door closed.

A metallic sound followed.

Locked.

Eden lay there, surrounded by the ruins of a night that was
supposed to mean something. Silk discarded on the floor.
Lace twisted. Candle flames guttering low, their light
flickering like it couldn't bear to stay.

Outside, the ocean still roared—indifferent, endless.

No music.

No love.

No beginning.

Only the truth, finally unmasked:

She was alone.

And she was no longer free.

Chapter Twenty-Two

Time no longer moved the way Eden remembered.

It folded in on itself, days collapsing into one another until she couldn't tell where one ended and the next began. Weeks passed. Maybe months. She stopped trying to count after realizing it didn't matter.

The seasons changed without her.

She knew only because the clothes Daniel laid out for her shifted—heavier fabrics in winter, lighter ones in spring. Long sleeves, always. High necklines. Shoes chosen not for comfort but for appearance. Each morning, the outfit waited on the bed like a decision already made.

She learned quickly that hesitation counted as disobedience.

At events, she was perfect.

She stood at his side on red carpets, fingers curled delicately around his arm. She smiled for cameras, laughed at the right moments, nodded when donors spoke. When photographers caught her glancing at him, it was with admiration carefully calibrated—not too much, not too little.

The mayor's wife.

Graceful.
Devoted.
Untouchable.

At home, the performance ended.

Daniel never raised his voice. He didn't slam doors or break things. His anger was precise, controlled, delivered in the same calm tone he used in press conferences.

That made it worse.

He hurt her in ways that could be hidden. He chose locations with care. He marked her where silk and tailoring would cover. And when she stood in front of the vanity mirror afterward, he stood behind her, correcting.

"Higher," he would murmur, guiding her wrist. "You missed the edge of that one."

She learned not to flinch when his fingers brushed her jaw.

He would smile at their reflection as if they were sharing a private joke.

Once—just once—she tried to resist.

She didn't say no. She didn't scream or fight. She only tensed, leaning away when his hand reached for her.

The sound came before the pain.

She didn't fall until after.

The next morning, a velvet box waited on her pillow. Inside, a necklace—diamonds, cold and brilliant.

"For the cameras," he said, already adjusting his cufflinks.

She wore it.

Inside, she was disappearing.

She tried sometimes to remember who she'd been before him.

The girl who loved old books and peach tea.
Who wrote late into the night just to see what her thoughts
looked like on paper.
Who believed in quiet mornings and bare feet and choosing
her own life.

That girl felt like a story she'd read once. A character whose
name she could no longer recall.

There were days Daniel locked her inside the house without
explanation.

Days he didn't come home at all.

And then there were the rules.

They weren't written. They didn't need to be.

She learned them through repetition.

Don't leave dishes in the sink.
Don't look tired.
Don't speak too long to other men.
Don't draw attention.
Don't make him uncomfortable.

When she failed, the punishment was immediate.

"You think anyone would believe you?" he asked one night,
fingers tight around her jaw, thumb pressing into the bruise

blooming beneath her skin. "They'd say you cracked under pressure. That the spotlight broke you."

Her breath shook as she stared at him.

Then his voice softened.

"Do you know what they said about Claire?"

Her body went rigid.

He smiled.

"Car accident," he continued lightly. "Slick roads. Very tragic. I gave a beautiful eulogy."

The words barely made it past her lips. "You killed her."

He leaned in, lips brushing her ear.

"I solved a problem."

Her blood turned to ice.

"I will not let you become one," he said calmly. "And if you ever try to make me look like a monster to those people out there—" he gestured toward the city beyond the window, "— I'll make sure you're remembered the same way."

A pause.

"A tragedy," he finished. "A footnote."

He kissed her cheek.

Then he left her standing alone, makeup smeared, hands shaking.

Weeks passed.

She learned not to cry when it hurt.
She learned to wear long sleeves in summer.
She learned how to smile without her eyes.

Most of all, she learned the most important rule of all:

Never give him a reason.

Still, there were moments—rare and dangerous—when her thoughts drifted to the locked door down the hall. The one he disappeared behind on nights he didn't touch her. The one she was forbidden to approach.

Every time she passed it, her skin prickled with dread.

She didn't know what was inside.

She only knew it wasn't meant for her to see.

And she knew better than to ask.

Chapter Twenty-Three

The gala blurred together.

Crystal chandeliers. Piano music. Silk and diamonds and carefully curated smiles. Eden wore the blue gown Daniel had chosen, the fabric clinging in all the right places. Her arms were bare—bruises hidden beneath layers of airbrushed foundation applied with clinical precision.

She stayed close to him.

Always close.

She hadn't eaten all day. At lunch, he'd glanced at her plate and said she looked bloated. Told her to tighten up before tonight. The champagne hit her too fast, warmth spreading through her limbs, dulling the edges just enough to make everything feel slightly unreal.

It happened quickly.

She was returning from the restroom when she lost sight of Daniel in the crowd. A man stopped her—young, polite, forgettable. A senator's aide. He complimented her dress.

She smiled. Said thank you.

When he offered to walk her back to her husband, she laughed once—a soft, reflexive sound meant to smooth the moment over.

A camera flashed.

Daniel didn't say a word on the drive home.

His jaw stayed tight, fingers rigid around the steering wheel. Eden kept her hands folded in her lap, spine straight, breathing shallow. She knew better than to apologize first. Apologies were admissions. Admissions invited consequences.

At the house, he didn't take her upstairs.

He led her down the long hallway instead—past rooms she'd learned not to look at—to the door at the very end.

The locked one.

Tonight, it stood open.

"Inside," he said.

She hesitated.

His voice lowered. "Now."

She stepped through.

The room was nothing like the rest of the house.

No windows. No marble. Cold stone and concrete. The air smelled sharp—antiseptic and metal. The walls absorbed sound, swallowing her footsteps whole. In the center of the room sat a chair, bolted to the floor, leather worn dark with age.

Her heart began to hammer violently.

"What is this?" she whispered.

Daniel closed the door behind them. The lock engaged with a heavy, final sound.

"My first wife," he said calmly, circling her, "had trouble remembering her place too."

Eden froze.

"I tried to be patient with you," he continued. "Tried to protect you from yourself. But you embarrassed me tonight."

"I didn't—"

The interruption came swift and stunning. Not loud. Not theatrical.

The blow came without warning.

Enough.

Her vision flared white. Her breath left her body in a sharp, involuntary sound as she stumbled back, the wall biting cold against her shoulder blades.

"You laughed," he said evenly. "At another man."

She shook her head, words tangled in terror.

"I wasn't—please—"

"I kept this room from you," Daniel continued, almost conversational. "Because I believed you might be different."

He gestured toward the chair.

He didn't raise his voice.

He didn't need to.

It wasn't dramatic.

It wasn't angry.

It was administrative—like assigning her a seat.

Eden didn't move.

Her legs locked. Her body refused the instruction the way it might refuse to step off a cliff.

Daniel waited.

That, more than anything, terrified her.

He didn't rush. Didn't threaten. Didn't repeat himself.

He simply watched her, eyes cool and assessing, as if noting a delay in compliance.

"I don't enjoy repeating myself," he said.

When he moved, it was efficient. Impersonal. A hand at her elbow—not rough enough to leave marks, not gentle enough to be mistaken for care. The chair waited in the center of the room, already prepared.

Leather restraints. Positioned with intention.

Understanding arrived too late.

"Please," she whispered.

Daniel sighed faintly. "You're going to make this harder than it needs to be."

He removed obstacles before he removed dignity.

Her clothes were not torn. That would have implied urgency. Instead, they were stripped away with methodical precision, each piece taken like a privilege being revoked. He didn't look at her body with desire. He looked at it like it was territory.

Exposure isn't about intimacy, it is about ownership.

What followed wasn't chaos.

It was procedure.

The lights hummed overhead—too bright, too close. Eden focused on the smallest things because it was the only way to survive the moment without shattering.

The crack in the wall behind him.
The smell of metal and leather.
The sound of her own breathing—ragged, uneven, hers.

Time stopped behaving normally.

Her body remained present while her mind withdrew, slipping somewhere unreachable, somewhere untouched. Pain blurred into abstraction. Sensation fractured into pieces she refused to assemble.

At some point, her head fell forward.

She wasn't sure how long passed before she felt the absence of pressure. The return of air. The hollow quiet that follows something irreversible.

Daniel straightened, adjusting his cuffs like he was finishing a negotiation.

He crouched in front of her.

His face was composed. Calm. Almost kind.

"If you ever humiliate me again," he said quietly, "there won't be a body for anyone to misunderstand."

His fingers brushed her cheek.

The touch was intimate. Casual. Disgustingly gentle.

"Do you understand?"

Her nod was barely perceptible.

Once.

Satisfied, he pressed a kiss to her forehead—paternal, claiming, obscene—and stood.

The lights stayed on.

The door locked.

Eden was left alone, restrained, staring at the blank wall ahead of her.

Her body hurt.

Her mind felt scattered, raw, stripped of illusion.

But beneath the fear—beneath the numbness—something else began to take shape.

Not a scream.

Not tears.

A decision.

Chapter Twenty-Four

The days did not announce themselves.

They arrived quietly, one after another, until Eden stopped measuring them at all.

She woke before dawn—not because she wanted to, but because the house did. Engines hummed beneath the estate, low and constant, like something breathing underground. Doors opened somewhere far away. Footsteps passed the hallway outside her room, soft and purposeful. Voices murmured—male, unfamiliar, clipped.

Daniel was gone.

He had kissed her temple before leaving, already dressed, already distant.
Back late, he had said. Be good.

The words lingered.

She lay still until the sounds faded, then slipped from the bed and padded barefoot to the door. It was unlocked today.

That alone made her stomach tighten.

The hallway felt different this early. Less ornamental. Less polite. She followed the noise—not down the main stairs (she knew better than that), but through the service corridor she had learned to use when she wasn't meant to be seen.

The walls here were plain. The floors colder. The air smelled faintly of disinfectant.

It led to a door she had never noticed before.

It stood ajar.

Inside, the room was small and windowless. A desk. Two chairs. A bank of monitors mounted along one wall.

She froze.

The screens showed different angles of the house—hallways, stairwells, exterior gates. And then—

A room she recognized.

Cold cement. No windows. The chair.

Her chest tightened as she realized there wasn't just one feed.

There were multiple.

Each showing a different room.

Each nearly identical.

Eden backed away slowly, bile rising in her throat.

She bumped into someone.

A woman stood behind her—young, maybe early twenties. Dark hair pulled back tight. Plain black dress. No jewelry. No phone.

Staff, Eden thought automatically.

But the woman's eyes flicked to the screens and then away, quick and practiced. Her expression was closed, hollowed out.

"You shouldn't be here," she said quietly.

"I— I got lost," Eden whispered.

The woman's gaze dropped to the ring on Eden's finger. Something like recognition—or pity—flickered across her face before disappearing.

"Go back to your room," she said. "Before someone notices."

Eden hesitated. "What… what is this place?"

The woman's jaw tightened.

"It's not for questions," she said. Then, softer, "And it's not just for you."

Footsteps echoed from the hall.

The woman stepped back instantly, head lowered.

Eden retreated, heart pounding, and didn't stop until she had locked herself inside her bedroom again. She pressed her back to the door, breath shaking.

Not just for you.

The words circled endlessly.

Later that afternoon, Daniel returned.

He was in a good mood.

He brought her a gift—a bracelet this time, thin gold, delicate. He clasped it around her wrist himself, thumb brushing her pulse.

"You've been quiet today," he said mildly.

She forced a smile. "Just tired."

He studied her for a moment too long, then nodded. "We're hosting tonight. Small gathering. Friends."

Friends.

She watched staff move through the house—not the usual ones. Different faces. Silent. Efficient. Avoiding eye contact.

At dusk, cars arrived.

Black. Tinted. Unmarked.

Men stepped out. Well dressed. Confident. Laughing.

They didn't look like politicians.

Daniel greeted them like brothers.

Eden stood at his side, smiling, arm looped through his, the perfect wife.

She noticed things now that she hadn't before.

The way certain doors stayed locked.
The way some women were guided, not invited.
The way no one ever used last names.

One man's gaze lingered on her a second too long.

Daniel's hand tightened at her waist.

"She's not available," he said pleasantly.

The man chuckled. "Yet."

Daniel smiled back. "Enjoy the evening."

Later, as music drifted through the house and glasses clinked, Eden slipped away to the restroom. She locked the door and stared at herself in the mirror.

Her reflection looked composed. Elegant.

Her eyes looked haunted.

This wasn't just about her.

It never had been.

And for the first time since the honeymoon suite, something cut through the fear—sharp and electric.

Not hope.

Understanding.

Daniel didn't hurt because he could.

He hurt because it was organized.

Because there were rules.
Roles.
Rooms.

And she was just one piece of something much larger.

When she returned to the party, Daniel caught her gaze across the room and smiled—slow, satisfied.

As if he knew.

As if he had been waiting for her to figure it out.

Chapter Twenty-Five

Three months had passed since the locked room.

Since her body had stopped fully healing between bruises. Since pain no longer arrived as a single event but as a constant undertone—something that lived beneath her skin, flaring when she moved the wrong way or breathed too deeply. Since her voice had narrowed into a small, reliable set of phrases she could deploy without thinking.

"Yes, Daniel."
"Of course."
"I'm sorry."

She said them automatically now, the way one recited a prayer long after faith had faded—not because she believed in the words, but because the ritual itself kept her safe.

Daniel allowed her to leave the house again, but only selectively. Strategically. Only when her presence benefited him. Fundraisers. Galas. Political rallies where her image mattered more than her silence. Where cameras could catch her at the right angle, smiling softly, arm looped through his, the picture of devotion.

"Damage control," he called it, once, without irony.

Eden called it survival.

Her face was always perfect. Her arms always covered. Her posture always composed. At home, the rules were absolute. Silence. Submission. Schedule. The house functioned like a living thing now—security systems humming invisibly through the walls, cameras lining every hallway, locks sealing every door. Daniel controlled everything: her phone, her laptop, the security feeds she was never meant to see. Even messages intended for her mother had once passed through him, screened and filtered, until he decided she no longer needed that distraction.

She hadn't spoken to Tonya since before the wedding.

"She was a bad influence," Daniel had said easily one night, adjusting his cufflinks in the mirror. "Always filling your head with nonsense."

Once, almost casually, he had mentioned the shelter—how funding could disappear overnight if Tonya became a problem. He said it like a fact, not a threat. But Eden understood the difference.

Daniel believed people disappeared quietly.

Tonya did not.

So Eden waited.

She watched patterns the way she once watched troubled kids at the shelter—quietly, patiently, cataloging what others overlooked. She learned routines. Counted seconds between glances. Noted which guards lingered and which drifted. Which cameras swiveled automatically and which relied on manual control. Which doors locked on timers and which depended on human habit.

She practiced looking empty while staying alert.

And she planned.

The donor meet-and-greet was held at the city library, a building designed to impress without feeling intimate. Marble floors reflected light too cleanly. High ceilings carried sound farther than expected, making even quiet conversations feel exposed. It was the kind of place where people felt watched even when they weren't.

Wine flowed freely. Cameras flashed, though not with the same intensity as before. Less press. More staff. More people who blended easily into the background.

Eden stayed glued to Daniel's side, her hand looped obediently through his arm, her smile precise and practiced. She laughed when he laughed. Nodded when he spoke. Played the role perfectly, down to the tilt of her head and the softness of her gaze.

Until she saw it.

A junior campaign staffer—a woman named Riley, barely out of college—set her phone down on the counter while pouring herself a glass of wine. She turned away for only a moment, distracted by someone calling her name.

That was all it took.

Eden didn't hesitate. She stepped away—one stride, then another—and slipped the phone into her clutch with practiced ease. Her heart slammed violently against her ribs, but her face never changed. She walked calmly down the hall, heels clicking at an unremarkable pace, and pushed into the nearest restroom.

She locked the door behind her.

Only then did her body react.

Her hands shook so hard she nearly dropped the phone. Her breath came shallow and sharp, each inhale scraping against her lungs. She pressed her palms to the counter, staring at her reflection until the room steadied enough for her to move.

She typed the number from memory.

Tonya answered on the second ring.

"Its me." Eden said quietly

"…Eden?"

"Don't say my name," Eden whispered. Her voice fractured despite her effort to keep it steady. "I only have a minute. I need help. Please. I can't—I don't know how much longer I can—"

"Okay," Tonya said instantly. All humor gone. All sharpness focused. "I've got you. Breathe. Listen to me."

Eden pressed her forehead to the cool mirror, eyes squeezed shut.

"You need to call someone," Tonya continued. "Her name is Alice."

Eden's breath stuttered.

"She's been watching. Waiting. She doesn't move unless the timing is right—and you just made it right."

The words settled differently than reassurance. Not comfort. Recognition.

"She'll believe me?" Eden asked, barely audible.

Tonya didn't hesitate. "She already does."

Something inside Eden cracked open—not relief, not hope, but understanding. This hadn't begun with her. She wasn't alone in it, not the way Daniel had made her believe.

Tonya rattled off the number.

Eden didn't write it down. She memorized it, burning it into her mind the way she once memorized emergency protocols and crisis scripts—something you carried with you because you might not get another chance.

Footsteps echoed outside the restroom door.

"I love you," Tonya said quickly.

"I know," Eden whispered.

She ended the call, deleted the number, and dropped the phone into the trash. She washed her hands carefully. Adjusted her lipstick. Smoothed her dress.

When she stepped back into the hall, she looked exactly as she should.

Daniel was waiting by the bar.

His gaze swept over her—not affectionate, not curious. Assessing.

"You were gone a while," he said.

"Restroom line," Eden replied smoothly. "Long."

His jaw tightened. For a moment, she thought he would press.

He didn't.

Later that night, he pressed her into the mattress and called her his perfect little puppet.

Eden said all the right things. Made the right sounds. Kissed him like she meant it.

But inside her head, she repeated the number.

Over and over.

Like a spell.

Like a promise.

Like a door that finally—finally—had a way out.

Chapter Twenty-Six

The invitation arrived on thick black cardstock, heavier than it needed to be, sealed in wax with a gold-embossed emblem Eden didn't recognize. Daniel slid it across the breakfast table without looking up from his espresso, the porcelain cup steady in his hand, his movements already finished with her before she'd had a chance to speak.

"You'll work the party," he said.

She blinked, the word catching. "Work?"

"You'll serve," he clarified, tone flat, dismissive. "Smile. Stay quiet." He took a sip, then added, as if it were an afterthought, "And you'll wear what I give you."

Eden didn't argue. By now, she understood the cost of hesitation.

The stylist arrived that afternoon, brisk and impersonal, eyes skimming over Eden the way someone assessed inventory rather than a person. She deposited a garment bag on the bed, murmured nothing, and left without explanation. Inside was a dress that barely qualified as clothing—sheer fabric, delicate straps, cut to expose rather than adorn. Eden's hands shook as she touched it, the material sliding too easily beneath her fingers. When she hesitated, standing frozen beside the bed, the stylist paused in the doorway long enough to say, "This isn't optional," before disappearing down the hall.

Eden dressed in silence.

The event wasn't held in the house. It was held beneath it.

They passed locked doors she had never been allowed near, corridors that smelled faintly of antiseptic rather than polish. An elevator she hadn't known existed descended far longer than felt reasonable, the hum of machinery loud in the enclosed space. Two guards stood watch when the doors opened, faces blank, hands resting casually near concealed weapons, as if violence were simply another tool they carried.

The room beyond felt unreal. White marble floors veined in gold reflected the glow of chandeliers suspended too low to be accidental. Classical music drifted through the air, elegant and deliberate, smoothing the edges of something sharp beneath it. Guests moved easily through the space in tailored suits and couture gowns, champagne flutes lifted in casual celebration.

She recognized some of them. A foreign dignitary. A tech mogul. A sitting U.S. senator.

At the center of it all stood Daniel—radiant, relaxed, entirely at ease in a world that had been built to accommodate him.

"This is where you stay," he told her, guiding her to a position near the bar with a hand at her elbow. "You're decoration. Nothing more."

Then he left her there.

Time lost its shape after that. Men watched her without speaking, their gazes lingering just long enough to register intent before sliding away. Conversations lowered when she passed, voices smoothing themselves into something careful. A few looks lingered longer than they should have, appraising rather than admiring. Eden kept her eyes down, her hands steady on the tray she carried, every movement measured.

At one point, a man murmured something to Daniel— something Eden didn't need to hear clearly to understand. Daniel's response was casual, dismissive.

"Not tonight."

Laughter followed, low and knowing. Eden's fingers tightened around the tray until the edges bit into her palms.

Later, a woman with too-bright eyes told her she was needed downstairs to help "reset." Eden followed without question. The air changed as they descended—colder, cleaner, stripped of warmth. The walls turned to glass and steel. The lighting shifted from flattering to clinical.

The rooms stopped her cold.

They were enclosed. Monitored. Identical. Beds made with surgical precision. Chairs positioned deliberately in the center of each space. And inside them were girls. Young women. Some stared at nothing, faces emptied of expression. Some trembled. Some were so still they barely seemed alive. They wore dresses chosen for access rather than comfort. Each wrist bore a band—tagged, numbered, cataloged. Countries listed.

Along one wall, monitors displayed every room. Along another, rows of velvet chairs faced a small raised platform.

Understanding hit her in a wave so violent she nearly stumbled. Eden backed away before anyone noticed her reaction, before her face betrayed what her body already knew.

That night, Daniel was pleased—at first. He told her she had looked beautiful. That she had carried herself perfectly. That she had understood what was required of her. His praise came quiet and proprietary, delivered like a performance review she had passed.

"You did well," he said, brushing his thumb along her jaw. "You represented me exactly the way I needed you to."

Relief loosened something in her chest. It didn't last.

Later, when the house had gone quiet and the guests were gone, his movements sharpened. The affection fell away.

"They looked at you," he said suddenly.

Eden stiffened.

"At the bar. When you walked past," he continued, voice calm but coiled tight beneath the surface. "They asked about you."

She kept her eyes down. "I didn't say anything."

"That's not the point," he snapped. "You made them think they could."

The hypocrisy was dizzying. He had chosen the dress. He had placed her there. He had allowed the stares. But his anger needed somewhere to land.

It always did.

When it was over, Eden curled inward, silent, waiting for the aftermath to pass. She didn't fight anymore. She survived.

Much later, when his breathing finally evened out, she lay awake in the dark. Her body ached, but her mind was painfully clear. She saw the glass rooms again. The numbered bands. The empty eyes. She understood now—fully, finally.

If she stayed, she wouldn't be spared. She wouldn't be special. She would be folded into the system the same way the others were—cataloged, controlled, erased.

The number returned to her mind, sharp and insistent. Not as a plan. As a lifeline.

For the first time since the wedding, Eden allowed herself one dangerous truth: she didn't need to save anyone yet.

She needed to get out.

<h1 style="text-align:center">Chapter Twenty-Seven</h1>

Eden waited until his breathing slowed, until the rise and fall of his chest evened out and the bruises along her ribs throbbed in time with the steady ticking of the antique clock on the dresser. She waited until she was absolutely certain he was asleep.

Only then did she move.

She slipped from the bed with painstaking care, muscles protesting as her feet touched the cold floor. Her lip still burned. Her cheek was swollen. The metallic taste of blood lingered at the back of her throat. Pain radiated through her body, sharp and insistent—but her mind was clear in a way it hadn't been in months. Focused.

She crossed the room barefoot, avoiding the places she knew creaked, moving through the space like a guest in her own life. The closet door opened soundlessly. Behind the rows of tailored suits and pressed shirts sat the safe.

She knew the code.

She had known it for months, memorized during one of his rare careless moments, when whiskey had loosened his tongue and arrogance had made him sloppy.

5–8–2–4.

The keypad emitted a soft beep. The door clicked open.

Her breath stuttered, but she didn't stop. Not now.

She retrieved the phone, hands trembling just enough that she had to brace herself against the wall. She stared at it for one second—feeling the weight of it, the danger—then dialed.

The line rang. Once. Twice. Three times.

A voice answered, low and cautious.

"…Hello?"

Eden swallowed hard. "Alice?"

There was a pause, then a calm reply. "Yes."

"My name is Eden," she whispered. "Tonya gave me your number. She said… she said you help people disappear."

"I know who you are," Alice said quietly. "I've been waiting for this call."

Something inside Eden finally gave way. She pressed her hand over her mouth as her breath broke free, shaking despite her effort to stay silent.

"I need out," she whispered. "This time… I'm ready."

Alice didn't ask questions. She gave her a date, a location, a time. She told her not to bring anything that tied her to him. No phone. No jewelry. No identification.

"You get one chance," Alice warned. "If he realizes what you're doing—"

"I know," Eden said, steadier than she expected.

When the call ended, Eden stood there a moment longer, heart
pounding so loudly she feared it would wake him. She
replaced the phone. Closed the safe. Turned the dial until it
locked.

Then she returned to the bed, slipping beneath the covers
without disturbing him.

Sleep never came.

She lay there, staring at the thin bands of light creeping
through the blinds, listening to the house wake itself around
her.

For once, the future didn't feel like a wall closing in.

It felt like a narrow opening.

Dangerous. Uncertain. Real.

For the first time in a very long time, Eden didn't feel
helpless.

She felt ready.

Chapter Twenty-Eight

She counted the days.

Three.

That was all Alice had given her. Three days to disappear without leaving a shadow behind. Three days to undo a life that had taken months to cage her.

By morning, she had a plan.

It was small. Quiet. Built on the same instinct that had kept her alive this long. Nothing abrupt. Nothing reckless. Nothing that would make him suspicious. Survival had taught her that sudden movement was dangerous. Careful erosion worked better.

She started with the pills.

The painkillers he kept her on — *for your nerves*, he'd said, sliding them into her palm like a kindness — were the first to go. One at a time. Spaced over hours. Flushed down the toilet when he was distracted, when he was asleep, when he paced the study barking orders into his phone at donors and campaign managers and men who never saw the bruises beneath her sleeves.

She needed her mind clear.

She needed to feel everything.

The fog lifted slowly, reluctantly. Pain surged back in waves — ribs, jaw, the deep ache that never fully left her body — but clarity came with it. Memory sharpened. Fear did too. But fear was useful now. Fear kept her awake. Fear reminded her what was at stake.

She began taking cash.

A five here. A ten there. From his wallet. From coat pockets he never checked because he had never needed to. She hid the bills inside a tampon box beneath the bathroom sink.

He had never looked there.

Her bruises faded from purple to yellow. Her split lip scabbed over. She let herself stand in front of the mirror longer than usual, cataloging what still belonged to her. What he had not yet taken. Her eyes. Her breath. Her resolve.

On the second day, she packed a bag.

Then unpacked it.

Then packed it again.

Alice had been clear. Don't bring anything that ties you to him. No identification. No phone. No jewelry. No paper trail. Nothing he could trace, claim, or twist into leverage.

But what did that even leave?

The closet was full of clothes he had chosen. Dresses he liked. Shoes that hurt but photographed well. Makeup he approved. Perfume he bought because it made her *smell like someone worth looking at*.

In the very back, she found a pair of jeans she barely remembered owning. Soft with age. Familiar in a way that made her chest ache. A plain black hoodie. A pair of tennis shoes with frayed laces.

No jewelry. No makeup.

Just the cash. A hair tie. And a scrap of paper with Alice's address, memorized and then burned over the stove until nothing remained but ash.

The third night, he didn't come home.

At first, she told herself it was a gift. One last mercy.

Then the paranoia crept in.

Was it a test?

A trap?

Did he already know?

She didn't sleep. She paced the bedroom barefoot, every sound amplified. Every headlight outside made her heart seize. She waited for the rumble of his car. For the slam of a door. For his voice calling her name like a summons.

He never came.

When dawn broke — pale and cold — she dressed quickly.

She braided her hair tight. Pulled on the hoodie. Slipped the tampon box into her pocket. She hesitated at the door, just for a second, then left it unlocked.

Wide open.

Let him wonder.

Let him think she'd been taken.

Let him rage and search and tear holes through the city looking for her.

She stepped outside and did not look back.

Not at the house.

Not at the life she was leaving.

Because she knew now — with a certainty carved into her bones — that if she had stayed, she would not have survived.

And for the first time since she met him, since love had become fear and safety had become a cage, Eden wasn't running blindly anymore.

She was running *toward* something.

Toward breath.

Toward silence that didn't hurt.

Toward a life that belonged to her.

Even if she had to rebuild it from nothing.

Even if it cost her everything she had ever known.

She walked into the morning empty-handed.

And free.

Chapter Twenty-Nine

Eden pulled the black hoodie tight around her face, the fabric rough against her cheek. The hood cast her features into shadow, turning her into just another shape moving through the city before dawn. The jeans she wore were scuffed and worn, softened by years she barely remembered now.

They were the only clothes that still felt like hers.

The tampon box was strapped inside her waistband, awkward but secure. It pressed against her hip with every step — a small, ridiculous thing holding everything she had left. Crumpled bills lifted from his wallet, from coat pockets he never checked, from a life he'd built on power and fear.

It wasn't charity.

It wasn't rescue.

It was hers.

Money he would never notice missing. Money he had taken from others without consequence. She had stolen it back one quiet bill at a time, reclaiming something that had never truly belonged to him.

The box bumped against her skin as she walked, grounding her. Proof that she had planned. That she had survived long enough to think ahead. That she was capable of more than obedience.

For the first time in years, she carried something of her own — not a dress he'd chosen, not a name he'd claimed, not a role he'd scripted.

Just enough to run.

She moved fast, but not frantic.

Frantic got you noticed.

She stayed close to buildings, slipping through the margins of the street where light didn't linger. Streetlamps flickered overhead, casting long, trembling fingers across the pavement that felt like hands reaching for her ankles. Every passing car made her flinch. Every engine slowing sent panic spiking through her chest.

She didn't look at faces.

Faces could recognize her.

Faces could belong to him.

She cut through an alley that smelled of old rain and rot, then ducked into a twenty-four-hour convenience store when her lungs began to burn. Fluorescent lights buzzed overhead. The clerk didn't look up.

She grabbed a bottle of water and paid in cash, hands shaking as she waited for change.

No mirrors. No cameras. No lingering.

Outside again, the cold bit through her hoodie. She forced herself to slow her breathing — short inhales, longer exhales

— grounding herself the way she'd once taught kids at the shelter.

You're here. You're alive. One step at a time.

She couldn't use her phone. She knew better.

Anything electronic was a leash. Daniel didn't just track devices — he anticipated behavior. The number Alice gave her burned behind her eyes, memorized until it felt carved into her skull.

But first she needed noise. Movement. A place where she could disappear without explanation.

The bus station loomed ahead, already humming with early-morning life.

Perfect.

No one questioned a woman in a hoodie here. No one looked twice. Everyone was tired, desperate, distracted. She blended into the current easily, bought a ticket with cash, avoided the self-serve kiosks and their blinking cameras.

She chose a seat near the back.

Always near the back.

The bench was cold beneath her thighs as she waited, ears tuned to everything — the scrape of metal, footsteps passing too close, laughter that felt too loud. She imagined Daniel's hand closing around her arm, his voice low and furious in her ear.

Not now. Not here.

The bus arrived with a hiss of air brakes and yellow headlights that split the dark open. She climbed aboard without looking at the driver, slipped into her seat, pressed her forehead briefly against the glass.

When the bus pulled away, the city began to recede — brick and steel blurring into distance.

Only then did she let herself breathe.

Not relief.

Not peace.

Just breath.

She knew better than to believe this was over. Daniel had power. Money. Men who owed him favors and men who didn't yet know they did. He would look for her. He would rage. He would lie.

But for the first time since the wedding, since the locked door, since the room beneath the house —

She was moving.

Not frozen.

Not waiting.

Running.

And somewhere ahead — beyond highways and forests and names she would have to learn again — was Black Hollow.

A place Alice said swallowed people whole.

A place where Eden could disappear.

A place where survival might finally turn into something else.

She tightened her grip on the tampon box, closed her eyes, and let the bus carry her forward.

For now, that was enough.

Chapter Thirty

The bus hissed as it pulled away, leaving Eden alone on the edge of cracked pavement. There was no station — just gravel, pine needles, and the lingering stink of old diesel fumes.

Black Hollow.

The name settled heavy in her chest, like something half-remembered and half-warned against. The town didn't exist on most maps. It was the kind of place you only heard about in backwoods gossip or horror stories meant to scare city girls out of wandering too far. Which made it perfect.

Eden pulled her hoodie lower over her brow and started walking, boots scuffing against gravel and pine needles as the road curved toward town. When she reached the sign — **WELCOME TO BLACK HOLLOW / POPULATION 1,208** — she stopped.

Now 1,209.

Out of all those people, only one knew who she really was.

The thought loosened something in her chest. Relief slid through her, slow and careful, like maybe — just maybe — she could breathe for the first time in months.

The town itself was small. A narrow stretch of road hemmed in by trees. A gas station with one lonely pump. A diner with a flickering neon sign. A handful of buildings that looked like they'd been standing longer than anyone still living inside them.

As she walked, her stomach clenched, sharp and insistent. She hadn't eaten since the night before. Her mouth felt dry, her tongue thick. The bus ride had been long and silent, her body locked tight the entire way — waiting for someone to recognize her. To stop her. To say her name.

No one had.

The diner sign buzzed faintly overhead — **THE HOLLOW FORK** — its neon struggling to stay alive. The windows were fogged with heat, the inside glowing warm and dim.

Food first, she told herself. *Then the key. Then the cabin.*

The bell above the door jingled as she stepped inside.

The smell hit her immediately — grease, coffee, sugar just past the point of burning. Heat wrapped around her like a blanket she wasn't sure she deserved yet. The diner looked like it hadn't been updated since the eighties, which meant they probably accepted cash and didn't ask many questions.

Conversation dipped just enough to register her existence, then resumed.

"Table or counter?" the waitress asked without really looking at her.

"Counter," Eden said softly.

The waitress nodded toward the stools and kept moving. Eden slid onto the nearest open seat, head down, hands tucked deep into the sleeves of her hoodie. The red vinyl creaked beneath her weight.

"Coffee?" the waitress asked, already reaching for a mug.

"Yes," Eden said.

The mug appeared. Coffee poured. Sugar and creamer slid across the counter. Eden wrapped both hands around the cup, letting the heat soak into her palms, grounding her. She drank slowly, ordered toast, forced herself to eat even when her stomach twisted in protest.

She could feel the town's attention — not hostile, just alert. New faces were rare here. Rare enough to be cataloged quietly. Remembered later.

The bell jingled again.

The air shifted.

Eden froze.

No one else seemed to notice. Not the way she did.

He was tall — too tall to go unnoticed — yet somehow moved like a shadow. Quiet. Deliberate. Dark hair fell into his eyes like he hadn't bothered to tame it. A week-old beard carved his jaw. His eyes — gray-blue, cold as winter steel — cut across the room and landed on her.

She looked down fast, fingers tightening around the coffee cup.

Don't stare. Don't be seen.

He walked past her, boots heavy against the tile. Even after he moved on, she could still feel him, like the air hadn't recovered yet.

She recognized that kind of presence.

Daniel had carried it too.

She didn't turn. She kept her eyes down. She knew better.

He sat a few stools away, shrugging off his coat and setting a book on the counter. She didn't see the title, but something about it tugged at her attention.

The waitress changed instantly — subtly enough to be practiced. Her smile brightened. Her voice lifted. Her posture softened.

"Coffee and pie?" she asked, already pouring.

He nodded once.

Of course she already knew what he wanted. He was the kind of man people remembered without trying to.

Eden kept her eyes on the counter, but she saw everything anyway — the way the waitress leaned too close, the way her fingers lingered near his cup, the laugh offered at nothing. Eden even noticed the undone button at the waitress's collar.

He didn't smile. He didn't flirt back.

But he didn't stop her.

Eden slid a few bills onto the counter and reached for the door.

Then his voice cut through the diner.

"Black Hollow doesn't get many passersby."

Low. Calm. Certain.

Her hand froze on the handle.

Slowly, she turned.

"I'm new in town," she said — too quickly — and knew immediately it had been a mistake.

She didn't wait for a response.

Outside, the air felt colder. Thinner.

Eden pulled her hoodie tighter and walked away, pulse pounding until the diner was well behind her.

Behind the building, the world went quiet.

The phone booth stood where Alice said it would — rusted, forgotten, glass cracked and webbed with ivy. Eden slid the door open, heart hammering, and reached beneath the broken coin return.

Cool metal pressed into her fingertips.

The key.

She closed her fist around it and didn't breathe again until she was walking.

The road to the cabin stretched farther than she expected —
nearly a mile past the last flickering streetlamp, down a gravel
path lined with thick pines leaning like sentinels. Every step
sounded too loud in the stillness. Every shadow felt alive.

She didn't slow.

When the cabin finally came into view, it looked wrong and
right all at once — sagging porch, moss creeping up the roof,
a cracked window like it had once tried to escape and failed.

But it was quiet.

And quiet was everything.

She unlocked the door, stepped inside, and closed it behind
her.

The air smelled of dust, mothballs, and forgotten stories. Not
fear. Not control.

Eden leaned back against the door, eyes closed, breathing
shallow but real.

She had followed Alice's instructions.

She was here.

She was alone.

And for the first time in a long time, the silence didn't feel
like a threat.

Chapter Thirty-One

The cabin barely qualified as a house.

It was a guest cabin tucked behind a farmhouse that looked like it hadn't hosted company since the Clinton administration. The floors were worn wood, dulled by decades of use, smelling faintly of pine sap baked in over time. One bedroom. No internet. No cell signal.

Just trees. Quiet. Distance.

It was perfect.

Eden stood just inside the door for a long moment, listening — not for footsteps or voices, not for the sound of a man deciding what she was allowed to do next.

Nothing came.

The absence hit her all at once.

She reached for the light switch. The bulb flickered, then steadied, bathing the room in soft yellow light.

Electricity.

The relief was sharp enough to steal her breath. She sat down hard on the couch, chest rising and falling unevenly. She hadn't realized how tightly she'd been holding herself until now.

The cabin was simple. A couch that had lived several lives. A narrow table with mismatched chairs. A kitchenette with chipped counters and a sink that groaned before giving up clean, cold water.

And best of all — no cameras. No locks she didn't control.

She slipped out of her hoodie and let it fall to the floor, standing there in jeans and a T-shirt, arms bare. The bruises along her ribs had faded to yellow. Her wrist still ached when she moved it wrong.

But she didn't feel exposed.

No one was watching.

She moved slowly, fingertips grazing the back of a chair, the windowsill, the worn spine of a book left on a shelf. Paperbacks — dog-eared, mismatched. Westerns. A battered book of poetry. A torn-cover copy of *The Secret Life of Bees*.

She traced the pages as if they might disappear.

Upstairs, the bedroom was small but clean. A narrow bed. A quilt folded at the foot. A single window looking out into trees instead of streets. Instead of glass towers. Instead of eyes.

Eden sat on the edge of the bed and waited for the panic.

It didn't come.

What came instead was exhaustion — deep, heavy, earned. The kind that followed survival.

She lay back fully clothed, staring at the ceiling as the cabin settled around her. Wood shifting. Wind brushing branches.

No one knew where she was.

Not the press.
Not Daniel.
Not the version of herself that had learned to disappear to stay alive.

Just her.

And Alice.

And a town that hadn't asked her for anything yet.

A truck slowed on gravel.

Eden sat up, pulse quickening — but not spiraling. She moved to the window and peeked through the curtain.

An older pickup idled near the farmhouse. A man stepped out.

Even at a distance, she recognized him.

The same presence. The same quiet weight. The man from the diner.

He didn't approach right away. Checked the side of the house. The spigot. Like he was following a list.

Then he knocked. Once.

"Hey," he called easily. "Alice sent me. Said the pipes like to freeze if you look at them wrong."

Eden hesitated, then opened the door partway.

"Yes?"

"Micah," he said. "Maintenance. Alice is my mother."

She studied him, then stepped aside.

He didn't linger. Checked valves. Adjusted the heater. Built a small fire without asking.

When he finished, he wiped his hands on his jeans.

"Welcome to Black Hollow," he said.

Then he left.

No questions. No curiosity.

Just help.

Later, Eden found a notebook in a drawer. Blank pages. A pen that still worked.

She sat for a long time before writing.

Then she wrote one sentence.

I'm here.

She closed the notebook and set it beside the bed.

That night, Eden slept.

Quietly.

Chapter Thirty-Two

The house was still the next morning.

Not the tense, coiled stillness Eden had learned to fear—but the kind that simply existed. No cameras humming. No locks clicking into place. No footsteps pacing overhead. No voice calling her name like a leash tightening.

Just wind in the trees. The soft complaint of old floorboards. Silence that didn't demand anything from her.

She pulled on her jeans and hoodie, twisted her hair into a tight knot beneath the hood, and slipped a few folded bills from the tampon box into her pocket before stepping outside.

The air was sharp enough to sting her lungs. She welcomed it. Let it hurt. Let it remind her that this was a place where pain came from weather, not people.

Black Hollow was barely a town by most standards. One main road. A few side streets branching off like afterthoughts. Wooded. Weathered. Forgotten on purpose. Most people didn't walk with their phones glued to their palms. Conversations happened face to face. News traveled over fences and coffee cups, not screens.

She moved with her head down, cataloging faces without meeting eyes—not from fear, exactly. Habit. Instinct didn't dissolve overnight.

The consignment shop came first. **Second Chances**, wedged between the post office and a bakery that smelled faintly of burnt sugar. A bell chimed as she stepped inside.

"Morning, hon," the woman behind the counter said.

Eden nodded and drifted toward the racks.

She chose clothes that didn't ask to be noticed—two pairs of jeans, sweaters worn soft with age, a coat with deep pockets, a scarf that could disappear up around her throat. She paid in cash, murmured thanks, and left before conversation could find her.

The grocery store was small and narrow. Bread. Peanut butter. Granola bars. Coffee. Powdered creamer. Shampoo. Fruit she could eat with one hand while walking.

Outside, the wind cut sharper. She wrapped the scarf tight and kept moving.

The library occupied what used to be a church, stained-glass windows dulled by time. Inside smelled like dust and paper and secrets that had outlived their owners. She wandered the stacks—*Jane Eyre*, *Walden*, mysteries missing covers. The librarian, a woman with round glasses and a careful stoop, nodded once and returned to her desk.

Eden didn't linger.

The diner sat at the corner of Main, windows glowing amber against the gray afternoon.

Warmth met her at the door. Coffee. Grease. Something sweet just shy of burning on the griddle.

It wasn't crowded—locals hunched over mugs, a waitress moving between tables with the ease of someone who'd done this a long time. Eden paused just long enough to let the room register her and move on.

That's when she noticed the woman behind the counter.

Salt-and-pepper braid. Strong arms. A face shaped by work rather than softness. The woman glanced up, took Eden in with one efficient look, and nodded—not curious. Not suspicious. Just acknowledgment.

"Sit wherever," she said, already pouring coffee. "It's fresh."

Eden slid onto a stool near the end of the counter—the same one as last night. Hood still up. Vinyl creaked beneath her weight.

The mug landed in front of her. Black.

"Thanks," Eden said.

The woman gave a grunt that might have meant *you're welcome* and moved on.

Eden drank slowly, letting the heat settle her. She didn't rush. Didn't stare. Tried not to make herself memorable.

When she stood to leave, the woman glanced at her coat.

"Good choice," she said. "It gets cold here once the sun drops."

The comment landed softer than Eden expected.

Outside again, she took the long way back—past the frozen pond, the abandoned mill, houses that looked like they'd learned to keep their stories quiet.

No one stopped her.

No one asked her name.

By the time she reached the cabin, dusk had settled thick and blue. She set the groceries on the counter, hung her coat, and sat on the edge of the mattress.

Her hands rested uselessly in her lap—not from fear, but from the strange realization that nothing was required of them.

She had walked the town. Bought what she needed. Spoken when spoken to. Been seen—and then dismissed.

Eden exhaled, slow and deliberate.

This place didn't care who she had been.

And for the first time in a long while, neither did she.

That night, sleep came quickly—and violently.

She was back in the Whitmore house.

Not the ballroom. Not the bedroom. The hallway beneath the house—the one without windows, the one where sound disappeared. The walls were closer now. Narrower. She walked barefoot, the floor cold enough to bite.

Daniel's voice carried from somewhere ahead of her.

Calm. Familiar. Certain.

"Come here."

Her body moved before her mind could stop it.

She reached the chair and found it empty. The straps lay open, waiting. She turned, heart hammering—and he was behind her, close enough that she could feel his breath warm against her ear.

"You ran," he said softly. Not angry. Amused.

She tried to scream.

She woke instead, choking on air, hands clawing at the quilt. Her heart slammed so hard it hurt. The cabin was dark. Quiet. Still.

No locks.

No footsteps.

No voice.

She stayed awake until dawn, reminding her body—over and over—that he was not here.

Chapter Thirty-Three

The next morning, Eden woke to the sound of tires on gravel.

Her eyes snapped open, body already braced—heart sprinting, lungs tight, the quilt twisted around her legs. For one panicked second, she didn't know where she was. The ceiling was low and water-stained. The air smelled like old wood and cold ash. Morning light cut through the grimy window in slats of gold.

Then the cabin came back to her.

Not the Whitmore house.
Not marble.
Not cameras.

This.

Footsteps crunched on the porch.

Eden sat up too fast, pain flashing sharp along her ribs. She pressed a hand to her side, swallowing the sound clawing up her throat. Another step. Another. The porch boards complained under someone's weight—unhurried. Certain.

A knock hit the door.

Sharp. Controlled.

Eden froze.

Another knock. A pause. Three beats of silence. Then two
more.

Her stomach dropped. The pattern lodged itself somewhere
deep and feral in her chest. She slid off the mattress and
moved barefoot toward the door, every instinct screaming
don't. Not to open it. Not to trust anyone.

But Alice had been the difference between a locked house and
a bus ticket out.

Eden cracked the door open.

The woman on the porch was older than she'd expected—
mid-sixties, maybe—but straight-backed, immovable. Dark
red lipstick. Hair braided tight down her back. A denim jacket
worn thin at the seams. A pale scar traced her jaw, neat and
deliberate, like someone had once tried to mark her and failed.

Alice's gaze swept over Eden—hair, hands, posture—
cataloging without judgment.

"You gonna let me in," Alice asked, "or are we doing this with
the wildlife?"

Eden opened the door.

"I'm Alice," she said, stepping inside without hesitation. She
held two steaming mugs of coffee, setting one down on the
table like she'd always belonged there. "Figured you'd want
something hot."

"Thank you," Eden said, voice hoarse. "It's… perfect. The
cabin."

Alice nodded once, as if she'd expected nothing else.

They sat at the small table. Alice pulled a manila envelope from her bag and slid it across the wood.

"I pulled some strings," she said. "Congratulations. You're Eliza Moore."

The name landed hard.

A life she hadn't lived. A woman who had never stood beside Daniel Whitmore under chandeliers and flashbulbs, smiling while her stomach turned to ice.

Alice continued, practical as a ledger. "Born in Spokane. Raised in rural Montana by a very dead grandmother. Social. Birth certificate. Temporary license. I'll get you a real ID in a few weeks."

Eden stared at the envelope like it might explode. "How did you—"

"People owe me favors," Alice said, sipping her coffee. "You needed clean papers. I made calls."

Alice pulled a folded slip of paper from the envelope and slid it across the table with the rest of the documents.

"And before you ask," she said, already sipping her coffee, "yes. I handled work."

Eden looked down at the paper.

The Hollow Fork
Morning shift.
Ask for Nell.

Her throat tightened. "You—"

"I don't relocate people without giving them a way to eat,"
Alice said flatly. "Diner doesn't run background checks worth
a damn. Cash tips. Locals mind their business. You show up
on time, keep your head down, and don't cause trouble, you'll
be fine."

"I don't have experience," Eden said automatically.

Alice's gaze sharpened. "You know how to pour coffee. You
know how to smile when you're supposed to and disappear
when you're not. You've been trained for this your whole
life."

The words landed heavier than Eden expected.

"She's expecting you," Alice added. "Hair up. No stories.
You're Eliza, and you're passing through whether you stay or
not."

Eden folded the paper carefully and slipped it back into the
envelope, hands unsteady. The idea of work—of routine, of
expectation that wasn't wrapped in threat—made something
ache behind her ribs.

"I don't know how to thank you."

Alice's gaze sharpened. "Then don't. Just don't screw it up,
and don't go falling for anyone in town."

Eden let out a breath that sounded almost like a laugh. "Falling for someone is the last thing I need to be worrying about right now."

"I believe you," Alice said. Then, almost idly, "But things have a way of happening anyway."

She leaned forward.

"Listen to me," Alice said, voice flattening. "If you screw this up, he will find you. And you will die."

The words were delivered like weather. No drama. No emphasis.

"Daniel Whitmore isn't just rich," Alice continued. "He's connected. Politicians. Judges. CEOs. Your face is still floating around in his world. One wrong name, one careless moment—he'll bury you before I can blink."

Eden nodded once. Anything more might shatter her.

"You're not a headline anymore," Alice said. "You're not a wife. You're not a symbol. You're a ghost who eats, sleeps, and stays quiet."

Alice slid a phone across the table. Old. Forgettable.

"No social media. No laptops. No accounts that remember your face. One number's saved. Mine."

"And… Tonya?" Eden asked quietly.

Something flickered behind Alice's eyes—gone almost as soon as it appeared.

"She'll stay quiet," Alice said. "She always does."

Eden swallowed. "Am I allowed to talk to her?"

"No."

The finality hit harder than the word itself.

"Any contact with Eden Whitmore is a risk," Alice said. "Phones get traced. Patterns get noticed. You don't get to half-disappear."

"My mom—"

"Cannot know," Alice said, gentler but immovable. "Not yet. I'll handle it. Carefully."

Silence stretched.

"This isn't forever," Alice said at last. "But it is everything right now. And staying alive is the first step to getting anything back."

Alice stood.

"Oh—Eliza?" she said, testing the name.

Eden looked up.

"Get a haircut," Alice added. "Dye it. You look too much like her."

Then she was gone.

The cabin settled into quiet again.

Eden opened the envelope with shaking hands.

Eliza Moore.

The name didn't fit yet.

But it would have to do.

Chapter Thirty-Four

The bathroom mirror was cracked at the corner, clouded from years of steam and neglect. Eden stood barefoot on the cold tile, scissors resting in the sink. The cabin was quiet except for the low hum of the heater and the distant rustle of trees shifting in the wind. Morning light crept in through the small window—pale, undecided, like it hadn't made up its mind yet.

Her hair hung down her back in soft blonde waves.

Too soft.
Too visible.

He had loved it like this. Had run his hands through it in public, claimed it with a familiarity that looked like affection to everyone else. Said it made her look warm. Approachable. Like something worth reaching for.

Hair held onto things. She knew that now. It absorbed years the way fabric did—scent, memory, touch. It remembered dinners and galas and hands that never asked permission. It remembered being arranged, praised, pulled.

She stared at her reflection and waited for doubt.

It didn't come.

She gathered a thick handful of hair in her fist and lifted it. The weight surprised her—not because it was heavy, but because it was full. Loaded with years she didn't want to carry anymore.

She closed her eyes.

The scissors cut through with a blunt, unmistakable sound.

The first lock dropped into the sink.

Her breath hitched—not in fear, but in release. Like something inside her had finally been allowed to exhale.

She didn't stop.

The cuts came faster, uneven and impatient. Hair fell in pale clumps against the porcelain, sliding down her arms, sticking briefly to her skin before dropping away. This wasn't about style. This wasn't about looking good.

This was about removal.

About taking back something that had been chosen for her.

When she finished, her hair barely brushed her jaw. Her neck felt cold. Exposed. Honest. The air touched skin that hadn't felt it in years.

She leaned closer to the mirror.

The woman staring back looked sharper. Older. Less ornamental. Her face wasn't softened by length or shine anymore. There was nothing decorative about her.

She didn't look pretty.

She looked awake.

The dye came next.

She'd bought it the afternoon before at the general store—ash brown, cheap, forgettable. The kind of color no one complimented. The kind that didn't invite memory.

She mixed it in the sink, the sharp chemical smell filling the small bathroom, and worked it through her hair with bare fingers. Blonde vanished beneath brown. Light swallowed by something steadier. Quieter.

When she rinsed it out, the water ran muddy down the drain, carrying the last of it away.

She dried her hair with a towel and looked again.

Eden Whitmore was gone.

Eliza Moore stared back at her—dark hair, blunt cut, eyes too alert, mouth set like someone who had learned how to survive without asking permission first.

She didn't smile.

That night, sleep came quickly—and badly.

She dreamed of marble floors slick beneath her bare feet. Of lights too bright, humming overhead. Of a voice calling her name from behind a locked door, calm and patient, as if he knew she would come eventually.

Eliza, the voice said, wrong in his mouth.

She woke with her jaw clenched so hard it ached, her heart pounding like she'd been running. The room was dark and quiet. The cabin intact. The door still locked—by her.

She pressed a hand to her throat until her breathing slowed.

He hadn't followed her.

But her body hadn't learned that yet.

She lay awake until the fear drained back into something manageable, listening to the wind move through the trees like it was standing guard.

In the morning, she dressed carefully.

Jeans that fit without clinging. A soft gray sweater. A jacket worn thin at the elbows. Shoes meant for standing, for moving, for staying upright on her own.

Nothing new.
Nothing memorable.

She pulled her hair back into a low ponytail, slipped the burner phone into her pocket, and stood in the doorway of the cabin for a moment, letting the quiet settle.

First days mattered.

She locked the door and started the walk into town.

The gravel road crunched beneath her boots. Pine needles lined the shoulder like warnings she didn't need anymore. The cold bit through her sweater—sharp, grounding. With each step, her body loosened. Not because she was safe.

Because she was choosing to move.

The diner came into view slowly.

She pushed the door open.

The bell jingled.

The waitress—the same one from the night she arrived—looked up. Her eyes paused. Recognition flickered.

Then slid away.

"Morning," the woman said. "You here for the shift?"

"Yes," Eliza said, steady. "I'm Eliza."

The name landed clean. No echo. No resistance.

"Apron's back there," the waitress replied, already turning away. "Coffee's fresh. Don't disappear and we'll get along fine."

Eliza tied the apron around her waist, fingers clumsy at first. Her hands shook when she poured her first cup of coffee, but she didn't spill it. She wiped the counter. Learned the rhythm. Learned who wanted cream without asking. Who tipped well. Who talked too much.

No one asked where she was from.
No one asked why she was here.

And halfway through the morning rush, something unfamiliar settled in her chest.

Pride.

She was tired. Her feet hurt. Her shoulders ached.

But she was here.

Working. Existing. Unowned.

At one point, she caught her reflection in the chrome of the coffee machine—dark hair pulled back, apron smudged, eyes clear.

She didn't see Eden anymore.

She saw Eliza.

Chapter Thirty-Five

By the end of the week, Eliza learned the diner's rhythms.

Mornings belonged to the same four men who claimed the counter every day—boots tracked with mud or chalk dust, coffee black, conversation spare. They talked about weather and livestock and school board nonsense with the weary familiarity of people who had known each other too long to bother posturing.

Midday brought teachers from the high school, a road crew that smelled like diesel and cold air, the librarian with her wrist still wrapped in a brace. Afternoons slowed enough that Eliza could breathe.

She learned how to keep her head down without disappearing.

How to smile without offering more than courtesy.

How to exist in a room without bracing for impact.

No one asked where she'd come from. In Black Hollow, curiosity had edges. People noticed new things, stored the information quietly, then waited to see if it mattered.

She mattered just enough.

At night, she walked back to the cabin with sore feet and a grounding sense of earned exhaustion. She cooked simple meals—eggs, toast, soup—and read until the words blurred together. The books came from the library: old paperbacks with cracked spines, stories that didn't ask her to be anything.

Sleep, however, was unreliable.

Some nights she drifted off easily, wrapped in quiet. Other nights she woke with the echo of a voice she couldn't quite hear, her hands clenched into fists, heart racing for reasons she couldn't immediately name. Once, she woke certain someone was standing just outside the door, listening.

There was no one there.

She checked the lock anyway.

She started carrying the notebook with her again.

At first, it held lists. Hours worked. Groceries she could afford. Things she needed to remember.

Then sentences crept in.

Not memories. Not explanations. Small things. Images. A line about steam rising off coffee cups. A paragraph about a woman who lived alone in the woods and learned the language of quiet. A few jagged lines of poetry that didn't rhyme and didn't need to.

She wrote until her hands stopped shaking.

Friday afternoon came loud.

A high school game had let out early, and the diner filled fast—teenagers buzzing with relief, teachers tired but indulgent. Eliza moved through it with practiced efficiency, pouring coffee, clearing plates, steadying herself in motion.

She was wiping down the counter when someone stepped into her line of sight—not crowding her space, not rushing her. Just there.

Tall. Broad-shouldered. Worn boots dusted with chalk.

Micah.

He waited until she looked up.

"How's the water holding up?" he asked easily. "Still running clear?"

Something loosened in her chest.

"Still hot," she said. "No surprise icicles yet."

"Good." He nodded. "If you need wood for the stove, let me know. Alice keeps meaning to restock out there and never does."

She smiled despite herself. "I've noticed."

He glanced at her hair then—not lingering, not intrusive. Just noticing.

"The cut suits you," he said. "The color too."

Her fingers tightened briefly around the rag.

"Thanks."

No appraisal. No expectation. Just a statement offered and left alone.

He slid a folded piece of paper across the counter. "That's my number. For pipes. Or wood. Or if the heater starts making noises it shouldn't."

She looked at it, then at him.

"Thank you," she said.

"Anytime." He paused. "You settling in okay?"

"Yes," she answered—and realized she meant it.

He smiled, small and genuine, then stepped aside to let someone else order. No questions. No fishing. No pressure to explain herself.

Eliza noticed, distantly, that her shoulders hadn't crept up toward her ears the entire time he'd been standing there.

When he left, she watched him cross the gravel through the window—steady, unhurried—and felt something settle into place.

Not attraction.
Not hope.

Trust.

Someone who noticed without claiming. Someone who offered without demanding.

That night, in the quiet of the cabin, Eliza opened her notebook.

She didn't write lists.
She didn't write his name.

She wrote a page—messy, imperfect—about a woman learning how to stay.

When she finally lay down, sleep came softly. And when it fractured—because it still did—it wasn't with terror, but with the memory of a voice growing fainter, less certain it would ever be answered again.

She turned onto her side, pulled the quilt higher, and let the cabin hold.

For now.

Chapter Thirty-Six

Six months had passed since Eden stepped off the bus into Black Hollow and became Eliza, and though she could still remember the sound it made pulling away—the hiss of air, the sensation of a door sealing shut behind her—that memory no longer lived in her chest. It had moved farther back, dulled by repetition, softened by time, replaced by other sounds that now defined her days: wind moving through trees, coffee cups clinking against chipped saucers, boots on gravel, her name spoken easily and without hesitation.

Eliza.

The name fit now in a way Eden never had at the end.

Spring arrived slowly, stubbornly, as if the land itself needed convincing. Snow lingered at the edges of roads before finally melting into mud, which gave way to patches of green that seemed to push through the soil by sheer will. The town softened—not dramatically, not all at once—but enough that Eliza noticed it when she walked, enough that the air felt different against her skin. She noticed it most in her own body, in the way she no longer flinched at sudden sounds, no longer felt the need to catalog every exit in every room.

Her hair had grown past her shoulders again, and she caught herself brushing it back without thinking, letting it hang loose more often than she tied it up. The sharp edge of the cut she'd given herself was gone, replaced by something fuller and softer, something that moved when she walked and rested against her neck in a way that felt familiar rather than threatening. She liked it—not because it made her feel pretty, but because it felt like hers.

The cabin felt lived in now, not borrowed or temporary. Her boots stayed by the door without being lined up. Books stacked unevenly on the table. A sweater permanently draped over the back of the chair. She knew which floorboard complained and which window stuck if you didn't lift it just right. Alice stopped knocking when she came by—just let herself in, set something warm on the counter, stayed as long as she felt like. They didn't talk about the past much, and they didn't need to. The silence between them had weight, but not menace.

Eliza worked full time at the diner and knew all of its rhythms by heart. She knew who wanted coffee before sitting down, who tipped in exact change, who needed to talk and who preferred silence. Her body no longer stayed braced through entire shifts, no longer waited for punishment to follow a mistake. She laughed sometimes—real laughter, quick and unguarded—and the sound no longer startled her when it came out.

People knew her name.

Not as a newcomer. Not as someone passing through. Just Eliza.

Joe at the market asked how her week was going and meant it. Shelby texted her photos of terrible thrift-store finds. Ms. Delaney waved her over at the library to recommend books she thought she'd like. She wasn't watched. She was expected, and that distinction mattered more than she'd realized it could.

She'd gone on a few dates—not because she was searching for anything, but because she was allowed to try. Coffee with a guy from the road crew. Dinner with a man who owned too many flannels and talked mostly about himself. A long walk with someone whose name she forgot as soon as it ended. They were fine. Pleasant. Easy. And when they didn't turn into anything more, she didn't feel disappointment or relief— just clarity. She was allowed to say yes. Allowed to say no. Allowed to change her mind without explanation.

Micah became part of her life quietly, without announcement or expectation. He showed up with firewood after storms, texted to check if the heater was behaving, walked with her through town when their schedules overlapped. In addition to handling maintenance jobs around Black Hollow, he worked full time at the high school teaching English literature, and their conversations often drifted from books to authors they loved, to ones they couldn't stand, to nothing at all. He never asked her to explain herself. Never rushed the shape of whatever they were building. She trusted that, and the trust itself felt like something earned.

Alice noticed. Pretended not to.

At night, Eliza wrote—not as proof of survival anymore, not as a record she might one day need to justify herself, but because it felt good. Pages filled with poems and short pieces she didn't outline or edit to death. Scenes that didn't ask permission to exist. She wrote about towns that felt like this one, about women who stayed, about quiet moments that mattered more than the loud ones. She didn't reread much. Writing had shifted from necessity to pleasure, and the difference surprised her.

One afternoon, walking through town, someone called her name—Eliza—and she turned without thinking. Without scanning faces. Without bracing. The realization came later, soft and startling, settling into her bones with quiet certainty.

This wasn't hiding.

This was living.

And she loved it.

Chapter Thirty-Seven

Eliza didn't plan to listen. It just happened the way so many things did now—quietly, without announcement, slipping into her awareness while she was busy doing something else. The late-morning lull settled over The Hollow Fork in that familiar, unguarded way, the rush long gone, plates stacked, coffee cups lingering full because no one felt like leaving yet. Eliza wiped down the counter slowly, her body moving on instinct while her thoughts drifted somewhere loose and unmoored.

That was when two women slid into the booth by the window.

"Poor Mrs. Grady," the one with the scarf said, easing herself into the seat with a careful wince. "Slipped right off her porch. Broke her hip clean through."

"That's what happens when you refuse to get your steps fixed," the other replied. "Doctor says she'll be out at least a month. Maybe longer depending on how therapy goes after surgery."

Eliza's hand stilled on the rag without her noticing right away. She kept her head down, kept moving, but the words lodged somewhere beneath her ribs.

"That leaves the Business Ed kids screwed," the first woman continued. "They can't find a sub willing to stick it out. Seniors this close to midterms? No one wants that mess."

Business Ed.
High school.

Eliza turned away before either woman noticed she'd been listening, focusing instead on the sink, on the steady rhythm of rinsing and stacking plates. The conversation drifted on without her, dissolving into weather complaints and quiet town gossip, but the thought didn't follow. It stayed.

She told herself it didn't matter. She wasn't Eden Whitmore anymore—degrees and résumés, a life that could be verified and traced. She was Eliza Moore. A waitress. A woman who had chosen quiet on purpose, who had built something good out of small, careful days. She had a job, a place to sleep, a body that felt like her own again. Evenings that didn't require permission. Mornings that belonged only to her.

That should have been enough.

But the wanting didn't fade.

Because this wasn't about escape anymore. It was about use— about the parts of herself she had carried through everything without ever losing, even when she thought she had. Listening. Patience. The ability to hold space for people when they didn't know how to ask for it. The shelter in New York came back to her in fragments: kids hunched over folding tables, trust built slowly and quietly, the satisfaction of knowing she mattered in ways that had nothing to do with how she looked or who she stood beside.

Teaching wasn't the same.

But it was close.

And close felt like oxygen.

The thought followed her through the rest of her shift, through the walk back to the cabin, through dinner eaten standing at the counter because sitting felt too still. It wasn't sharp or desperate. It was steady, persistent, the kind of wanting that didn't demand but didn't leave.

That night, Eliza pulled her notebook from the drawer. She didn't write poetry. Didn't write memories. She wrote a sentence instead.

I miss being useful.

She stared at it for a long moment, then crossed it out—not because it wasn't true, but because it wasn't quite right. She tried again.

I want to build something here.

That one stayed.

Her fingers hovered before she reached for her phone. Alice answered on the second ring.

"Eliza, it's kind of late," Alice said. "Everything okay?"

"I overheard something at the diner," Eliza said quietly. "The school needs a long-term substitute."

Silence stretched across the line.

"You remember what I said about standing out," Alice replied at last.

"I do," Eliza said. "And I'm not trying to. My life here is good. I'm not looking to change that."

Another pause.

"But," Alice said.

"But this could make it fuller," Eliza said. "I worked in a youth shelter. I have a degree in social work. This isn't me reaching for something dangerous—it's me using what I already am."

The line stayed quiet long enough for Eliza to wonder if she'd pushed too far.

"You want papers," Alice said finally.

"Yes."

"That's not a small ask."

"I know." Eliza's fingers dug into her thigh. "And I wouldn't ask if I didn't believe I could do it quietly. Correctly. Without drawing eyes."

Alice exhaled, slow and deliberate. "You always had terrible timing."

Relief hit Eliza hard enough that she had to sit down.

"I can make it work," Alice continued. "Transcript. Degree. Emergency substitute license. New York isn't hard if you know which doors to knock on."

"When?" Eliza asked.

"Soon," Alice said. "But listen to me. Schools remember faces. Kids remember names. You make one wrong move and someone looks too closely—I can't pull you back."

"I understand."

"No," Alice said. "You understand the risk. What you don't understand is the cost if Daniel ever connects you to a school full of minors."

The warning settled heavy—but it didn't erase the resolve.

"I won't screw it up," Eliza said.

Another pause.

Then, softer, almost reluctant, Alice said, "You were good with the kids at the shelter. I'm sure you'll be good at the school."

Eliza closed her eyes.

"Thank you."

The line went dead.

Eliza set the phone down and leaned back against the wall, staring at the ceiling. For the first time in a long while, the future didn't feel like something she was outrunning. It felt like something she was choosing.

Chapter Thirty-Eight

Alice arrived just after dusk.

Eliza heard the truck before she saw it, the low, familiar growl of an engine easing down the gravel drive. Tires crunched. The sound didn't spike her pulse anymore. She didn't freeze or count seconds or reach for the lock. She was sitting at the small kitchen table, a mug cooling beside her, when the screen door opened and closed.

Alice let herself in.

"You eat?" Alice asked, shrugging off her coat and hanging it on the hook by the door like she owned the place—which, in a way, she did.

"Yeah," Eliza said. "There's soup on the stove if you want it."

"I'll take coffee," Alice replied, already setting her battered leather satchel on the table.

The bag looked heavier than the last time Eliza had seen it, more worn, like it had been carried longer than planned. Alice didn't sit.

"This took longer than I wanted," she said. "Which is a good thing."

Eliza straightened, fingers curling loosely around her mug. Alice unzipped the satchel and pulled out a thick manila folder, its edges softened from handling. She placed it on the table between them but didn't slide it forward yet.

"Before you touch this," Alice said, "you need to understand something."

Eliza nodded. She didn't brace anymore—but she listened.

"This isn't just a name on paper," Alice continued. "This is a public role. Schools mean databases. Background checks. Administrators with too much time and a savior complex."

Alice met her gaze. "If anyone pulls too hard on a thread, it leads back to me. And if it leads back to me, it leads back to you."

"I won't give them a reason," Eliza said.

Alice's mouth twitched, not quite a smile. "Everyone says that."

She opened the folder.

The documents lay inside with quiet precision: a New York driver's license bearing the name Eliza Moore; a bachelor's degree in Human Services from a mid-sized state university; official transcripts; an emergency substitute license stamped and signed; a background check so clean it looked freshly scrubbed. Clipped neatly at the front was a printed email confirming emergency coverage, complete with a start date and instructions to report to the front office at 7:15 a.m.

Eliza stared. It didn't feel fake. It felt earned.

"You worked in a youth shelter," Alice said. "That part's true. Your degree lines up. If anyone asks, you bounced around after graduation—contract work, short stays. You don't talk about it because it wasn't glamorous."

"And if they call the university?" Eliza asked.

"They won't," Alice said. "And if they do, they'll talk to someone who was paid very well to remember you as competent—and forgettable."

That settled heavier than reassurance ever could.

Alice slid the folder toward her. "You don't quit the diner. You don't announce this like it's a new life. You switch shifts. You stay tired. You let this look temporary and practical."

The Hollow Fork. School during the day."

Alice studied her. "That's two full-time jobs."

"I know," Eliza said. "I want it."

The silence that followed wasn't tense. It was measuring.

"This isn't about running anymore," Alice said.

"No," Eliza replied. "It's about building something. I like my life here. I just want more of it."

That earned her a nod.

"One more thing," Alice said, already reaching for her coat. "If Daniel ever resurfaces—news, rumors, investigations— you tell me immediately. You don't get curious. You don't get brave."

"I won't."

"And Eliza?" Alice paused at the door. "Those kids don't need saving. They need consistency. Be calm. Be boring. Be kind."

She left without ceremony.

After Alice was gone, the cabin didn't feel empty. Eliza sat at the table and opened the folder again, running her fingers over the ink and seals that said she existed cleanly and quietly, without a past anyone could trace back to blood or bruises.

She wasn't Eden Whitmore. She wasn't anyone's wife.

She was Eliza Moore.

And in a few days, she would walk into a school as someone trusted with other people's children. The thought didn't scare her. It grounded her.

She slid the folder into her bag and reached for her phone, already planning how she'd ask Nell for the shift change, already calculating sleep and coffee and exhaustion. It would be a lot.

But it would be hers.

That night, she set her alarm earlier than usual—not because she was afraid, but because tomorrow she would keep choosing the life she was building, one ordinary, demanding, hopeful day at a time.

Chapter Thirty-Nine

Eliza woke before her alarm.

Not because of fear. Not because of habit.

Because she was ready.

Morning light filtered through the thin curtains, pale and tentative, catching on the edges of the quilt and the worn wood floor. The cabin was quiet in the way she had come to love—not empty, not lonely. Just still. The kind of quiet that waited patiently for you to step into it.

She lay there for a moment, one hand resting on her stomach, listening to the birds beginning their morning negotiations in the trees outside. Spring was trying. You could feel it in the air—softening the cold, loosening winter's grip inch by inch.

Today mattered.

The thought didn't tighten her chest the way it used to. It didn't come with dread or obligation. It felt clean. Intentional. Something she had chosen rather than something being demanded of her.

She sat up, stretched the stiffness from her shoulders, and swung her legs over the side of the bed. Her hair—longer now, brushing past her shoulders again—fell forward in a way that still surprised her sometimes. She ran her fingers through it absently, a small, private smile tugging at her mouth.

There had been a time when mirrors felt like threats. When she'd checked them compulsively—bruises, posture, expression—measuring herself against invisible rules. This morning, she didn't rush to the bathroom mirror. She didn't need confirmation.

She showered quickly, letting the hot water ground her, rinsing away sleep and nerves alike. Steam fogged the mirror, and she left it that way, toweling off without clearing the glass. She didn't need to see who she was to know.

She dressed carefully but without anxiety—a flowy floral skirt that fell just below her knees, a soft sweater, boots she trusted to get her where she needed to go. Practical. Comfortable. Hers. She packed her bag with the quiet precision of someone who knew what she was doing: notebook, pens, lunch wrapped in foil, the folder Alice had delivered days ago after reminding her—more than once—to breathe.

Before leaving, she paused at the door.

Not to brace.

Just to take it in.

Then she stepped outside.

The walk to Black Hollow High took just under forty minutes, winding through quiet roads and thinning trees. Snow still lingered in stubborn patches along the ditches, but crocuses had started pushing through the softened earth, purple and yellow like secrets daring themselves into daylight.

As she walked, Eliza felt it—that subtle shift between being unseen and being known.

People passed her now and nodded. A man walking his dog lifted a hand in greeting. A woman she recognized from the diner called out a casual, "Morning, Ms. Moore."

Ms. Moore.

The name settled easily, without resistance. Without echo.

The school came into view slowly, brick and wide and familiar in the way public buildings always were. It wasn't impressive. It didn't need to be. It existed to hold people, to give them somewhere to go.

The parking lot was already alive with students spilling out of cars, laughter and music cutting through the crisp air. Eliza slowed just slightly at the edge of it, letting herself feel the moment instead of rushing past it.

She had missed this.

Not the noise. Not the chaos.

The possibility.

Inside, the front office buzzed with the low-grade urgency unique to schools everywhere. Phones rang. A printer complained. A secretary waved her toward the sign-in clipboard without looking up.

"Eliza Moore?" she asked, glancing at the schedule. "Business Ed. Room 214. You're early."

"I like early," Eliza said.

"That'll wear off," the woman replied dryly, then smiled. "Glad you're here."

The hallway smelled like floor cleaner and pencil shavings. Lockers slammed. Sneakers squeaked. The day moved whether you were ready or not.

Room 214 waited.

Eliza set her bag down, looked around, and felt something steady click into place. The posters. The desks. Mrs. Grady's handwriting still faint on the board like an echo.

She picked up the marker and added her own beneath it:

Good morning. I'm Ms. Moore. Let's get started.

When the bell rang, students poured in, eyes sharp and curious, measuring her the way teenagers always did. Eliza met them calmly, one by one, her voice even, her posture relaxed.

They tested her.

She didn't flinch.

They listened.

Halfway through the period, a familiar presence appeared in the doorway.

Micah leaned against the frame, coffee in hand, watching the room with quiet interest. No announcement. No interruption.

Just him.

Eliza caught his eye and felt herself smile before she could stop it. The reaction startled her—not because it was intense, but because it was unguarded.

"Thought I'd check on you," he said once she gave a small nod of permission. "Make sure they hadn't staged a coup."

"Not yet," she said. "Still early."

A couple of students perked up immediately.

"Mr. Hale!"

Micah acknowledged them with a quick lift of his mug, then lowered his voice. "You're doing good. They're settled."

"Feels right," she admitted.

"Yeah," he said softly. "It does."

He set a folder on her desk. "Extra copies. And if you need anything—anything—you know where my room is."

"I do," she said.

"You stopping by the diner later?"

"Yeah."

He smiled. "You look like someone who's going to need pie tonight."

She laughed quietly. "You have no idea."

He lingered just a second longer, eyes warm, steady—then stepped away without needing reassurance.

She watched him go and felt the absence of tension more than the presence of attraction.

That felt important.

<hr>

By the end of the day, her body was tired and her heart was full.

She walked back out into the afternoon light with ink on her fingers, voices echoing behind her, and a sense of belonging she hadn't rushed or forced—only allowed.

Tonight, she would work the diner.

Tomorrow, she would come back.

And for the first time in a long time, the future didn't feel like something waiting to happen to her.

It felt like something she was already living.

Chapter Forty

The dinner shift moved slower than the morning rush, thick with the smell of grease and coffee that had been sitting too long on the burner. Eliza tied her apron tighter at the waist and leaned into the rhythm—wipe, pour, carry, repeat.

Her body was tired in layers now. Feet sore from standing all day. Shoulders tight from holding space for thirty teenagers and then an entire town's worth of small needs. It was a lot.

But it was hers.

Nell worked the grill with her usual steady focus, spatula snapping against the flat top. Shelby breezed past Eliza with a tray balanced on one hip, eyes bright with curiosity.

"So," Shelby said, dragging the word out. "Ms. Educator. How was your big first day?"

Eliza reached for the coffee pot. "It was fine."

Shelby laughed. "That wasn't the question. Fine like *I survived*, or fine like *I might actually be good at this*?"

Eliza paused just long enough to choose honesty without inviting interrogation. "Fine like… I'll keep going back."

"That's huge," Shelby said. "Most subs don't make it past day three."

The bell over the door jingled.

She didn't have to look to know who it was. She felt it instead—the room shifting, not dramatically, just subtly, like something familiar settling into place.

"Hey," Micah said, sliding onto his usual stool.

"Hey yourself," Eliza replied, already reaching for the coffee pot. "You're late."

"Parent-teacher emails," he said. "They multiply when you're not watching."

She snorted and poured his coffee. "That sounds illegal."

"Feels illegal," he agreed. "Also, I was promised pie."

She shook her head, smiling despite herself. "Blueberry or apple?"

"Dealer's choice."

She slid the plate toward him and leaned her hip against the counter for a heartbeat longer than necessary. The closeness didn't spark alarm. It didn't send her scanning for exits.

That was new.

"So," he said, fork in hand. "How'd day one go?"

She exhaled. "No one flipped a desk. Only one kid tried to argue that credit scores are fake."

"That's a solid start."

"I think I scared them a little."

He looked at her. "You? Doubt it."

She met his eyes. "I have a look."

He smiled around his bite of pie. "You do. It works."

They sat in companionable quiet for a moment—Micah eating, Eliza working, the space between them easy instead of charged. She noticed how he didn't track her movements. Didn't lean in when she leaned away. Didn't fill silences that didn't need filling.

"You working here tonight and tomorrow?" he asked.

"Yeah," she said. "I switched to nights once the school thing started. Temporary insanity."

He nodded. "You always do that. Stack things until you forget how tired you are."

She glanced at him. "You make it sound like you know me."

"I've been paying attention," he said simply. "I do see you almost every day, after all."

Shelby passed by and shot Eliza a look. Eliza ignored her.

Micah wiped his mouth with a napkin. "So. End of the week. You'll have survived your first week teaching."

"Bold assumption."

"When you survive," he corrected, "I was thinking we could do dinner. Friday night. Celebrate."

Eliza paused.

Not because she was unsure.

Because the moment deserved care.

Dinner meant intention. It meant being seen in a different context. It meant choosing to let someone take up space in her life without shrinking herself to accommodate them.

"Dinner like… dinner," she said carefully, "or dinner like you're being sneaky right now?"

He laughed softly. "Probably both."

She considered him—not the idea of him, not the promise of something else—but the man sitting in front of her, patient, unassuming, not asking her to become anything she wasn't.

"Yeah," she said. "Okay."

His smile softened—not surprised, just pleased. "Good."

She picked up the coffee pot again. "You asking me out, Hale?"

"I am," he said. "Finally."

She rolled her eyes. "Took you long enough."

He stood, leaving bills on the counter. "Friday. After your shift?"

"Friday," she confirmed.

As he headed for the door, he glanced back. "You're doing good, Eliza. I know you don't always see it."

The bell jingled as he left.

Eliza stood there for a moment, heart warm and steady—not racing, not guarded.

Just open.

Nell glanced over from the grill. "You look happy."

Eliza lifted the coffee pot. "I think I am."

And she meant it.

Later, when the shift ended and the lights dimmed, she stepped outside into the cool night air. The stars hung bright and unconcerned above Black Hollow.

She walked home slowly, tired and full and quietly looking forward to Friday.

That felt like something worth holding onto.

Chapter Forty-One

She returned to the school for her second day and noticed immediately that the classrooms felt different.

Not friendly, exactly—but familiar.

The students weren't testing her in the same way they had yesterday. The questions came quieter now, edged with curiosity instead of challenge. They knew her name. They knew she followed through. They knew she didn't bluff.

That mattered.

Eliza moved through the morning with a steadiness that surprised her—attendance, lesson plans that required improvisation, a discussion that wandered and then found its way back. A senior asked if she'd be there tomorrow. A junior asked if Mrs. Grady was ever actually coming back.

"I don't know," Eliza said honestly. "But I'm here today."

That seemed to be enough.

By lunch, her shoulders ached in that familiar, earned way. She washed her hands, smoothed her cardigan, and checked her reflection without flinching—hair pulled back, face open, eyes alert but calm—before heading toward the teachers' lounge. She didn't love the room. Too many voices. Too many opinions ricocheting off the walls. But she didn't avoid it either.

Progress.

She took a seat at the end of the table, unwrapped her sandwich, and let the room exist around her.

"You're settling in."

The voice came from her left.

Eliza looked up.

He was tall and broad-shouldered, with the solid confidence of someone who worked with his hands. Dark hair, an easy grin, sleeves rolled to his elbows like he didn't believe in formality longer than required.

"Second day," she said. "Still standing."

He laughed. "That already puts you ahead of the last two subs."

"Low bar."

"Painfully."

He didn't sit—just leaned casually against the table, close enough to be present without crowding her space. She noticed that immediately. Noted it.

"Luke," he said. "Shop."

"Eliza."

"I've seen you around," Luke continued easily. "The diner. Now the school. Feels like Black Hollow's trying to make a point."

She took a bite of her sandwich, unbothered. "It's a small town."

"Sure," he said. "But some overlaps feel intentional."

She glanced at him then—really looked—and caught the spark behind his smile. Not aggressive. Just confident. Curious.

"Would you want to grab dinner or drinks sometime?" he asked. "We can celebrate you officially joining the CTE department. We are, after all, the best department in the school."

"I already have plans," she said evenly. "Dinner. Friday."

Luke blinked, then grinned wider. "Already?"

She shrugged lightly. "Apparently I'm very popular."

He laughed, hands lifting in mock surrender. "All right. Fair enough." Then, amused, "Who's the lucky guy?"

She hesitated just long enough to enjoy it.

"Micah Hale."

Luke stared at her for half a beat, then barked out a laugh. "You're kidding."

She smiled. "Nope."

"My brother," he said, shaking his head. "Of course it is. That's painfully on brand."

She blinked. "Brother?"

"Different dads," Luke said easily. "Same mother. Alice didn't mention?"

Eliza huffed a quiet laugh. "Alice doesn't mention a lot of things."

"Yeah," he said fondly. "That tracks."

He straightened, still smiling, no bitterness in it. "Guess that means I'm officially late to the party."

"You didn't do anything wrong," Eliza said. "Timing matters."

Luke nodded, surprisingly sincere. "It does."

He pushed off the table. "For what it's worth—welcome to the school. And the family, apparently."

She laughed. "I'll try not to cause trouble."

"No promises," he said. "We're not built for boring."

He headed out, leaving behind a faint trace of sawdust and amusement.

Eliza finished her lunch feeling light. No tension. No second-guessing. Just the simple relief of being honest and having it land cleanly.

The afternoon passed smoothly—a quiz, a discussion that almost unraveled and didn't, a room full of students slowly deciding she was worth listening to. When the final bell rang, she gathered her things and stepped outside into the sharp spring air. Snow still lingered in patches, but the sun had teeth now. The promise of thaw.

That night at the diner, someone mentioned the school in passing.

"She holding up?" a man asked.

Nell shrugged. "Seems steady."

That was enough.

When Eliza finally locked up and started the walk back to the cabin, she didn't replay the conversation with Luke. Didn't wonder if she'd said too much or too little. She had been honest. She had been comfortable. She had been herself.

And that—more than anything—felt like the real victory.

Chapter Forty-Two

By the end of the first week, Eliza stopped feeling like a guest.

The bell rang sharp and metallic, echoing down the hallway like punctuation, and the students shuffled in with the practiced indifference of teenagers who had already decided how much effort the day deserved. Eliza stood at the front of the room, hands loose at her sides, watching them settle.

They knew her name now.

Not all of them liked her. That was fine. She wasn't here to be liked. She was here to be steady.

She wrote the agenda on the board in clean, deliberate strokes and turned back toward them. A few heads lifted. A few didn't. One boy in the back rested his forehead against his desk like gravity had finally claimed him.

"Morning," she said, calm and unforced. "Let's get started."

She didn't raise her voice. She didn't threaten. She didn't bargain.

Somehow, that worked better.

The lesson wasn't flashy—budgeting basics, credit myths, the quiet danger of assuming future-you would magically be smarter than present-you—but Eliza taught it like it mattered. Because it did. She asked questions that made them think instead of perform. Let silences stretch until someone filled them. Corrected gently. Praised effort instead of volume.

Halfway through the period, she felt the shift.

Not attention.

Respect.

After the bell, a girl lingered near the door, hoodie sleeves pulled over her hands, eyes darting toward the hall like she might disappear if someone looked at her too long.

"Ms. Moore?" the girl asked.

Eliza waited. Didn't rush her.

"My mom says credit cards are a scam," the girl said. "But she also says we need one to get an apartment. So… which is it?"

Eliza leaned back against the desk, folding her arms loosely. "Both," she said. "And neither. It depends on how much power you give it."

The girl frowned, thinking.

Then nodded.

"Thanks," she said, hesitating. "You explain things better than Mrs. Grady did."

It wasn't a compliment Eliza had expected.

It followed her through the rest of the day.

Lunch came and went in the teachers' lounge, the air thick with reheated leftovers and burnt coffee. Eliza ate quietly, listening more than speaking, learning the rhythms—who complained, who joked, who watched. She wasn't invisible anymore, but she wasn't on display either.

Someone slid into the chair across from her.

"Well," he said pleasantly, "you've survived your first week."

She looked up.

Early forties. Glasses slipping down his nose. Sweater vest. A bow tie that looked permanently amused.

"So far," she said.

He smiled. "That's better than most subs."

"I'm Dan—Mr. Meyer," he added, tapping the table lightly. "Music."

"Eliza."

"You planning on being back next week?" he asked, casual but hopeful.

"Yes."

"Good," he said. "The kids could use consistency. And they seem to like you."

Eliza smiled, the kind that reached her eyes before she realized it.

That afternoon, Principal Carver stopped her in the hallway.

"Mrs. Grady's recovery is taking longer than expected," he said, hands clasped behind his back. "Surgery hit her harder than she anticipated."

Eliza kept her expression neutral, posture open.

"We'd like you to stay on," he continued. "At least until she's cleared. No clear timeline yet. If that works for you."

It did.

She said yes.

She walked out of the building with tired legs and something warm and unfamiliar blooming in her chest.

She was needed.

That mattered.

That evening, back at the cabin, Eliza stood in front of the bathroom mirror longer than usual.

She'd been plain since she arrived—clean, practical, unremarkable on purpose. Minimal makeup. Hair pulled back. Clothes chosen for function, not feeling.

Tonight was different.

Not because she needed to impress Micah.

Because she wanted to feel beautiful.

She let her hair down, surprised by how much it had already grown back—softer, fuller, no longer something she tried to disappear. She applied makeup slowly, carefully. A little color in her cheeks. Mascara. Lipstick just dark enough to feel intentional.

When she stepped back, she barely recognized herself.

A woman with purpose. With a job she mattered in. With a date waiting.

She changed into a dress she hadn't worn yet—simple, flattering—and slipped on boots that made her feel grounded instead of small. She caught her reflection once more and smiled, just a little.

Later, she opened her notebook.

Not to list. Not to observe.

She wrote one sentence and didn't cross it out.

Today, I mattered.

Then she closed it, turned off the light, and let herself look forward to the evening ahead.

Chapter Forty-Three

Micah knocked exactly once.

Not tentative. Not demanding. Just enough to be heard.

Eliza took a breath she hadn't realized she'd been holding and crossed the cabin, pausing with her hand on the door for half a second—not out of fear, but anticipation. That was new enough to feel strange. When she opened it, Micah stood on the porch with dusk settling behind him, the last of the light catching in his hair. He'd cleaned up—dark jeans, a button-down with the sleeves rolled just past his forearms, a jacket slung over one shoulder like he hadn't overthought it.

He looked at her and stopped.

Not dramatically. Just long enough to take her in.

"You look really nice," he said, quiet and sincere, like it wasn't a line he practiced.

Heat bloomed low in her chest. "You do too."

His mouth curved, just a little. "Ready?"

She grabbed her coat and locked the door behind her, the click familiar and unremarkable. They walked down the porch steps together, shoulder to shoulder, the space between them comfortable instead of charged. His truck waited just off the drive—nothing flashy, clean, lived-in. He opened the passenger door without ceremony.

On the drive into town, the radio played low—something acoustic, familiar but unobtrusive. The road was dark, trees pressing close, and Eliza found herself relaxing into the seat in a way she hadn't expected.

"So," Micah said after a minute, "first week survived."

"Barely," she said, smiling. "I'm pretty sure I aged five years."

"That's generous. Seniors will do that to you, especially this close to graduation."

She glanced at him. "You're enjoying this."

"Immensely." He paused. "But I meant what I said. You're good with them. They need someone who doesn't flinch."

Something tightened gently in her throat. "Thanks."

He nodded, like that was enough.

They didn't go somewhere flashy. He took her to a small restaurant just outside town—warm lights, wood tables, quiet enough to hear yourself think. A place people came to talk, not be seen. Inside, he held the door, let her go first, and didn't rush the moment when the hostess led them to their table.

Once they sat, something shifted.

Not tension.

Permission.

They talked easily—about books, teaching, the strange
assumptions people made about small towns. Micah told her
stories about students who surprised him, about why he
stayed. She laughed more than she expected to. He listened
like her words mattered, like he wasn't waiting for his turn.

At one point, she caught him watching her—not her body, not
her face alone, but the way she spoke when she got animated,
hands moving, eyes bright.

"What?" she asked.

He shook his head. "Just thinking how different you are
tonight."

She raised a brow. "Different how?"

"Not guarded," he said gently. "Still careful. But… here."

The word settled softly between them.

Here.

Dinner stretched comfortably. No rush. No pressure. When
they finished, Micah paid without comment and stood,
offering his hand—not to pull her anywhere, just to connect.
She took it.

Outside, the air had cooled, the sky clear and star-heavy. They
walked slowly toward the truck, neither eager to end the night,
neither forcing it to continue.

"I'm glad you said yes," he said as they stopped beside the
door.

"So am I."

He hesitated, then stepped closer, enough that she could feel his warmth without being crowded.

"I don't want to make assumptions," he said quietly. "But I'd like to do this again."

Her answer came without hesitation. "I would too."

Relief crossed his face before he masked it, honest and endearing.

He didn't kiss her right away. Instead, he brushed his thumb along her cheek, a question without words. Eliza leaned in.

The kiss was soft, unrushed, careful in the way only someone who respected boundaries could be. No claiming. No urgency. Just lips meeting, parting, meeting again—confirmation rather than conquest.

When they pulled back, she rested her forehead briefly against his chest, surprised by how natural it felt.

"Thank you," she said.

"For dinner?" he asked.

"For... tonight."

He smiled—the real one. "Anytime."

The drive back was quieter but not awkward. When he pulled up to the cabin, he cut the engine and turned to her.

"Text me when you get inside."

"I will."

He didn't follow her to the door. Didn't linger. Just watched until she unlocked it and stepped inside, then gave a small wave and drove off.

Inside, Eliza leaned back against the door, hand pressed to her mouth, heart steady but full.

Chapter Forty-Four

Eliza woke to light instead of alarm.

Sun filtered through the thin curtains in pale bands, warming the quilt at her feet. For a moment she lay still, listening to the cabin breathe—the soft creak of wood, the distant hush of wind through branches. Her body felt loose in a way it hadn't the day before. Or the day before that. The kind of ease that arrived quietly and stayed if you didn't startle it.

Her phone buzzed on the nightstand.

She reached for it without expectation and found everything.

Micah:
Morning. Hope I didn't wake you.
There's an author reading at the bookshop around ten.
Thought of you.
Coffee after, if you want.

She smiled before she could stop herself. Not the careful smile she wore for strangers, but the real one—the kind that surprised her.

Eliza:
You didn't. And yes—coffee sounds perfect.

The reply came almost immediately.

Micah:
Good. I'll meet you there.

She set the phone down and sat up, heart steady, warm. No rush. No nerves twisting her stomach. Just anticipation—the gentle kind that didn't ask to be managed.

She showered and let the hot water loosen her muscles, lingering beneath the spray longer than necessary, letting herself feel good in her body without rushing away from it. Steam fogged the mirror, and she didn't wipe it clear. She didn't need to check who she was. When she dressed, she didn't reach for the same soft sweater she always did. She chose a simple top that skimmed her curves without announcing them, jeans that fit instead of hid, flats worn smooth from being walked in with intention. She brushed her hair until it fell loose around her shoulders and paused at her reflection—not to critique, not to fix, but to acknowledge the quiet spark there.

She smiled at herself, small and genuine.

Not because she needed to impress him.

Because she wanted to show up as someone who felt good being seen.

You're allowed to enjoy this, she told herself, and believed it.

The walk into town felt different. Spring had settled in fully—no snow clinging to corners, no gray slush underfoot. The ground was dark and soft, dotted with early flowers pushing up wherever they could. Trees wore a faint green haze, leaves not quite grown but confidently on their way. The air smelled warm and alive, like earth and rain and the promise of long evenings that didn't end too soon.

She breathed it in and smiled without meaning to.

The bookshop sat halfway down Main, narrow and deep, its front window cluttered with handwritten signs and mismatched displays. Inside, it smelled like paper and coffee and time.

Micah was already there, leaning against a shelf near the back with a paperback in his hands. When he looked up and saw her, his face softened—open, pleased, unguarded.

"You made it," he said, like it mattered.

"So did you."

They took seats in a small cluster of folding chairs near the front just as the reading began. The author—a woman with silver hair and a voice like gravel and honey—read from a collection of essays about grief, place, and becoming someone you didn't plan to be. Eliza found herself leaning forward without realizing it. Micah noticed but didn't comment, just stayed close, shoulder nearly brushing hers, presence steady.

When the reading ended, applause filled the room—earnest and unpolished. The author answered a few questions. Someone asked about fear. About starting over.

Eliza swallowed.

They drifted toward the coffee counter together, moving easily, like this was already a rhythm they understood.

"You okay?" Micah asked softly as they waited.

"Yeah," she said. "That was… exactly what I needed."

"I thought it might be." He smiled. "You have good taste."

She laughed. "Says the English teacher who brought me here."

"Fair."

They took their coffees and stepped back outside, choosing a bench near the window. Sunlight hit the glass just right, warming their backs.

"So," Micah said, blowing on his cup, "how does it feel being off for a morning?"

"Strange," Eliza admitted. "Good strange."

He glanced at her. "You're allowed that too, you know."

She met his gaze. "I'm starting to believe you."

They talked about books they loved, characters who felt like old friends, about writing—what it meant to put pieces of yourself on a page and let strangers hold them.

"I used to write," Eliza said quietly.

Micah didn't jump on it. He waited.

"Not for anyone," she continued. "Just… to make sense of things."

"Do you miss it?"

"Yes," she said, surprised by how quickly the answer came.

He nodded. "Then you should start again."

She smiled into her coffee. "You make it sound easy."

"It's not," he said. "But it's worth it."

They sat longer than they planned. The town moved around them—cars passing, people waving, life continuing in small, ordinary ways. When Micah glanced at his watch and sighed, it was reluctant, not rushed.

"I should let you go."

"Probably."

They stood, neither eager to end the morning, neither forcing it to last.

"I'm glad we did this," he said. "Not just because of the books."

"Me too."

He leaned in and kissed her—soft again, familiar already. This time she kissed him back without thinking, hands resting easily against his chest. When they parted, he rested his forehead against hers for a brief second.

"See you tonight?" he asked. "If you're working."

She nodded. "I'll save you pie."

His smile widened. "I'll hold you to that."

As she walked home, coffee warmth still in her hands, Eliza realized something quietly profound.

She wasn't bracing for the moment to end.

She was letting it carry her forward.

Chapter Forty-Five

The dinner shift had settled into its familiar rhythm by the time Eliza tied her apron and stepped behind the counter. The air was warm and heavy with butter and coffee, the faint sweetness of pie lingering near the register where someone had set it too close to the heat. The windows were open now—spring confident enough to stay—and voices drifted in from the sidewalk along with laughter and the distant thrum of a radio playing too loud somewhere down the street.

Micah was already there.

He sat near the end of the counter, a book open beside his coffee, jacket draped over the stool next to him like he expected to stay awhile. When he looked up and saw her, his smile came easily—unguarded, familiar. The kind that didn't ask anything of her, didn't pull or claim.

"Hey," he said.

"Hey," she answered, and only noticed after that her voice sounded lighter than usual.

She slid his mug toward him and moved down the counter to wipe up a spill, aware of him watching—not her body, not her face alone, but the way she moved. Like he was simply glad she existed in the same room.

The bell over the door jingled.

Luke didn't hesitate. He walked in with the confidence of someone who never questioned whether he belonged where he stood, jacket unzipped, boots still dusted from the shop. His grin was already in place when he spotted Micah.

"Well, I'll be damned," Luke said, dropping onto the stool beside him. "Pie and a book. You really are predictable."

Micah didn't look up. "You say that like you didn't come here hoping for pie."

Luke smirked. "I came for the waitress."

Eliza arched a brow as she set down a plate. "That so?"

Luke's attention shifted fully to her—easy, unapologetic. "I was wondering if you'd changed your mind."

"About what?" she asked, though she already knew.

"Letting me take you out," he said. "Dinner. Drinks. Something that doesn't involve grading papers or pretending coffee counts as a meal."

Micah closed his book slowly, finally meeting his brother's eyes. "You don't quit, do you?"

Luke shrugged. "Why would I? She's interesting."

Eliza leaned lightly against the counter, unbothered. "You know I've been seeing Micah."

Luke flicked a glance at his brother, then back to her. "Sure. But that's casual, right? Nothing official."

She hesitated—just long enough to register the shift—then glanced at Micah. "I guess," she said honestly.

Luke laughed under his breath. "Then I still have a shot."

Micah exhaled. "Don't make it weird."

"Oh, I'm absolutely making it weird," Luke said cheerfully. Then, to Eliza, "You sure you don't want to try the better brother?"

Micah snorted. "Debatable."

The sound that came out of Eliza surprised her—a real laugh, loose and unguarded. Not tense. Not defensive.

"You two are exhausting," she said. "And for the record? I didn't pick based on who tried harder."

Luke lifted his hands. "Fair enough. Had to ask."

He ordered pie, paid, and stood a moment later, tapping the counter. "No hard feelings, Ms. Moore. I admire commitment. Even when it's annoying."

Micah shot him a look. "Get out."

Luke grinned. "See you at Sunday dinner."

That earned a groan.

When Luke finally left and Micah followed not long after—coffee finished, book tucked under his arm—the diner felt quieter. Not empty. Just settled.

Nell wandered over from the grill, wiping her hands on a towel. "Didn't know we were hosting family drama tonight."

Eliza shook her head, smiling. "They're ridiculous."

"They're brothers," Nell said. "It's required." She tilted her head. "Alice know about this?"

Eliza paused, then shrugged. "Probably."

Nell hummed. "That woman always does."

Eliza finished her shift with tired feet and a warm chest—the kind of exhaustion that came from being present instead of braced. When she stepped outside, the night air was soft and clear, stars scattered bright above Black Hollow like they'd been waiting for her to notice them.

She walked home slowly, not replaying conversations, not questioning her choices.

Just letting herself enjoy the fact that she had been wanted—

and that she was the one who got to choose.

Chapter Forty-Six

The rain started sometime after noon.

Not a storm. Not the kind that demanded attention. Just a steady, patient spring rain—the kind that soaked into the ground instead of running off it, that made everything smell alive again.

Eliza opened the windows and let it in.

Cool air drifted through the cabin, carrying the scent of wet earth, budding leaves, and something green she didn't have a name for. The fire burned low in the hearth, just enough to chase away the chill, its crackle soft and companionable. She curled one leg beneath her on the couch, a mug warming her palms—cocoa this time. Wine felt like celebration. This felt like returning.

For once, she wasn't waiting for anything.

No shift to get to.
No lessons to plan.
No expectations pressing against her ribs.

Just a Sunday.
Just rain.
Just quiet.

The notebook sat on the coffee table where she'd left it earlier, closed but not ignored. It had been there for weeks now—

present, patient. Lately she'd filled its pages with fragments. Observations. Images. Sentences that didn't yet know what they were becoming.

But today felt different.

Today, the quiet didn't feel empty.

It felt like an invitation.

She reached for the notebook and opened it, fingers tracing the faintly rough paper. She stared at the blank page longer than she meant to—not frozen, not afraid. Just remembering.

Micah's voice from the bookshop drifted back to her.

You should write again.

She had smiled then. Deflected. Safer to keep things light.

But alone, with the rain tapping softly against the windows and the fire breathing low behind her, the truth settled in her chest without resistance.

She didn't just miss writing.

She missed telling the truth.

Not the polished version. Not the one shaped to survive headlines and sympathy. The real one. The one that lived in her body. The one no one had ever asked for.

Her pen hovered.

Then she wrote.

I used to belong to a man who taught me how to disappear in plain sight.

The words landed heavier than she expected. Not painful.

Solid.

She kept going.

She wrote about the beginning—the charm, the attention, the way being chosen had felt like proof of worth. She wrote about how love didn't curdle all at once, how it arrived in corrections and expectations, in small punishments disguised as care.

She wrote about learning to measure herself.

Her voice.
Her laughter.
Her hunger.
Her ambition.

She wrote about how nothing looked broken from the outside.

The rain picked up slightly, a soft percussion against the roof, like it was urging her on.

Her hand cramped. She didn't stop.

She wrote about the night she understood staying would kill her—not quickly, not dramatically, but in pieces. How survival had stopped meaning living. How leaving meant becoming a ghost.

She wrote about the bus.
The diner.
The cabin.

She wrote about cutting her hair and watching pieces of herself fall into the sink like evidence she was done carrying.

At some point, tears slid down her cheeks—not sobs. Not collapse. Just release. She wiped them away with the back of her hand and kept writing, ink blurring slightly where the page caught her breath.

This wasn't a diary.

It was a record.

A map of where she had been—and how she had escaped.

When her hand finally slowed, when the words tapered into silence, Eliza leaned back against the couch and closed her eyes.

The fire popped softly.
The rain softened again.

Her chest felt open in a way that startled her—not raw. Not wounded.

Open, like a window after a long winter.

She understood something then, quietly, without ceremony.

This wasn't just healing.

This was evidence.

Someday, she would need this.

Someday, the truth would need a place to stand.

And when that day came, she would already have the words.

Eliza closed the notebook carefully and set it back on the table—not hiding it. Just letting it rest. She finished her cocoa and listened to the rain until the fire burned low and afternoon slipped toward evening.

For the first time in a long while, she didn't feel like a woman hiding her past.

She felt like a woman documenting it.

And that made her smile.

Not because she was safe—

but because she was finally powerful in a way no one could take from her.

Chapter Forty-Seven

Alice's house smelled like coffee and rain-soaked earth.

The windows were cracked despite the chill, curtains lifting and falling with the breeze as if the house itself were breathing. Outside, the trees dripped steadily, the ground dark and saturated from the storm that had passed through earlier. Alice sat at the kitchen table with her laptop open, sleeves rolled to her elbows, eyes narrowed at the screen like whatever she was reading had already irritated her more than once.

Eliza lingered in the doorway longer than necessary.

She didn't feel afraid.

She felt full. Charged. Like something inside her chest had finally aligned and was humming quietly because of it.

Alice glanced up. "You're pacing."

Eliza exhaled and stepped inside, shrugging out of her jacket. "I didn't mean to be."

Alice tipped her chin toward the chair across from her. "Sit. Whatever you came here to say has weight on it."

Eliza sat.

For a moment, she didn't speak. She watched the rain slide down the glass, the way the world outside looked softened by it—edges blurred, colors deeper. Six months ago, she wouldn't have trusted a silence like this. Wouldn't have believed it could exist without consequence.

Now she did.

"I've been seeing Micah," she said finally.

Alice didn't react. Not surprised. Not curious.

"I figured," she said. "He's been uselessly careful."

The words pulled a small, unexpected smile from Eliza. "He really has."

"And Luke," Eliza added. "He's been asking me out too."

That earned a twitch of Alice's mouth. "That sounds like Luke."

Eliza hesitated, then said quietly, "I wanted you to hear it from me. Not because I think I'm doing anything wrong—but because I don't want secrets between us anymore."

Alice closed the laptop halfway and leaned back, giving her full attention. "You're allowed to have a life," she said. "You always were. You just weren't safe enough to live it before."

Eliza swallowed. "I'm not hiding from it anymore."

Alice studied her for a long moment, something sharp and thoughtful moving behind her eyes. Then she nodded. "Good."

Eliza took a breath. "There's more."

Alice nodded once. "I assumed."

The rain tapped harder against the windows, a steady punctuation.

"I want to know what story Daniel told," Eliza said. "What the world thinks happened to me."

Alice didn't soften the moment. She turned the laptop fully toward Eliza. "We'll do it here. My network. Nothing touches you."

Eliza nodded, bracing.

Alice typed a name.

Not Eliza Moore.

The other one.

Eden Whitmore.

The headlines appeared immediately.

Mayor Whitmore Requests Privacy Amid Personal Family Matter
Sources Close to the Mayor Confirm Wife's 'Emotional Breakdown'
A Tragic Strain of Public Life: When First Ladies Disappear

Something cold slid through Eliza's veins.

Alice scrolled.

A photo of her filled the screen—carefully chosen. Soft lighting. Concern curated into her expression. The version of herself she'd been trained to present.

"She entered a private recovery facility," Alice read aloud, flat. "'Out of state. At her request.'"

Eliza let out a short, humorless breath. "Of course."

"Daniel positioned himself as patient," Alice continued. "Devoted. Heartbroken but respectful."

"Martyr," Eliza whispered.

"Yes," Alice said. "That."

Eliza stared until the words stopped meaning anything. Until the story flattened into noise.

Then she said, quietly, "I want to stop him."

Alice went still.

Not shocked. Not alarmed.

Interested.

"He didn't just hurt me," Eliza said, her voice steady in a way that surprised even her. "There were women. Parties. The basement. The things he paid to keep quiet. He's still doing it. I know he is."

Alice folded her hands. "I know."

Eliza looked up sharply. "What?"

"I've been watching him for years," Alice said.

The silence that followed was absolute.

"That's how I knew who you were," Alice continued. "Before Tonya ever called me."

Eliza's chest tightened. "Tonya?"

Alice exhaled slowly. "This is the part that's going to hurt."

Eliza's hands curled into fists in her lap.

"Tonya is my daughter," Alice said. "And she didn't meet you by accident."

The room tilted.

"No," Eliza said. "She was my friend."

"She was," Alice said gently. "That part was real."

Eliza stood abruptly, the chair scraping back. "You used her. You used me."

"I protected her," Alice said evenly. "She knew exactly what she was walking into."

Hot, furious tears burned instantly. "She watched me break. She held my hands. She let me trust her."

"Yes," Alice said. "Because trust is what Daniel exploits. And because Tonya needed to be close enough to see everything."

Eliza shook her head, breath coming fast. "You planted her."

"I gave her a choice," Alice said firmly. "She chose to help expose him. And when you married him and she couldn't reach you anymore, she chose you."

Eliza pressed her palms to the table, grounding herself. "Was any of it real?"

"All of it," Alice said without hesitation. "That's why she called me instead of disappearing you herself."

Eliza laughed—a sharp, broken sound. "Jesus."

"And before you ask," Alice added, "Micah and Luke don't know what I do."

Eliza looked up, eyes red. "They're not lying to me too?"

"No," Alice said. "They know I help people. They don't know how. They don't know Daniel. And they don't know who you were."

She paused. "Micah cares about you. He talked about you before you ever noticed him."

Eliza blinked. "He did?"

"He gave you space when he wanted more," Alice said. "That tells me everything."

Eliza sank back into the chair, shaking. "I don't know how to feel."

Alice softened, just slightly. "That's because you're finally allowed to feel all of it."

Eliza wiped her face. "I want to help you take him down."

Alice's gaze sharpened. "That's not a small decision."

"I know," Eliza said. "But I'm not afraid anymore."

Alice studied her for a long, quiet moment.

Then she nodded.

"All right," she said. "Then we do this the right way."

The rain slowed outside. The air felt charged, alive.

"You don't go back to being a ghost," Alice said. "You become a witness."

Chapter Forty-Eight

Eliza didn't have a plan, she left Alice's farmhouse with her head full and her chest too tight to sit still, the night air cool against her flushed skin. The truths she'd learned clung to her like static — Daniel's lies, Tonya's betrayal, the long shadow Alice had been standing in for years.

But underneath all of it was something else.

Relief.

Micah wasn't a lie.

He wasn't watching her. Wasn't placed. Wasn't part of the web.

He had been careful because he cared.

The thought undid her.

She drove into town without thinking it through, tires humming against the road, hands steady on the wheel even though her pulse wasn't. Micah's apartment sat above a converted storefront on the quieter side of Main — old brick, a single light on in the upstairs window.

She parked. Sat there a moment.

Then she went inside.

The stairs creaked under her boots. She stopped at his door, lifted her hand, hesitated — not from fear, but from the weight of what she was choosing.

She knocked.

Micah opened the door in socked feet and a soft T-shirt, hair still damp like he'd showered recently. Surprise flickered across his face — then concern.

"Eliza?"
His voice gentled instantly. "Hey. Are you okay?"

That was all it took.

She nodded, once, sharp. "Can I come in?"

"Of course."

His apartment was warm and lived-in — books stacked on every flat surface, a mug abandoned on the counter, a lamp on instead of the overhead light. It smelled faintly of coffee and clean laundry.

He closed the door behind her but didn't touch her. Didn't crowd. Just waited.

She crossed the room slowly, then turned to face him.

"I went to Alice's tonight," she said. "She told me some things."

Micah's expression didn't change — but his attention sharpened, complete and unwavering.

"Okay," he said. "Do you want to tell me? Or do you want me to listen?"

Her throat tightened.

"Listen," she said.

So he did.

She didn't tell him everything. She didn't say Daniel's name. She didn't explain the web or the danger or the past in full.

But she told him enough.

That she'd been lied to.
That someone she loved hadn't been who she thought.
That she was angry and hurt and relieved all at once.
That she needed to be somewhere she didn't have to guard every word.

Micah didn't interrupt. Didn't try to fix it. Didn't ask for details she didn't offer.

When she finished, she realized her hands were shaking.

He noticed too.

"Hey," he said quietly, stepping closer now — slow, deliberate, giving her time to pull away if she wanted. "You don't have to hold yourself together here."

The words broke something open.

She exhaled hard, a sound halfway between a laugh and a sob, and pressed her forehead into his chest. He wrapped his arms around her without hesitation, solid and warm, one hand settling between her shoulder blades like it belonged there.

She melted.

Not collapsed. Not disappeared.

Melted.

He held her until her breathing evened out, until the tension drained from her shoulders, until the world narrowed to the steady rhythm of his heart.

When she pulled back, she didn't step away.

She looked up at him instead.

"I needed to know you were real," she said.

His thumb brushed gently along her jaw. "I am."

She believed him.

She rose onto her toes and kissed him.

It wasn't rushed. It wasn't clumsy or desperate. It was deliberate — her mouth warm and sure against his, like she was testing something she already knew the answer to. Micah froze for half a second, not from surprise, but from respect — giving her space to change her mind.

When she didn't, when she leaned in instead, he kissed her back.

Slowly.

His hands came to her waist, firm but careful, thumbs brushing the fabric of her shirt like he was learning the shape of her instead of claiming it. The kiss deepened in quiet increments — a breath caught, a soft sound she didn't realize she'd made until it was already gone, his mouth tilting to meet hers more fully.

Her body responded before her thoughts could interfere.

Heat unfurled low in her belly, familiar but different — not edged with fear or performance, not sharpened by expectation. Just warmth. Want. Presence.

Micah's forehead rested against hers when they finally broke apart, his breath unsteady now too.

"We can stop," he murmured, voice rougher than before.
"Any time."

"I know," she said.

The knowing mattered.

She slid her hands up his chest, feeling the solid reality of him
beneath her palms, the way his breath stuttered when her
fingers brushed the back of his neck. She kissed him again,
slower this time, and felt the moment tip — not into urgency,
but into inevitability.

He followed her lead.

They moved together toward the bedroom without haste,
pausing as clothes were shed piece by piece — her shirt first,
then his, hands warm against newly bared skin. She felt
exposed in the best way, her body remembered not as
something to endure but something to inhabit.

Micah's gaze never felt hungry.

It felt reverent.

Like he was seeing her — not a version of her, not a role —
but her.

When he touched her, it was with intention. Fingers tracing her spine, her hips, the curve of her waist, mapping her like she was somewhere he meant to return to. She breathed him in — clean skin, faint soap, something uniquely him — and let herself be held without bracing for what might follow.

She hadn't realized how long she'd been waiting for that.

They came together slowly, bodies fitting in a way that felt earned rather than taken. She pressed her face into his shoulder, a quiet sound escaping her when sensation flooded in — not sharp, not overwhelming, just deep and grounding.

Micah stayed close, whispering her name like a promise, moving with her instead of over her, reading every shift in her breath, every subtle change in her body.

For the first time in years, she didn't disappear inside herself.

She stayed.

Every sensation anchored her — the press of his hands, the steady rhythm between them, the way her body responded not out of habit but desire. When release came, it did so without violence, without fear — a wave that carried her instead of crashing over her.

She laughed softly afterward, surprised by herself.

Micah smiled into her hair, arms firm around her, holding her like she wasn't something fragile that might break if he let go.

Later, wrapped in his sheets, her head resting on his chest, she listened to his heartbeat slow beneath her ear. His hand traced lazy, absent-minded patterns along her arm, grounding her in the quiet aftermath.

She stared at the ceiling and felt something settle — not safety, exactly.

Ownership.

Of herself.

She hadn't come here to be saved.

She'd come because she was ready to choose.

And choosing him — choosing this — felt like stepping fully back into her body, her life, her desire.

Not as Eden.

Not as Eliza hiding.

But as a woman who knew exactly where she was — and why.

Chapter Forty-Nine

Morning didn't rush them.

Eliza woke with her cheek pressed to Micah's chest, the steady rhythm of his breathing beneath her ear anchoring her in place. For a few seconds she floated in that half-space between sleep and awareness—not startled, not afraid—just wrapped in softness. Then memory settled gently into place. His apartment. His arms. Last night.

She shifted slightly, and his arm tightened around her in response, instinctive and sure. Protective without being possessive.

"Hey," he murmured, voice rough with sleep.

"Hey," she whispered back, smiling before she could stop herself.

He brushed his thumb slowly along her spine, a familiar path already learned. "You okay?"

"I am," she said, and meant it. "I just… didn't want to move yet."

"Then don't."

They stayed like that for a while, tangled and quiet, the light creeping higher along the walls as responsibility nudged its way in without urgency. There was no rush here, no need to perform the morning or hurry toward the next obligation.

"We're going to be late," she said eventually, not sounding upset about it.

"Worth it," he replied without hesitation.

She laughed softly, the sound warm and unguarded, and leaned up to kiss him. It started gentle—lingering lips, shared breath—but deepened quickly, hunger blooming where comfort already lived. He rolled them easily, careful and attentive, checking in without words, reading her the way he always did.

When they finally pulled apart, both breathing heavier now, Micah rested his forehead against hers.

"Shower?" he asked. "Before we do something irresponsible."

She studied him, eyes bright. "We're already doing something irresponsible."

That grin again—crooked, fond. "Fair."

The bathroom filled with steam almost immediately, the mirror fogging until the world beyond it disappeared. They stepped under the spray together, warmth cascading over skin still sensitive from the night before. Micah's hands slid over her back, familiar now, confident but unhurried.

He kissed her shoulder. Her neck. The place just behind her ear that made her shiver.

Eliza leaned back against him, eyes closing as water slicked between them, heat loosening something deeper than muscle. She turned, palms pressing to his chest, meeting his mouth again—slower this time, fuller, like they were choosing each other all over again.

Nothing about it felt rushed. Nothing felt taken.

It was connection—bodies fitting together, breath and touch and trust, the sound of water muffling everything else. When it crested, it wasn't explosive. It was grounding. Like settling back into herself inside someone else's arms.

Afterward, they stayed beneath the spray, foreheads touching, both quiet.

Micah brushed wet hair back from her face. "You don't ever have to be ready for more than this," he said softly. "I'm not going anywhere."

Her throat tightened—not with fear, but gratitude. "I know."

They dried off and dressed quickly, lingering in small touches—fingers brushing, smiles exchanged—before heading out into the cool morning air.

Micah drove her back to the cabin, the world bright and clean beyond the windshield. When they pulled up, she paused, hand resting on the door.

"Wait here," she said. "I want us to go to work together."

Inside, she changed—comfortable but thoughtful, hair brushed, a touch of color on her lips she hadn't bothered with in a long time. When she stepped back outside, Micah looked at her like he was trying not to stare.

"You look…" He stopped himself, smiling. "Happy."

"I am."

They drove into town together, parked at the school, and walked in side by side—easy, unselfconscious.

And that was when Luke saw them.

He was leaning against the lockers near the main hallway, coffee in hand, mid-conversation with another teacher. His eyes flicked up casually at first—then sharpened.

Micah greeted him without breaking stride. "Morning."

Luke's gaze moved to Eliza, then back to Micah, something amused and competitive sparking there.

"Well," Luke said slowly, a grin spreading. "Guess that answers a few questions."

Eliza raised an eyebrow. "Good morning to you too."

Luke chuckled. "Didn't realize I was losing to my own brother."

Micah squeezed her hand once before letting go. "You weren't losing. You were just late."

Luke laughed, shaking his head. "Cliché as hell."

Eliza smiled—unbothered, unashamed.

"See you later," Micah said quietly, brushing his thumb once over her knuckles before heading down the hall.

Luke watched him go, then looked back at her. "Huh," he said. "Didn't see that coming."

She met his gaze calmly. "I did."

Chapter Fifty

Eliza had just settled into her prep period when there was a knock on the open classroom door.

Not tentative. Not intrusive. Just present.

She looked up from the stack of worksheets she'd been half-grading and felt the now-familiar shift in the air.

Luke.

He leaned against the doorframe, one boot crossed casually over the other, shop jacket unzipped, sleeves rolled like he'd come straight from the welding bays. He didn't smile right away.

"Hey," he said.

She set her pen down slowly. "You're not supposed to wander into Business Ed during prep. That's how rumors start."

He huffed a laugh. "Pretty sure those already did."

She didn't smile. "Luke."

"Relax," he said, lifting his hands. "I'm not here to cause trouble."

"That depends on your definition."

He stepped inside anyway but stopped a respectful distance from her desk. That mattered.

"I saw you come in with Micah this morning," he said plainly.

"Yes," she replied. "You also commented on it."

"And I meant what I said then," he continued. "I'm losing to my brother."

She sighed. "This again?"

"Let me finish," he said, more serious now. "I'm not trying to steal you. I'm not trying to undermine him. And I'm not pretending I don't know you're seeing him."

"Then why are you here?" she asked.

Luke held her gaze. "Because I don't want to wonder."

The words landed heavier than she expected.

"I've been clear," she said. "More than once."

"I know," he said. "And I also know you haven't known either of us that long. And that sometimes people choose safety before they choose truth."

Her spine straightened. "Careful."

"I am," he said quietly. "That's the point."

She studied him—not the flirt, not the confidence. The man standing in her classroom during his free period, risking rejection in a place where pride usually mattered more than honesty.

"You want me to go out with you," she said.

"One date," Luke replied. "That's it."

She shook her head. "You saw me with your brother."

"Yes."

"And you're still asking."

"Yes."

"Why?"

Luke exhaled slowly, like he'd been holding it in since morning. "Because Micah is steady. He's safe. He's good." A pause. "I'm not asking you to choose me. I'm asking you to make sure you're not choosing him because he's easier to fall into."

That wasn't fair.

And it also wasn't entirely wrong.

"If you say no after one date," Luke continued, "I'll drop it. Completely. No more jokes. No more asking. No pressure."

"And if I say yes?"

"Then I'll show you who I am," he said. "Not compared to him. Just me."

Silence stretched.

"You understand how this looks," she said.

"I do."

"You understand I won't hide it from Micah."

"I'd be insulted if you did."

She leaned back against her desk, heart steady but loud. This wasn't danger. This wasn't manipulation.

This was choice.

"One date," she said.

Luke's expression shifted—not triumph, not smugness. Something quieter. Earned.

"One," he agreed. "Friday?"

She nodded once. "I'll talk to Micah first."

"I figured you would," Luke said. "That's part of why I asked again."

He stepped back toward the door, then paused. "And Eliza?"

"Yes?"

"This isn't a test," he said. "I just want you to know you had options."

When he left, the room felt different.

Not heavier.

Clearer.

That afternoon, she found Micah in the English wing, leaning against the copy machine with a stack of essays and the resigned expression of a man who had already lost this battle.

"Luke came by my room," she said.

Micah looked up immediately. "I figured."

"He asked me out again."

Micah didn't interrupt.

"I said yes," she continued. "One date. I told him I'd talk to you first."

Micah was quiet for a moment.

Then he nodded. "Okay."

"That's it?" she asked.

"That's it," he said. "I trust you."

She stepped closer. "You're not angry?"

"No," he said honestly. "I'd be angry if you felt cornered. Or guilty. Or like you had to pretend you didn't want to know."

"And if I decide…?" she trailed off.

Micah met her eyes, steady and sure. "Then I want it to be because you chose me. Not because you didn't give yourself permission to look."

Her chest tightened.

"Friday," she said softly.

"Friday," he echoed.

He smiled—not threatened. Not possessive.

Certain.

Chapter Fifty-One

Friday night came, and Luke picked her up in a truck that looked like it had lived a life.

It wasn't polished or new. The paint bore thin scratches along the side—not damage so much as memory—and the cab smelled faintly of sawdust layered with something citrusy that might have been cleaner or might have been gum. The radio was already on when she climbed in, loud and reckless, the kind of song that felt like motion for the sake of motion.

Luke glanced at her with a grin that was too easy to be rehearsed.
"You ready?"

She buckled her seatbelt, arching a brow. "For what?"

"That's the spirit," he said, laughing as he pulled away from the curb.

She laughed too, despite herself.

They didn't head toward town. They didn't head anywhere familiar. The road narrowed quickly, trees blurring past as the music pressed against her chest, the windows rolled down just enough for warm air to tangle in her hair. Luke drummed his fingers against the steering wheel, relaxed in a way that felt fundamentally different from Micah—less careful, more kinetic, like he trusted momentum to carry him where he needed to go.

"So," she said after a few minutes, watching the trees streak by. "You going to tell me where we're going, or is mystery part of the experience?"

Luke shrugged one shoulder. "If I tell you, it ruins it."

"That tracks."

When they finally turned into a sprawling gravel lot, it was lit with strings of lights and flickering neon that dared the night to keep up. Noise spilled outward—laughter, engines revving, the sharp clash of sound effects and music overlapping without apology.

An arcade.

Not the sad kind. The loud kind.

Racing games. Air hockey. Flashing screens. Teenagers and couples and groups of adults who had clearly decided growing up was optional tonight.

Eliza stared. "You're kidding."

Luke shut off the engine. "You look like someone who forgot how to play."

She opened the door slowly. "I did not agree to this."

"Too late," he said. "You're already smiling."

She hated that he was right.

Inside, it was chaos in the best possible way—color and noise and motion colliding into something alive. Luke dropped a stack of tokens into her palm.

"Rules are simple," he said. "No mercy."

"I don't even know what I'm doing."

"That's the point."

They started with racing games, Luke loud and competitive, Eliza yelling at the screen like it could hear her. She lost badly. Then won unexpectedly. Then demanded a rematch she insisted didn't count the first time.

Air hockey turned physical fast—hands colliding, bodies leaning too far over the table, laughter bursting out of her like something unburied. At one point, Luke leaned across the table, eyes bright, breath close.

"There you are," he said.

"Where?" she asked, breathless.

"Right here," he replied. "Not thinking. Just moving."

Something loosened in her chest at that.

They ate greasy pizza standing up, fingers dusted with flour and oil. Luke wiped a smear of sauce from the corner of her mouth without thinking—then froze.

"Sorry," he said quickly. "Too much?"

She met his eyes. "It was fine."

He nodded, accepted it, didn't push.

Later, outside beneath the string lights, the night had cooled enough to raise goosebumps along her arms. Luke shrugged out of his jacket and draped it over her shoulders without comment.

"Thank you," she said softly.

He leaned against the railing beside her, close but not touching. "I told Micah I wasn't trying to steal you."

She smiled faintly. "And?"

"He told me to stop being an idiot," Luke said. "In a very polite, very brotherly way."

She tipped her head back and laughed, the sound free and unguarded.

"You okay?" he asked.

"Yes," she said, surprised by the certainty of it. "I really am."

They stood there for a while, the noise behind them fading, the night stretching wide and forgiving.

Luke turned toward her then, without bravado or jokes. "This is where I ask if I can kiss you."

Her pulse flickered—not fear, just awareness.

She considered it honestly.
"Yes."

The kiss wasn't anything like Micah's.

It was playful. Warm. A little reckless. Luke's hand settled at her waist, grounding without claiming. When they pulled apart, he rested his forehead briefly against hers.

"Thank you," he said.

"For what?"

"For giving me the chance to know the answer."

The drive back was quieter, the music low, the road sliding past like it was holding its breath. When he pulled up near the cabin, he didn't get out.

"I meant what I said," Luke told her. "Whatever you decide— I'm good. No pressure. No games."

She nodded. "I know."

She opened the door, then paused. "You didn't try to win."

Luke smiled. "Didn't need to. Just needed to show up."

She watched him drive away with her heart steady and her mind clear.

Not torn.
Not confused.

Just informed.

And that felt like power.

Chapter Fifty-Two

The cabin was warm when Eliza got home.

Not overheated or stifling—just held. The fire she'd banked that morning had settled into a low, steady glow, casting soft light across the floorboards. Outside, rain tapped patiently against the windows, the kind of spring rain that smelled alive. Damp earth. New leaves. The promise of things still coming.

She kicked off her shoes by the door and stood there for a moment, letting the quiet gather around her.

The night with Luke lingered at the edges of her thoughts—not heavy, not intrusive. Laughter. Motion. The bright, uncomplicated rush of letting herself enjoy something spontaneous without apology. He had made her feel wanted in a way that was open and undeniable.

And Micah—

Micah felt different. Quieter. Like something that didn't need to announce itself to be real.

She didn't feel torn.

That surprised her.

Eliza moved to the kitchen, poured herself a small glass of wine, and carried it to the table where her notebook waited. The same notebook she'd been filling for weeks now. She sat, flipped to a page marked with a folded corner, and rested her pen against the paper.

For a moment, she didn't write.

Not because she was afraid—but because she was choosing where to begin.

Then she did.

I remember the first time I saw the basement.

The words came clean and steady. Her hand didn't shake.

She didn't write like a victim. She wrote like a witness.

She described the door—unmarked, soundproofed, hidden behind a locked storage room Daniel had called private. She wrote about the smell first. Chemical. Sweet and wrong. About the faint buzz of the lights and the way the room was designed to disorient. No windows. No clocks.

She wrote about the women.

Not names—she didn't have those—but faces. Ages. The way some avoided eye contact while others stared too hard, daring someone to see them. She wrote about bruises that didn't match the stories Daniel told at fundraisers. About how he called them guests. About the way he laughed when she flinched.

She paused only to breathe.

Then she kept going.

She paired dates as best she could. Events upstairs—galas, donor dinners, political meetings—with what she knew was happening below them. She wrote about nights he came to bed smelling like bleach. About threats delivered softly, like advice.

You're safer not knowing everything.
This is how power works.
You wouldn't survive without me.

Her jaw tightened, but her pen didn't slow.

This time, she didn't write how it made her feel.

She wrote what happened.

That was the difference.

When her hand finally cramped, she set the pen down and stared at the page. The rain had grown heavier now, drumming against the roof like punctuation.

She hadn't undone herself by writing it.

She felt clearer.

Eliza leaned back and took a slow sip of wine as the fire popped softly behind her. Somewhere beyond the trees, a frog croaked, oblivious to human ruin.

She thought of Alice. Of Tonya. Of the years this had been unfolding without her knowing.

She wasn't ready to confront all of it yet.

But she was ready to keep writing.

Not to relive it.

To preserve it.

She closed the notebook carefully, slid it into the false bottom of the drawer Alice had shown her months ago, and locked it. Then she moved to the window.

Rain streaked the glass, blurring the world into greens and grays. The cabin glowed behind her reflection—hair loose over her shoulders, face softer than it had been a year ago, eyes clear.

She liked her life.

That mattered.

She liked the school. The kids who looked at her like she might have answers. She liked the diner, the quiet approval in Nell's gruff nods. She liked Micah's patience. Luke's fire. The fact that she was allowed to feel both without shame.

She wasn't becoming Eden again.

She was becoming Eliza—fully.

And Eliza could hold two truths at once:

She was safe.
And she was not done.

Eliza turned away from the window, banked the fire, and climbed the stairs to bed.

Tomorrow she would wake early. She would teach. She would pour coffee. She would laugh at something small and stupid. She would text Micah. She would keep living.

And when the rain stopped—when the timing was right—

She would be ready.

Not to run.

To finish what had been started long before she ever stepped off that bus.

Chapter Fifty-Three

The email sat unopened for nearly five minutes.

Eliza stared at the subject line as if looking at it too long might change what it contained. She already knew it wasn't a routine update or an attachment she'd forgotten to print. It carried weight, the kind that settled in her chest before her mind could put a name to it.

She was alone in her classroom. Third-period prep stretched out ahead of her like a held breath. Sunlight spilled across the desks in long, uneven stripes, catching on scratched laminate and the faint smudge of yesterday's dry-erase marker. Chalk dust clung to the air in a way that always made her think of old schools and old lives. Outside the door, the building moved on without her—lockers slamming, laughter rising and falling, shoes squeaking down the hall—but in Room 214, it was quiet.

A quiet that waited.

She clicked the email open.

Her eyes skimmed once, fast and instinctive, as if speed might soften impact. Then she slowed—because she had to, because the words wouldn't let her keep running over them like they were nothing.

Mrs. Grady had decided to retire.

Not immediately. Not dramatically. Just finally, the way bodies did when they'd been asked for too much too long. Recovery had taken more than she'd wanted to admit. The effort of coming back, of proving she still could, had tipped the scales. She was choosing rest. She was choosing herself.

And they wanted Eliza to stay.

Not temporarily. Not until further notice. Not as a placeholder.

They wanted her—fully, officially, permanently.

Eliza leaned back in her chair and stared at the ceiling tiles like they might rearrange themselves into something holy. Her throat tightened. Her eyes burned—not with panic, not with fear, but with the strangest ache: recognition.

This wasn't adrenaline.

This wasn't the sharp terror of being found out.

This was being chosen.

This was permanence.

And the part of her that had learned to distrust anything that felt like stability tried—quietly—to flinch away from it.

But nothing hit. No punishment followed. No hand closed around her wrist. No voice corrected her for wanting too much. The room stayed still and bright and ordinary. The desks stayed where they were. The clock kept ticking.

She had earned this, and the world wasn't taking it back.

When Principal Carver called her down later that morning, she walked to the office slowly, letting her shoes echo down the hallway. For once, she wasn't bracing. She wasn't rehearsing how to make herself smaller. She wasn't planning a version of herself that would be easiest to accept.

She was just… walking.

Carver's office smelled like coffee and paper and whatever lemon cleaner the custodians used. He gestured her in, motioned to the chair across from his desk, and spoke with the careful steadiness of a man who understood that some offers carried more than salary.

He talked about student feedback. About stability. About how consistency mattered to teenagers who pretended they didn't need anyone. He explained numbers and contracts and timelines, but his voice softened when he said the part that mattered most.

"You have a way of making them feel seen without making it about you," he said. "That's not something we can teach."

Something in Eliza cracked open at that. A quiet, internal sound, like ice giving way to water.

Carver folded his hands, meeting her eyes. "I know you already read the email, but I'd like to officially offer you the position," he said. "Full-time. Business Education teacher. It's yours, if you want it."

Eliza didn't rush her answer.

She thought about the cabin at night—quiet and warm, not borrowed, not temporary. She thought about walking home after work instead of dragging herself into a second shift until her body felt like it belonged to exhaustion more than to her. She thought about evenings that were hers. Weekends that didn't feel stolen.

She thought about the students who looked at her like she might be steady enough to trust.

"I want it," she said.

And for the first time in longer than she could remember, wanting something didn't feel dangerous.

Carver smiled—not a grand gesture, just a small, satisfied curve of approval. "Good," he said. "We're lucky to have you."

The word lucky landed somewhere tender.

On the way back to her room, she passed Micah's classroom.

He looked up from a stack of essays, caught her expression, and stilled as if he'd felt the news before she said a word. She lifted the badge she'd been given that morning—clean and official.

MS. MOORE — STAFF.

Micah's smile bloomed slow and proud and unmistakably real, like this outcome had never been in doubt. He didn't speak through the glass. He didn't interrupt his students. He just lifted his mug in a quiet toast and held her gaze long enough to make her chest warm.

She carried that warmth with her the rest of the day.

That evening, she went to the diner with gratitude and closure humming beneath her skin like a second heartbeat. It wasn't dread. It wasn't guilt. It felt like stepping into a chapter she could close without bleeding.

Nell didn't miss a beat when Eliza told her. She flipped a burger, eyes on the grill, voice blunt as ever.

"Good," Nell said. "I'll be sad to see you go, but that place needs you more than I do."

Eliza swallowed hard at the simplicity of it. Nell didn't make her prove she deserved it. Nell didn't ask for a backstory. She didn't turn it into a lecture. She just acknowledged what was true.

Shelby squealed and launched herself at Eliza, hugging her hard enough to steal her breath.

"You better not disappear," Shelby warned into her shoulder. "I still expect you to come in for gossip and pie."

"I won't," Eliza promised.

And she knew she meant it. The diner had been a bridge. A place to land while she learned how to stand again. It had held her without asking for her whole story. Now she could cross the bridge without needing to burn it behind her.

When she untied her apron at the end of the shift, she didn't feel loss.

She felt closure.

Not the kind that slammed shut. The kind that settled—quiet, earned, complete.

The walk home felt different without the pressure of another day looming in her ribs. No second shift waiting. No clock chasing her down. The air felt open. Unrestricted. Like she could take a full breath without counting it first.

At the cabin, she cooked dinner properly—chopped vegetables, stirred a pot, opened the windows to let the evening air roll through. She ate sitting down, savoring the simple pleasure of not rushing.

Later, she curled up on the couch with her notebook.

Not the one filled with Daniel—this one was for her.

Lesson ideas spilled across the page in looping handwriting. Notes in the margins about budgeting without shame. About teaching kids that money could be a tool instead of a threat. About survival as something learned—not something you apologized for.

She was halfway through a thought when her phone buzzed.

Micah:
I already told you this today, but I'm saying it again—congratulations.

Her lips curved before she could stop them.

Eliza:
Thank you.
It still feels a little unreal.

A few seconds passed.

Micah:
Then let me take you out Friday.
We should celebrate properly.

Warmth moved through her—not nerves, not uncertainty, just
the ease of being seen.

Eliza:
Dinner sounds perfect.

She set the phone down, still smiling, and moved toward the
sink to rinse her mug.

That was when she heard gravel crunch outside.

Not hurried. Not unfamiliar.

She frowned slightly, wiped her hands on a towel, and opened
the door.

Micah stood on the porch.

Jacket shrugged open. Hair tousled by the breeze. One hand
held a paper bag of groceries, the other a loose bundle of
wildflowers—imperfect, unarranged, unmistakably chosen
with intention.

She blinked, then laughed softly.

"You were just texting me," she said, warmth blooming in her
voice. "You could've warned me."

Micah smiled—the kind that didn't ask for anything, just
offered.

"I wanted to make sure you were home," he said. "And I wanted it to be a surprise."

Her chest did that quiet, dangerous thing—the one that felt like trust settling in.

"Well," she said, stepping aside, "you succeeded."

He followed her in like he belonged there, setting the groceries on the counter. Fresh bread. Strawberries. A bottle of wine. Nothing extravagant. Everything thoughtful.

"I figured," he said, almost sheepish, "you've had enough temporary celebrations. Thought this one deserved to be real."

Eliza leaned back against the counter, watching him take in the space—the table, the books, the life she'd built here—as if it mattered.

"You didn't have to do this," she said.

"I know," he replied easily. "I wanted to."

Something in her loosened.

No grand gesture. No pressure. Just presence.

They cooked together—bumping shoulders, passing ingredients, moving in quiet sync. Music played low from her phone. The windows were open, the evening air drifting through with the scent of earth and things that stayed.

Later, they ate at the small table, knees brushing, wine warming her chest.

Micah lifted his glass. "To Ms. Moore," he said. "Who earned this."

She met his gaze, steady and full.

"To staying," she replied.

When he left, he didn't rush and he didn't linger too long. He kissed her once in the doorway, soft and sure, and then he was gone down the gravel drive like he trusted she wouldn't vanish in the night.

Eliza stood on the porch for a while afterward, flowers in a mason jar beside her.

She had a job.
A home.
Someone who showed up without being asked.

And beneath the calm, beneath the happiness, something steadier held her upright.

She hadn't forgotten what she was writing.
She hadn't forgotten who she was holding accountable.

She had simply built a life strong enough to carry the truth when it was time.

Her phone buzzed again.

Luke:
Heard the news.
Full-time suits you.

She smiled.

Eliza:
Thank you.
It feels… earned.

A beat.

Luke:
I'm guessing Hale beat me to the celebration.

She huffed a quiet laugh.

Eliza:
He came over with flowers and groceries and made us dinner.
You're late.

Luke:
Damn.
I knew I should've brought pie.

She could hear his voice in it—cocky, teasing, impossible to
take entirely seriously.

Then another message came through, slower, different.

Luke:
For what it's worth—I'm really happy for you.
You belong there.

That one landed deeper than the joke.

Eliza:
That means more than you think.

A pause—long enough that she wondered if that would be the
end of it.

Luke:
Doesn't mean I'm done competing.
Just means I'm playing the long game.

She laughed out loud this time, soft and unguarded, and set the phone facedown on the counter.

For once, she didn't feel pulled in opposite directions.

She felt steady—like she was standing inside her life instead of watching it from the edges.

Chapter Fifty-Four

By the time May crept toward Black Hollow, Eliza had found her groove.

The kids knew she was staying now, and they behaved like it mattered—some of them pretending it didn't while proving the opposite. Someone had decorated her door with a crooked banner that read CONGRATS MS. MOORE in glitter marker and tape that wouldn't stick. A few students had complained loudly about the extra work they'd "definitely" do now that she was permanent, then turned their projects in early anyway.

Room 214 felt lived in.

It wasn't just worksheets and posters anymore. It was continuity made visible—notes taped near the board reminding seniors about FAFSA deadlines, a whiteboard calendar counting down to finals, a chipped mug that said World's Okayest Teacher sitting on her desk like a quiet joke and a claim. She'd brought in a plant she kept forgetting to water, and somehow it stayed alive. She'd hung up a few quotes about money and choices and future selves. She'd made the space hers carefully, like she was teaching her body that this was allowed.

That morning, she stood at the front of the room, sleeves rolled to her elbows, hair pulled back loosely, watching students settle.

"Okay," she said, clapping once. "If you haven't turned in your budgeting project, this is your last warning before I pretend I don't know your name at graduation."

Groans erupted. Laughter. A chorus of Ms. Moore, come on.

She smiled despite herself.

She'd earned this.

Halfway through attendance, the door opened and the guidance counselor stepped in with a girl at her side.

"This is Marisol Reyes," the counselor said. "Transfer. Junior. Just moved into the district."

Marisol stood with her backpack slung over one shoulder, posture guarded in that unmistakable way city kids carried— alert, self-contained, eyes sharp. Dark hair, winged eyeliner done with confidence, sneakers that had never seen mud.

"Marisol just moved here from New York City," the counselor added. "Please make sure she feels welcome."

Eliza didn't clock it consciously. Didn't feel danger in it. The idea that someone—sixteen, brand new, bored enough to dig—could recognize her here didn't even register. Black Hollow felt like its own pocket of the world, sealed and quiet and safely irrelevant.

"Welcome," Eliza said warmly. "Grab a seat. We're starting with financial goals today, which I promise is more interesting than it sounds."

Marisol's eyes flicked up.

Just for a second.

Then away.

But something had shifted all the same.

Marisol didn't speak much that day.

She took notes. Asked one careful question. Watched Eliza with a focus that felt intense but not disruptive. Plenty of students watched teachers like that—sizing them up, deciding how much they could trust.

Eliza noticed it only in passing.

By the end of the period, she was answering questions about graduation requirements, signing off on missing assignments, reminding seniors that adulthood did not, in fact, come with a manual.

When the bell rang, Marisol lingered.

"Ms. Moore?" she asked.

"Yes?"

"Do you have any recommendations for budgeting apps?" Marisol asked casually. "Like… ones that don't assume your parents are rich."

Eliza snorted softly. "Yes. I'll write a few down."

Marisol thanked her and left.

Nothing about it felt wrong.

That was the problem.

That night, Marisol posted a TikTok.

It wasn't malicious. It wasn't dramatic. It wasn't even framed like a gotcha. It was the kind of curiosity that felt harmless until it wasn't—until it landed in the wrong algorithm, until strangers decided it belonged to them.

The video started with a shaky clip of a classroom whiteboard.

SMART SPENDING STARTS NOW.

A whisper over the footage: "Okay, so tell me I'm not insane…"

Then a blurry still photo from the back of the room. Eliza at her desk, laughing at something a student had said.

"My new teacher looks exactly like the missing mayor's wife from New York."

Text appeared on the screen:

am i crazy or???

Then side-by-side images pulled from Google.
Eliza Moore.
Eden Whitmore.

The similarities were impossible to ignore—bone structure, smile, the shape of her eyes even with different hair.

The comments ignited like gasoline.

That's her.
No way she just disappeared.

Why is she teaching in the middle of nowhere?

Someone check this town.

Tag the news.

Tag the mayor.

Tag the FBI.

It jumped from teens to true-crime accounts. From locals to strangers. From curiosity to obsession in a matter of hours.

By midnight it had tens of thousands of views.

By morning it had hundreds of thousands.

Eliza slept through all of it.

She found out the next day in a way that felt almost mercifully small at first.

Nell wouldn't look her in the eye.

"You okay?" Nell asked too carefully, sliding her coffee across the counter.

Eliza frowned. "Why wouldn't I be?"

Shelby burst in from the back with her phone already in hand, eyes wide, breath quick like she'd been running.

"Okay," Shelby said. "Don't freak out. But also maybe freak out."

Her voice cracked on the last word.

"This isn't actually you, is it?" Shelby asked, shoving the phone toward her. "This can't be true, right?"

Eliza took the phone.

Watched once.

Then again.

The world didn't shatter.

It tilted.

Her hands went cold so fast it felt like her blood had drained out of them. Something thin and sharp slid under her ribs, the old fear testing the door like it still had a key.

She sat down hard on the stool, the diner noise fading until it felt far away.

Micah called first.

"I'm coming over," he said. "Don't argue."

"I'm fine," Eliza said automatically, the words reflexive and useless.

"You're not," he replied gently. "And that's okay."

Alice called next, voice like steel.

"This is contained," Alice said. "For now. But it's moving fast."

"I didn't think—" Eliza started.

"I know," Alice cut in. "That's not a failure. It's just timing."

Eliza hung up and sat very still.

For the first time in almost a year, fear tried to crawl back into her bones.

Not because the town was dangerous.

Because the world was.

Because Daniel had lived in the world where headlines became weapons and stories became cages and people stopped being people the second they became a spectacle.

By afternoon, messages had started coming from numbers she didn't recognize. Strange friend requests. A woman she didn't know leaving a comment on a school district Facebook post with Eden's name like it was a dare.

The life Eliza had built didn't collapse.

It creaked.

And creaking was enough to make her feel sick.

It was nearly dark when she heard the car.

Not Micah's truck.

Not Alice's.

Something unfamiliar.

Eliza stood slowly, every muscle in her body tightening with a memory that didn't belong to this town. She walked toward the door, the fear arriving first as sensation—cold fingers at the back of her neck, a pressure in her ears, that old instinct to make herself quiet.

She opened it.

Tonya stood on the porch.

Hair shorter. Face harder. Eyes full of things Eliza wasn't ready to name—regret and fury and something that looked like grief twisted into a weapon.

"We have a problem," Tonya said.

The world went quiet.

And Eliza knew—truly knew—that the calm was over.

Chapter Fifty-Five

Tonya stood on the porch like she had been carved there by bad timing.

Not apologetic. Not frantic. Not even winded, though the gravel drive suggested she'd pulled in too fast. She looked tight with urgency—jaw set, shoulders squared, eyes tracking the edges of the clearing like danger might step out of the trees at any moment and call her name.

"We have a problem," she said again.

Eliza didn't answer right away.

Her body went still in the old way—not freezing, exactly, but locking into place, gathering itself behind her ribs and holding. It was the reflex she hated most because it belonged to a version of her that had survived by becoming smaller than the moment.

The porch light buzzed faintly overhead. The air smelled like wet pine and spring soil. Somewhere in the distance, a night bird called once, sharp and lonely.

"Come inside," Eliza said finally.

Tonya stepped in without hesitation. The cabin swallowed her, and when Eliza shut the door, the click of the latch sounded too final, like a decision being made on her behalf.

The space changed the second Tonya crossed the threshold.

The cabin had always been small, but it had felt like Eliza's small—warm, familiar, safe in its simplicity. Tonight it felt like a box.

Tonya paced once, as if she couldn't help it, then stopped near the table. She looked older than Eliza remembered. Sharper. Less forgiving. Whatever softness she'd once carried had been burned down to something harder—survival honed into muscle, eyes trained to see exits and threats and patterns.

"It's everywhere," Tonya said. "TikTok, Reddit, Twitter. Local news hasn't picked it up yet, but they will. Someone tagged a national outlet twenty minutes ago."

Eliza swallowed. Her throat felt paper-dry.

"A student," she managed.

Tonya nodded. "From New York. A transfer. Her aunt works in media." She dragged a hand across her mouth, like she was trying to keep herself from saying the rest too sharply. "She didn't mean harm. Curiosity went viral."

Eliza sank into the chair. The wood pressed cold against the backs of her thighs.

"I didn't think—"

"No one ever does," Tonya said, quieter now. Not cruel. Just honest. "That's how it works. People don't think about consequences. They think about attention."

The silence stretched—thick, charged, full of everything Eliza didn't want to imagine.

Then headlights cut through the trees.

Tonya stiffened.

Eliza stood so fast the chair legs scraped. Her pulse jumped—not because she didn't know the sound, but because she did.

"That's Micah," she said, and the relief in her voice betrayed her before she could stop it.

Tonya turned her head. "Micah?"

The knock came before Eliza could say anything else—firm, familiar, unafraid.

She opened the door.

Micah stepped in with concern already written across his face—until his eyes landed on Tonya.

Everything in him stopped.

The shift was immediate and instinctive. His shoulders tightened. His gaze sharpened. The air around him changed, like something protective had flicked on without asking permission.

"Tonya?" he said slowly.

Tonya's mouth twitched like she couldn't decide whether to smile or grit her teeth through it. "Hey, little brother."

The words cracked something open in the room.

Micah looked between them, then back to Tonya. "What are you doing here?" His voice stayed even, but there was a tremor beneath it—the kind that came when someone had walked into a memory they didn't want.

Tonya didn't soften. "If you don't already know, you're behind."

Eliza stepped forward, instinctively placing herself between them. "Micah—"

"No," he said gently but firmly, and the gentleness didn't make it less final. His eyes stayed on Tonya. "I need you to let me ask this."

Eliza's throat tightened. She nodded once.

Micah's attention didn't waver. "How do you know her?" he asked Tonya, the words deliberate. "And why are you at her cabin?"

Tonya crossed her arms, bracing herself like she expected the answer to land like a blow. "You're not going to like it."

"That's becoming a theme," Micah said, and there was something bitter in the attempt at humor.

Another set of headlights swung through the trees.

Then another.

Eliza's stomach dropped as the gravel drive filled with light and shadow.

Alice's truck pulled in first. Luke's right behind her.

The door barely had time to open before Alice stepped inside, already assessing, already braced, face hard in a way Eliza recognized. Not anger. Strategy.

"Well," Alice said flatly. "So much for timing."

Luke followed her in. He took one look at Tonya, then Micah, then Eliza—and let out a slow breath like the truth had finally caught up to him.

"Oh," he said under his breath. "This is bad."

Micah turned toward Alice, eyes sharp. "You want to start explaining," he said. "Right now."

Alice didn't deflect. Didn't soften. Didn't lie.

"Eden Whitmore," she said calmly, "has been under my protection."

Micah's head snapped toward Eliza so fast it looked like it hurt.

The name hit him like a slap he hadn't seen coming.

"No," he said. "No. That's not—"

"Eliza," Alice continued, not looking away, "is not her real name."

Luke swore under his breath, low and stunned.

Tonya spoke next, quieter than Eliza expected. "Eden Whitmore," she said. "The mayor's wife who 'disappeared.'"

Micah staggered back a step.

Eliza watched it happen—the moment his mind tried to reject what he'd heard, tried to find a loophole big enough to climb through. The way his eyes moved over her like he was looking for a seam, a place where the story could split into something easier.

He looked wrecked.

Not distrustful. Not furious.

Just devastated.

"You're—" His voice broke on the word. "You're her?"

Eliza stood.

She didn't flinch. She didn't shrink. She didn't hide behind the table or the apology she could have offered to make it easier for him to swallow.

"Yes," she said. "I am."

The silence that followed was absolute.

Even the cabin seemed to hold its breath.

Luke dragged a hand through his hair. "Jesus Christ."

Micah shook his head slowly, like the motion might reset reality. "You were hiding. I knew that. I knew you weren't running from nothing." He let out a short, broken laugh that didn't belong to humor. "But this?"

Eliza's chest ached. The hurt in his voice cut cleaner than anything Tonya had said.

"I didn't tell you because I didn't want you pulled into it," she said, careful, steady. "I didn't want you in danger because of me."

"You don't get to decide that alone," Micah said. He still wasn't angry. That was worse. Hurt had a longer echo than rage. "You don't get to… let me build my life around someone and not let me know what I'm standing next to."

Alice stepped in before Eliza could respond. "I do," she said. "That was my call."

Micah turned on her. "And you thought that was okay?"

Alice didn't blink. "I thought keeping her alive was more important than anyone's feelings."

Luke shifted, jaw tight, eyes flicking to Eliza like he was checking whether she was breathing.

Alice's voice stayed calm, but something hard lived under it. "I've been watching Daniel Whitmore and his family for years," she said. "Before Eden ever crossed his path. Before Tonya ever stepped foot near him."

Micah's gaze snapped to Tonya. "What does that mean?"

Tonya didn't look away. "It means I wasn't just her friend."

Eliza felt her stomach drop like the floor had vanished.

"I was placed," Tonya continued. "To get close. To listen. To confirm things Alice already suspected."

The words hit Eliza harder than the TikTok ever could have.

Because this wasn't strangers.

This was *her*.

"You were—" Eliza's voice cracked. "You were lying to me."

Tonya's eyes shone. "I was protecting you."

"You watched him hurt me," Eliza said, and the sentence came out quieter than it should have, like her body still didn't believe she was allowed to say it out loud.

Tonya's face tightened. "I watched him," she said fiercely, "because if I didn't, no one else could. And because when you finally ran, we had a path ready." Her breath shook. "You think I wanted to sit there and smile and hold your hand while he destroyed you? You think that didn't eat me alive?"

Micah stepped between them without thinking, body going instinctively protective—of Eliza, of the room, of whatever fragile thread was keeping this from turning into something irreparable.

"That's enough," he said.

Tonya swallowed hard and stepped back a fraction. Not because she'd been put in her place—because she respected him. Because she knew he wasn't wrong.

Alice nodded once. "This stops being compartmentalized now," she said, turning her gaze to Eliza. "No more pieces. No more pretending we can keep everyone separate."

Luke's voice came out low, blunt. "Are we in danger?"

"Yes," Alice said. "But not because of her." Her eyes flicked to Eliza. "Because of him."

Micah turned back to Eliza, voice lowered, as if softness could keep her from shattering. "Tell me one thing," he said. "Right now."

She met his eyes.

"Did you choose this life here," he asked, "or was it just another hiding place?"

Eliza didn't hesitate.

"It started as a hiding place," she said, and her voice didn't shake. "But it became more than that. I chose to make it what it is." She swallowed. "I chose you."

Something in Micah softened—fractured, then realigned. His eyes shone in a way he didn't seem to notice.

Alice cleared her throat, drawing them back into the reality that didn't care about tenderness.

"Daniel's story is unraveling," she said. "Eden's 'breakdown.' Her 'rehab.' His carefully mournful silence. It won't hold."

Luke straightened. "Then what's the plan?"

Eliza exhaled. Fear still lived in her, but it wasn't at the wheel anymore.

"I keep living," she said. "I keep teaching. I keep writing." Her hand lifted slightly, palm pressed to her chest like she could anchor herself there. "Everything he did. Everything I saw."

Tonya nodded, expression tight with resolve. "And I stop hiding."

Alice looked at her sons. "This is where I ask you something I never wanted to."

Micah didn't hesitate. "I'm in."

Luke glanced at Eliza, then Micah. His expression shifted—protective, resigned, loyal in the way only family could be.

"Yeah," Luke said. "Me too."

Alice's jaw tightened—pride and fear warring in equal measure.

"Then understand this," she said. "Once we move forward, no one is untouched."

Eliza reached for Micah's hand.

He took it.

His grip was firm, steady—still him, still present, even while his world rearranged itself around the truth.

Eliza didn't disappear again.

She stood her ground.

And Daniel Whitmore had no idea what was coming.

Chapter Fifty-Six

Eliza sat at the kitchen table long after the cabin had gone quiet.

The lights were off except for the one over the sink, casting a tired pool of yellow across the counter and the worn wood floor. The window was cracked open just enough to let the night air in—cool and damp, carrying the sound of insects and the distant hush of the trees. Normally, the quiet calmed her.

Tonight it pressed in.

Micah sat on the arm of the couch, elbows on his knees, hands clasped like he was holding himself together with them. Luke stood near the door, arms crossed, jaw tight, restless in a way Eliza didn't usually see in him. Tonya hovered by the counter as if she didn't know where to put her guilt, shifting her weight, eyes flicking toward Eliza and then away.

Alice didn't move at all.

She stood across from Eliza with her hands braced on the table, gaze sharp, expression focused in the way that meant she was already ten steps ahead of everyone else in the room.

"They'll fire me," Eliza said, and the words slipped out before she realized she'd spoken them.

Her voice didn't sound like panic. It sounded like reality. Like the one thing she couldn't afford to lose.

Micah's head lifted slightly, eyes tightening.

Luke's posture changed—subtle, protective.

Tonya's face pinched like she wanted to take it back for Eliza, as if she could.

Alice didn't blink.

"They can't," Alice said.

Eliza let out a hollow laugh that carried no humor. "Alice, I taught their kids under a name that isn't mine."

Alice tilted her head, just slightly. "Incorrect."

Eliza blinked. "What?"

"You taught under a name that is legally valid," Alice said, calm as a ledger. "You didn't forge anything. You didn't lie on an application. You were hired under an emergency authorization using credentials that exist."

Luke frowned. "You're saying the papers were real."

"I'm saying," Alice replied, "that no crime was committed."

Eliza's chest tightened, breath catching on the edge of hope she didn't want to trust. "But when this hits the school board—when parents start calling—"

Alice straightened, cutting her off. "The school board will see exactly what I want them to see."

She reached into her bag and pulled out a thin folder—not thick, not dramatic. Practical. The kind of thing that looked boring enough to hold power.

She slid it toward Eliza.

"This is the emergency substitute pathway you were hired under," Alice said. "It allows districts to place someone immediately when they're short-staffed, with credential verification finalized after the fact."

Eliza stared at it like paper could decide her future.

"That's… a loophole," Micah said slowly.

"No," Alice corrected. "It's a system designed for reality."

She opened the folder and pointed at sections as she spoke, voice steady, precise.

"You had a degree that matched. Work history consistent with student-facing roles. A clean background check. The district exercised discretion because they needed you."

Eliza swallowed. "And now?"

"Now," Alice said, "we convert."

The word landed like a door opening.

Alice looked directly at Eliza. "Mrs. Grady is retiring. The district already wants continuity. Parents are happy. Students are stable." Her gaze sharpened. "That gives us leverage."

Tonya spoke quietly, voice thick. "But the name—"

Alice nodded once, as if she'd expected the question and already had the answer.

"Which brings us to phase two."

She pulled out another document and set it on the table.

Eliza's hands trembled as she looked at it.

"A legal name consolidation," Alice said. "Eliza Moore becomes your professional identity. Eden Whitmore becomes a sealed former name attached to protected records only."

Eliza's throat tightened. "They'll ask why."

"They'll be told the truth," Alice said. "Enough of it, anyway."

She leaned forward slightly, and her voice lowered—not softer, but more deliberate.

"Domestic violence. Identity protection. Confidentiality request."

Micah went still.

Luke's jaw clenched.

Eliza felt something crack open in her chest—not fear, not shame, but grief. The kind that arrived when you realized you'd still been living inside rules you never agreed to.

"I don't want to be a problem for them," she whispered.

Alice's gaze sharpened. "You are not the problem."

Her voice didn't rise. It didn't need to.

"The problem is a man who built his power on silence," Alice said. "You don't get punished because you escaped him."

The room stayed quiet, but it shifted. Like everyone heard it— not just as comfort, but as a verdict.

Alice continued. "The district's lawyers will advise them not to touch this with a ten-foot pole. Terminating a qualified teacher under DV protection?" She let out a short breath. "That's a lawsuit they don't want. And it's bad optics they can't afford."

Eliza's voice came out small, even though she hated that it did. "So I don't lose my job."

"No," Alice said simply. "You keep it."

Micah exhaled slow and controlled, like he'd been holding his breath for hours. His eyes dropped to the floor, then back to Eliza.

"The kids," he said quietly.

"They don't lose her," Alice replied. "That's the point."

Eliza's eyes burned.

She had been temporary for so long it had turned into a belief. A truth she carried like a bruise: nothing lasted, nothing held, nothing stayed hers.

"I finally felt like I wasn't temporary," she said. The confession came out rough, torn from somewhere deep. "Like I mattered."

Alice softened—just slightly. The smallest shift in her face, like she couldn't quite keep the tenderness out of her eyes.

"And you do," Alice said. "That's why this matters."

Luke stepped closer, voice quieter now. "So what happens next?"

Alice straightened again, businesslike.

"Tomorrow, I make a few calls," she said. "The district finalizes the conversion. Eliza signs updated employment paperwork under her current legal name. The board is briefed without details."

"And Daniel?" Micah asked.

Alice's mouth curved—not a smile. Something sharper.

"He thinks exposure is a weapon," she said. "He's about to learn it's evidence."

Eliza looked down at her hands.

Ink stains from grading. A faint callus from chalk. The small markers of a life built honestly, quietly, without cruelty. Proof she belonged to herself.

"I don't want to disappear again," she said.

Micah's gaze lifted, and it hit Eliza then—how much he'd been holding. Not just shock. Not just betrayal. Fear, too. Fear of losing her. Fear of having been fooled. Fear that the last eleven months had been a dream he'd wake up from.

But his voice was steady when he spoke.

"Then don't," he said. "And don't do it alone."

Eliza's breath shuddered out of her, and she didn't bother to hide it.

Alice met her eyes. "You didn't build this life to abandon it at the first threat," she said.

Eliza nodded slowly.

She felt it then—not relief exactly, but something steadier.

Ground.

The cabin creaked softly as the wind shifted outside. The life she'd built didn't shatter.

It held.

And Eliza believed she could keep standing exactly where she was—

visible, legitimate, and unafraid.

Chapter Fifty-Seven

They didn't want to leave her alone.

Micah said it first, gently, like he was trying not to sound like he was afraid. He stood near the door with his jacket already on, hands shoved into his pockets like he didn't know what to do with them. His eyes stayed on her face—reading, checking, searching for something he could fix.

"You don't have to be brave tonight," he said. "Just… let us stay. One of us. I'll sleep on the couch. Luke can take the chair. Hell, I'll sleep on the floor."

Luke nodded immediately, fierce in that blunt, restless way of his. "Or both. I don't care. We'll take turns watching the damn trees if that's what it takes."

Tonya hovered near the sink, eyes red, arms wrapped around herself like she didn't trust her own body not to fall apart. Her voice came out small when she added, "Please. Just for tonight."

Alice watched Eliza instead of speaking. She didn't push. She didn't plead. She just stood there, steady as stone, waiting to see what Eliza would choose when no one was forcing her.

Eliza listened. She really did.

She felt the pull of it—the comfort of other people in the house, the safety of movement and voices, the way it would be easier to let someone else hold the sharp edge of the fear for her. It would have been so simple to say yes, to let Micah stretch out on the couch and Luke pace the windows and Tonya sit at the table like a witness who refused to leave.

But that wasn't what she needed.

"I'm okay," Eliza said.

Micah's brow furrowed. "You don't have to be."

"I know," she replied, and meant it. "But I am."

Luke shook his head. "That's not the point."

Eliza crossed the room and stopped in front of them, close enough to be heard without raising her voice. Her own calm surprised her—quiet, unshaking, not numb but clear. She could feel her heartbeat, steady and present, like proof that fear didn't get to own her anymore.

"If he comes," she said evenly, "it won't matter how many people are sleeping here." She let her gaze move from Micah to Luke to Tonya, making sure they heard her. "He won't knock. He won't ask permission. He won't play fair."

The cabin went very still.

Alice's eyes sharpened—not in disagreement, but recognition. Like she understood exactly what Eliza meant, and exactly what it had cost her to say it without trembling.

"I won't live my life barricaded," Eliza continued. Her voice stayed calm, but something iron lived underneath it. "I didn't survive all of that just to build a smaller prison with better lighting. I won't spend the rest of my life guarding doors like that's living."

Micah opened his mouth, then closed it again. He looked at her like he was searching for cracks and finding none. Like he didn't know whether to be proud or terrified.

"You'll call," he said.

It wasn't a question.

"Yes."

"And if anything feels wrong—if you hear something, see something—"

"I'll call," she repeated, steady as a promise.

Alice finally spoke, voice low and sure. "She's not reckless," she said. "She's resolved. There's a difference."

Luke let out a hard breath through his nose, frustration and love tangled together. "I hate this."

Eliza reached for his hand and squeezed once—small, grounding. "I know."

One by one, they accepted it.

Tonya hugged her first, too tight, like she was afraid Eliza might slip out of her arms the way Eden had slipped out of the world. Eliza held her back—not as forgiveness, not as reconciliation, but as something real. An acknowledgment of the mess and the history and the fact that Tonya was still here, still trying.

Luke was next. He didn't hug like Micah did. Luke held her briefly, firm and protective, then pulled back and looked at her with that familiar fire.

"If anyone shows up," he said quietly, "you call. I don't care if it's three in the morning."

"I will," Eliza promised.

Micah lingered the longest.

He didn't rush her, didn't perform comfort. He just stepped close, forehead pressing briefly to hers, breath catching as if he were memorizing the feeling of her being right here, alive, in front of him.

"I love you," he said.

Eliza didn't hesitate. She didn't weigh the words like they were dangerous. She didn't swallow them back out of habit.

"I love you too," she said.

Micah's eyes closed for a beat, like something in him unclenched.

Then he let her go.

When the door finally shut, the cabin settled into silence.

Not the heavy silence of fear.

The intentional kind—the kind she chose.

Eliza locked the door, then unlocked it again.

She turned off the lights, then turned one back on—the lamp by the table. She didn't do it because she was undecided. She did it because she refused to live like a hunted animal. A lock wasn't going to stop Daniel. Darkness wasn't going to hide her. If she was going to be afraid, she was going to be afraid in her own home, with her head up.

She sat.

Pulled her notebook toward her.

This one wasn't for school.

This one wasn't for poetry.

This one was for truth.

She flipped past pages already filled—memories, dates, patterns. The language of what he'd done. The details that made her stomach tighten even now: rooms that looked harmless until the door closed, laughter that turned sharp, the way power always wore the mask of normal.

She turned to a clean page.

At the top, she wrote a name.

Alice.

She didn't rush. She wrote carefully, deliberately—not instructions, not strategy. Gratitude. Understanding. The kind of words you wrote when you realized someone had shifted the trajectory of your life with their own hands.

Then she turned the page.

Tonya.

Her hand shook this time.

She paused, breathed, and kept going.

Love and anger tangled together on the paper. The ache of betrayal. The truth that Tonya had been both real and placed, both friend and instrument. The ugliness of that. The complicated, unbearable fact that Eliza still cared anyway.

Another page.

Micah.

She stopped.

Not because she didn't know what to say—because she knew too much.

She rested her forehead against the paper for a moment, eyes closed. The lamp hummed softly. The cabin creaked like it was alive. Somewhere outside, wind moved through the trees and the sound made her spine want to tighten.

When she lifted her head again, she wrote his name like it was something sacred.

She didn't censor it. She didn't protect him from the depth of it. She wrote what he had given her without knowing the whole story: gentleness without ownership, patience without expectation, love that asked instead of took.

Another page.

Luke.

Different words. Different gratitude. Respect. Challenge. The safety of someone who never tried to possess her, even when he wanted her. The relief of someone who saw her spine and admired it.

Only when the names were written did she turn to a fresh page.

This one had no heading.

Just a single line at the top.

If he finds me.

Eliza's hand steadied.

She didn't write fear.

She wrote intention.

If he comes, I will not run.
If he takes me, I will let him believe he has won.
I will survive long enough to end this.

The words didn't thrill her. They didn't make her feel brave. They made her feel prepared.

She wrote about watching. About listening. About patience. About how men like Daniel always needed to be admired, needed to feel in control—and how that hunger could be used against them. She wrote about the way he loved isolation because it made him feel like a god.

She wrote about the cabin he would romanticize.

The privacy.

The arrogance.

She wrote one final sentence and underlined it twice.

I will bring him down from the inside.

When she finished, she closed the notebook and set it carefully in the drawer beneath the table.

Then she stood, walked to the window, and looked out at the dark line of trees.

Her heart was steady.

Her life was real.

And if the storm came for her, she would not meet it empty-handed.

Eliza turned off the lamp.

And she went to bed—not because she thought she was safe, but because she refused to let fear steal sleep from a life she had fought to build.

Outside, the trees moved in the wind.

Inside, she stayed.

Chapter Fifty-Eight

Morning came the way it always did—too early, too bright, indifferent to whatever had happened in the dark.

Eliza woke before her alarm and lay still for a moment, staring at the ceiling while the cabin held its quiet around her. The air carried clean pine and the faint, dusty warmth of embers that had burned down hours ago. Rain had passed through sometime after midnight, soft and steady, the kind that left everything rinsed and honest. The porch boards would be damp. The gravel would be dark. The world outside would look brand new, like it hadn't heard a single rumor.

Her body didn't jolt awake. No spike of panic. No instant rush of blood that made her sit up and listen for footsteps.

That was what startled her most—not the absence of fear, but the way fear stayed where it belonged. Present, alert, but not driving. A low sound in the background instead of a siren in her bones.

She got up, padded into the kitchen, and poured coffee. The mug warmed her hands as steam curled upward and disappeared into the air. The window above the sink was cracked open, letting in birdsong and the damp, green smell of wet earth. Somewhere beyond the cabin, something shifted— a branch settling, a small animal moving through leaves—and her head turned automatically.

Her body still remembered.

She let herself look toward the sound without punishing herself for it. Then she turned back to the coffee as if it were the most natural thing in the world.

She wasn't undoing all her instincts.

She was learning to live with them.

Eliza dressed without ceremony. She didn't reach for anything dramatic—nothing that demanded attention, nothing that screamed confidence like armor. She chose what made her feel steady: dark slacks, a soft blouse she'd found at Second Chances because it looked like her, not like a disguise. A light cardigan because May in New York couldn't commit to anything, not even warmth. She brushed her hair back at the crown, fingers lingering like she was checking that she was real. Mascara, quick and careful. A small swipe of color on her lips—not for anyone else, not to be seen, but to remind herself she wasn't hiding.

She stood in front of the mirror a beat longer than usual.

Her face looked calm.

It wasn't a performance. It was a choice.

Yes, they know.
Yes, he will find out.
No, I'm not leaving.

She grabbed her tote—grades, a spare pen, a lunch she'd wrapped in foil out of habit more than hunger—and stepped outside.

The air felt open, freshly washed by rain. The trees glittered with droplets that caught the morning light like tiny, bright secrets. Somewhere, a bird argued with another bird over territory that didn't matter.

She locked the door.

Then, after a pause, she unlocked it again.

Not carelessness. Refusal.

If Daniel came, a lock wouldn't stop him. She wasn't going to let a deadbolt turn her home into a bunker. She wasn't going to start living like she was already captured.

She started walking.

The town moved slowly at this hour, awake in small increments. Joe at the market lifted the metal shutters, hands moving with practiced ease. A dog barked once behind a fence, then settled. A truck rolled past without urgency, tires hissing softly on the damp road. The gravel glittered in patches where rain hadn't fully soaked in yet.

Eliza didn't hurry.

She moved like she belonged to the morning, because she did.

Still—her mind worked the way it always had, the way it always would.

She noticed the silver sedan parked near the corner that hadn't been there yesterday. Not a town car, not one she recognized. Too clean. Too neutral. She noted the way it sat, angled like it hadn't been parked by someone who planned to stay long.

Two men near the post office stood too close to the wall to be waiting for anything legitimate. They talked low, heads dipped, and when she passed their eyes flicked up and away—not curiosity, not gossip. Assessment.

A woman in a windbreaker stood on the sidewalk with her phone raised like she was texting, but her thumb didn't move. Her gaze traveled over Eliza's face and slid off quickly, like she'd been warned not to stare too long.

Any one of those things could have meant nothing.

Together, they felt like a pattern trying to form.

Eliza didn't speed up. She didn't look down. She didn't shrink into her shoulders the way she used to.

She kept walking with the same steady pace and the same neutral expression, like the world had no right to make her small again.

Because it didn't.

Black Hollow High rose at the edge of town, brick darkened by years of weather and student fingerprints. The flag snapped once at the top of the pole, impatient with the breeze. The parking lot was already full—old cars with rust on the wheel wells, trucks that had lived through too many winters, the kind of vehicles you kept running because you had better places to spend money.

Eliza reached the front doors and paused with her hand on the handle.

Not fear.

Focus.

Then she stepped inside.

The hallway hit her with all its familiar life: floor cleaner, pencil shavings, yesterday's fries lingering in the air. Lockers slammed. Sneakers squeaked. Someone laughed too loud, like they were trying to prove something. Schools moved fast. They always had. They didn't pause for personal disasters or public scandals. They kept going whether your heart was steady or breaking.

She liked that.

It meant she didn't have to be the center of anything.

When she entered the front office, the secretary looked up and her expression tightened—just a fraction. Not unkind. Protective. The look of someone who knew the world had teeth and didn't want those teeth near her building.

"Morning, Ms. Moore," she said.

Eliza met her gaze and didn't flinch from the name.

"Morning," Eliza replied.

A beat passed. The secretary's shoulders eased, as if Eliza's calm had given her permission to breathe.

"Principal Carver wants you after fourth hour," she added, voice lowered. "Nothing bad. Just… a check-in."

Eliza nodded. "Okay."

She didn't ask if it was about the TikTok.

It was.

They both knew it.

But the office stayed busy—phones ringing, a kid waiting for an ice pack, another waiting for the counselor, a parent's voice sharp on the other end of a call. Life didn't pause for gossip. Eliza wasn't going to be the one who made it.

She turned and walked down the hall.

Room 214 looked exactly as she'd left it Friday: posters about budgeting and credit scores, a stack of worksheets too neat to be trusted, her mug on the corner of the desk like a small flag planted in ordinary ground.

She set her tote down and wrote on the board in clean, deliberate strokes:

DO NOW:
What is one money decision you've seen an adult make
that you swore you'd never make?
Be honest. No names.

The first bell rang.

Students filtered in slower than usual, like the building itself had taken a breath over the weekend and hadn't fully exhaled. They slid into their seats with practiced teenage indifference, but Eliza felt the undercurrent—the way eyes lingered, the way whispers traveled like sparks.

A boy in the back—messy hair, too confident, always testing—sat down and didn't immediately pull out his phone.

That was new.

A girl near the window stared at Eliza's face like she was trying to solve a puzzle she couldn't name. Another kid looked away too quickly, like looking at her was suddenly rude. A few stared with the same hungry curiosity people used online, like a person was only real if you could turn them into content.

Eliza didn't acknowledge any of it.

She moved through the room like she always did—handing out papers, tapping the board lightly with the marker, pausing at desks to point at a question or clarify an example. She kept her voice even, her posture relaxed.

"Good morning," she said. "Start with the Do Now. I'll come around."

Someone whispered, "That's her," like Eliza couldn't hear.

Eliza didn't turn.

She didn't harden either.

She stopped beside a desk where a student's pencil had snapped and they muttered a curse under their breath. Without comment, she set her spare pencil down next to their hand. The student blinked, startled—like kindness wasn't what they expected from a woman the internet had decided to dissect.

At another desk, a kid stared at the prompt and didn't write.

Eliza leaned down just enough to be heard and not overheard.

"Try," she said softly. "You'll be surprised what you already know."

The kid swallowed and picked up their pencil.

Eliza straightened and kept moving.

Second hour was louder. It always was.

More boys, more bravado, more restless energy that could tip into cruelty if you let it. The room carried a pressure-cooker hum, like everyone could feel the gossip pressing at the edges and wanted to be the one to name it first.

Halfway through, someone tossed the question out like bait.

"Are you, like… famous?"

A few snickered. A few leaned in. Phones stayed down— barely—but the attention in the room sharpened anyway.

Eliza didn't react as if she'd been hit.

She didn't smile either.

She kept her face neutral, as if she were considering a question about homework.

"I'm your teacher today," she said simply. "And the assignment is still due at the end of class."

A pause.

Then another voice—quieter, not mocking. Curious in a way that almost sounded like concern.

"But is it true? Like… are you—"

Eliza looked directly at the student who spoke. She let the silence stretch—not punitive, just heavy enough to mean something.

"If you have questions about my personal life," she said calmly, "you ask an adult you trust at home. Here, we're learning skills that will keep you from making decisions you regret later."

The room went still.

Not because they were afraid of her.

Because she didn't give them what they wanted.

No tears. No anger. No confession. No drama they could replay and repost.

Just a boundary.

Teenagers respected boundaries more than they pretended to.

"Now," Eliza continued, tapping the worksheet with her marker, "let's talk about interest rates. Because those will ruin you faster than gossip ever will."

A few laughs broke out—genuine, surprised.

The tension loosened, just a notch.

Eliza took it and moved forward like she'd never been asked anything else.

During her prep period, she stepped into the hallway to refill her water bottle, and there he was.

Micah leaned against the wall near the English wing with a stack of papers under one arm. His tie was loosened like he'd already fought a battle with the copier and lost. When he looked up and saw her, the change in his expression was immediate—no pity, no alarm.

Warmth.

Like seeing her was simply his favorite part of the day.

"Hey," he said.

Eliza's shoulders dropped before she even realized they'd been lifted.

"Hey," she replied.

Micah's gaze flicked over her—quick, careful. Checking, but not probing. The way someone looked when they cared about whether you were holding yourself together or only pretending.

"You okay?" he asked.

She nodded. "Yeah."

Micah exhaled slowly, as if her yes meant something he could set down inside himself.

"They being weird?" he asked, and the faint smile at the corner of his mouth said he already knew.

Eliza gave him a look. "They're teenagers. Weird is their love language."

Micah's mouth curved. "Fair."

He shifted the papers in his arm. "I was going to stop by later. But I remembered you said pie was your coping mechanism now."

Eliza huffed a soft laugh. "Did I say that?"

"You implied it," he said deadpan, then softened. "I'll come by tonight. If you want. I can grade while we eat like an old man."

"You're already an old man," she teased.

The way his eyes warmed at that—at her ease, at the fact she could still tease him after everything—hit her in the chest like a gentle ache.

"Okay," he said. "Old man with pie."

He stepped closer—not trapping, not crowding—just enough that his fingers brushed her wrist, a small touch that didn't claim her.

It reminded her.

She wasn't alone in this.

"I'm proud of you," he said quietly.

Eliza's throat tightened. She didn't look away.

"Thank you," she whispered.

Micah nodded once like that was enough, then tipped his travel mug in a mock salute—bright enough for anyone passing by to hear, intimate enough that it was only for her.

"See you later, Ms. Moore," he said.

Then he walked away, leaving her with her water bottle and the strange, steady warmth of being loved without being owned.

She was halfway back to her classroom when Luke appeared like trouble with good timing.

He came out of the shop wing with sawdust on his sleeves and a grin like he'd never met a boundary he didn't want to test—less because he wanted to break it and more because he liked watching things spark.

"Well," Luke drawled, falling into step beside her. "Look at you. Walking the halls like you owned the place."

"I'm just going to my classroom," Eliza said, not slowing.

Luke leaned closer, voice dropping. "Saw you talking to my brother."

Eliza side-eyed him. "And?"

Luke's grin sharpened. "And he looked like a man who was winning."

Eliza's mouth twitched. "Is this you being supportive?"

"This is me accepting defeat with dignity," Luke said.

"That's new," Eliza replied.

Luke put a hand to his chest like he was wounded. "I contained multitudes."

Eliza shook her head, but she was smiling—small, reluctant, real.

Luke's expression shifted just for a second, humor fading into something quieter. "You good?" he asked. "Like… actually."

Eliza studied him.

Luke wasn't Micah. He didn't move gently through the world. He didn't soften his edges to make you comfortable. But he cared in his own way—loud, stubborn, present.

"I'm good," Eliza said. "Just… aware."

Luke nodded once. Then the humor came back like he didn't want to sit in heavy things too long.

"Okay," he said. "Then I'm gonna do what I do best."

"And what's that?" Eliza asked.

Luke grinned. "Be annoying."

Eliza laughed under her breath.

Luke pointed down the hall. "Go teach. Be brilliant. Make them all realize you're not breakable."

Then he leaned in just enough to be heard and not overheard, his voice rough as gravel.

"And if anyone says something out of line," he added, "you tell me."

Eliza's smile softened. "I can handle myself."

Luke winked. "I know. Doesn't mean you have to."

Then he peeled away toward the shop wing, leaving her with the echo of his presence and a strange realization that made her chest tighten.

The people in this town didn't just notice her.

They cared.

After fourth hour, Principal Carver called her into his office.

Eliza sat across from his desk with her hands folded neatly in her lap, posture calm on purpose. Carver didn't waste time and he didn't perform concern.

"I'm not here to pry," he said. "And I'm not here to ask you for details you don't owe me."

Eliza held his gaze.

"But I need to know one thing," he continued. "Can you keep doing your job?"

"Yes," Eliza said.

No hesitation. No explanation. No apology.

Carver studied her for a beat longer, then nodded. "Good."

He slid a document across the desk. Not the contract itself— yet. Formal language. District wording. The kind of paper that meant systems were moving.

"We'll be finalizing your permanent position," he said. A pause, a faint edge of humor. "Alice was… persuasive."

Eliza's lips twitched before she could stop them.

Carver's mouth quirked in agreement. "Your name will be protected in the ways it needs to be. HR will walk you through it. And the board—" He paused. "They're not going to touch this. Not when you're doing well, and not when this could open the district to liability."

Eliza exhaled slowly, something in her ribs loosening. Not safety.

Space.

Carver's voice softened just slightly. "You're good for those kids," he said. "That's what I care about."

Relief hit her so cleanly it almost hurt.

"Thank you," she said quietly.

Carver nodded once as if he didn't want the moment to turn sentimental. "Go teach," he said. "And if you need a day—if you need a moment—ask."

"I will," Eliza said.

She left his office with the paper in her hand and something steady under her skin.

Not protection.

Position.

When the final bell rang, Eliza walked out of the building with the same calm she'd walked in with.

Kids spilled into the parking lot, laughing and shoving and living loudly. Teachers sighed and carried stacks of papers like badges of survival. The sky was open and clean, the kind of blue that made you feel like you could start over even if the past was screaming from the internet.

Eliza didn't look at her phone.

Not yet.

She didn't need to.

She could feel the world watching her, yes. She could feel the pull of it—the way curiosity turned into hunger, the way people reached for stories as if stories were owed to them.

But she could feel something else too.

Her own spine.

Her own choices.

The cabin. The school. The diner. The two men who cared for her in wildly different ways. The woman who had built an underground system out of grit and grudges and mercy. And somewhere beyond all of it—Daniel, moving toward her like a storm that believed it owned the sky.

Let him come, Eliza thought.

Not with bravado.

With certainty.

She wasn't waiting to be rescued.

And she wasn't waiting to be taken.

She was living.

And she was done being quiet.

Chapter Fifty-Nine

The cabin felt warm when Eliza got home.

Not just the heat—something deeper than temperature. The quiet wrapped around her instead of pressing in. It greeted her like it had been waiting, patient and familiar, the way a home did when you had earned it.

She set her bag down by the door, kicked off her shoes, and stood with her palm on the edge of the table for a moment, letting the worn wood steady her. She had made it through the day.

That thought carried weight now. Not relief. Pride.

She changed into soft clothes, pulled her hair back loosely, and poured herself a glass of water. Outside, the sky faded fast—blue deepening into indigo, the trees turning into silhouettes she knew by heart. She rinsed a mug and listened to the faint hush of the wind moving through branches.

Headlights swept briefly across the front window.

Eliza didn't tense.

She smiled.

A knock followed—easy and unforced, the kind that belonged here. When she opened the door, Micah stood on the porch with two white bakery boxes balanced in one hand and a stack of papers tucked under his arm. His hair was still slightly rumpled from a long day. His eyes softened the moment they found her, as if seeing her like this—safe and upright and here—mattered more than he ever said.

"I brought reinforcements," he said. "And pie. The good kind. Nell threatened me if I dropped it."

Eliza laughed quietly and stepped aside. "She did that."

Micah came in like he'd done it a hundred times, like he wasn't afraid of the threshold, like the cabin hadn't become precious and fragile in the last twenty-four hours. He set the boxes on the table and shrugged out of his jacket.

"I figured we could pretend grading was less awful if we did it together," he said.

"That logic was deeply flawed," Eliza replied, "but I appreciated the effort."

They sat across from each other at the table, papers spread between them, forks tapping softly against plates. The pie was still warm, cinnamon and sugar filling the room with something dangerously close to comfort. Micah graded with the kind of patience he brought to everything—deliberate, steady. Occasionally, he made a face at an especially creative student answer, then wrote a comment anyway, like he couldn't help being kind.

Eliza watched him when she thought he wasn't paying attention—the way he leaned back when he was thinking, the way his pen paused when something mattered, the way he had learned to exist without taking up too much room around her.

"This one tried to argue that interest rates were a government conspiracy," Micah said mildly.

Eliza smiled. "Did they cite sources?"

"No," he said, deadpan. "But they were very confident."

"That tracked."

Their knees brushed under the table—not accidental, not rushed. Just there. A quiet acknowledgment. A reminder that something gentle still existed in a world that had become loud.

"You were good today," Micah said after a while, not looking up.

Eliza's pen slowed. "You noticed."

"I always noticed," he replied simply.

Something in her chest softened—like a knot loosening by degrees rather than snapping. She reached across the table without thinking and brushed her fingers against his hand. Micah went still beneath the touch like he always did, like he never took it for granted. Like even now, after everything, her choosing him in small ways still felt sacred.

They didn't talk about the video.

They didn't talk about Daniel.

They didn't have to.

Later, when the papers were stacked and the plates were empty, Micah stood and pulled her gently into him. Eliza rested her forehead against his chest and listened to his heartbeat—steady, present, real. It grounded her more than any plan ever had. He kissed her slowly, not like he was trying to convince her of anything, but like he already knew the answer and simply wanted to meet her there.

They moved together without urgency, the cabin holding their quiet laughter and their closeness like it was meant for it. Clothes slipped away with ease. Touches stayed deliberate, reverent. Micah learned her again, and Eliza let herself be known—not as a secret, not as something fragile, not as a thing to be handled carefully like it might break.

When they finally lay together, breath tangled and bodies warm, Eliza traced the line of his shoulder with her fingertips and let herself anchor to the fact of him.

Micah pressed a kiss to her temple. "I love you," he murmured—not as a declaration, not as pressure. As a truth he'd been living for a while.

Eliza didn't answer with words.

She kissed him instead—deeper, slower—her hand sliding over his heart like she was memorizing where it lived.

Later, Micah dressed quietly, careful not to shatter the calm. He lingered at the door, pressed one last kiss to her mouth, then rested his hand briefly on her cheek like he needed to reassure himself she was still here.

"Text me in the morning," he said. "We'll grab coffee before work. I'll pick you up."

"I will," she promised.

"And Eliza?"

"Yes?"

His eyes held hers, steady. "I'm not going anywhere."

She smiled, and the smile didn't wobble. "I know."

He left.

The cabin settled again.

Eliza locked the door out of habit more than fear, then moved through the small space, turning off lights one by one. She went to bed with the window cracked, night air cool against her skin. Her body felt loose, warm, pleasantly heavy. She drifted toward sleep thinking about nothing in particular.

That's when the dream started.

At least, she thought it was a dream.

The room felt… wrong. Too quiet. The air shifted, pressure changing like something had entered it. Like the cabin itself had noticed before she did.

"Eden."

Eliza's eyes fluttered open.

For one heartbeat, she smiled.

Micah, she thought—half-asleep, soft with warmth.

Then she saw him.

Daniel stood at the foot of the bed.

Not a shadow. Not imagined. Solid. Real.

Her breath caught—not in a scream, not yet, but in disbelief so sharp it stole sound from her lungs. Her mind tried to reject him on instinct, tried to shove him back into the category of nightmares where he belonged.

"This isn't real," something in her insisted. "This is panic. Memory. Fear wearing his face."

Then he stepped closer.

And she smelled him.

Cologne—familiar, controlled. The scent of power and polish. The kind of expensive that always came with teeth.

Reality slammed into her.

Eliza sat up too fast, the room tilting. "You're not—" Her voice broke. "You're not here."

Daniel smiled.

God, that smile.

"I've missed you," he said softly. "You look… different. Stronger."

Her heart hammered, but beneath it, something else steadied—something she had built on paper, sentence by sentence.

This is it, she thought.

This is the moment I planned for.

Daniel moved fast.

He covered her mouth. His weight drove her back into the mattress. Her body reacted on instinct—fear slicing hot and bright through her—but she didn't thrash.

She didn't scream.

She went still.

The stillness confused him.

He leaned closer, voice low, intimate, cruel. "Did you really think you could belong to someone else?"

Tears slid hot and silent into her hair, but her eyes stayed open, sharp and cataloging.

The way he positioned himself.

The words he chose.

The confidence.

The arrogance.

Just like she'd written.

Just like she knew.

When he pulled her from the bed, her feet barely catching the floor, Eliza clenched her jaw and held onto one truth as tightly as she could:

They will know.

Micah will notice.

Tonya will understand.

Alice will move.

Luke will not hesitate.

Daniel's mouth brushed her ear as he dragged her toward the door. "I watched you with him," he whispered, venom wrapped in velvet. "You never should've made me jealous."

Eliza didn't answer.

She let him believe he had won.

Because this time, she wasn't alone.

And this time—

She was ready for him.

Chapter Sixty

Daniel didn't rush her.

That was the worst part—how calm he was. How controlled. He moved through the dark like a man who believed the world still bent to him, even here, even now. One hand locked around her wrist, the other steady at her back as he guided her through the trees behind the cabin. The night swallowed sound. The branches scraped softly against their clothes. The ground was damp from recent rain, and the air smelled like pine and earth and something colder underneath.

"Eden," he murmured whenever she didn't respond fast enough, as if the name itself was a leash he could tighten.

She didn't correct him.

She saved her breath.

The SUV waited just beyond the tree line—black, expensive, wrong in this place. Its engine idled with quiet confidence. Daniel opened the rear door and produced rope with the casual efficiency of a man who had rehearsed this in his head long before he ever stepped into her room. He tied her wrists with practiced cruelty, tightening until her hands tingled and her pulse throbbed against the knot.

"You always were bad at listening," he said, almost gently. "This will help."

When her foot caught on the gravel and she stumbled, the correction came fast—controlled, familiar, meant to remind her where she stood in his world. The air left her lungs in a sharp rush. Her vision sparked at the edges.

He opened the trunk.

Cold darkness waited there, smelling of rubber and oil and stale metal.

He shoved her inside and shut it.

The latch snapped, final as a period.

Eliza curled instinctively, cheek pressed to the hard surface, every sense sharpened to a blade. The car lurched forward. Gravel spat under the tires. The world narrowed to vibration and motion and her own breath.

She didn't scream.

Not because she wasn't afraid.

Because she couldn't afford it.

She counted turns. Time. The subtle rise and fall of the road. She tracked the long stretches that felt like highway and the rougher patches that suggested back roads. She listened for voices, for music, for anything that could give her a landmark later.

She held onto the only thing that mattered:

Survive long enough to make this evidence.

When the trunk finally opened, the air hit her like a slap—
colder, thinner, pine-heavy. Daniel hauled her out and dragged
her toward a cabin, dark and half-hidden by the trees. It
looked old, but not neglected. Maintained. Prepared. The kind
of place someone called private when they meant
untouchable.

Then she realized where they were, his father's cabin.

A retreat where no one asked questions.

Inside, a single lamp glowed near the corner, turned low like
someone preferred shadow to light. The room smelled like
woodsmoke and old leather. A fire had burned down to
embers. The air held that peculiar stillness of a place that
waited.

He tied her to a chair in the center of the room with
methodical care, binding wrists and ankles until she couldn't
shift without rope biting into her skin. The chair legs were
looped and cinched in a way that told her everything she
didn't want to know:

He'd done this before.

Not as improvisation.

As routine.

"You don't get to flinch," Daniel said calmly when she
reacted. "You don't get to react. You lost those privileges."

Eliza tasted blood and swallowed it. She tried to sit up
straighter. The rope snapped her short. Her knees were cold

through her jeans. The floor beneath her was rough plank, unforgiving.

A memory rose sharp and useless—Micah's mouth against her temple. Warm pie between them. Two stacks of papers side by side like a life could be ordinary if you arranged it carefully enough.

Her throat tightened.

No.

Not now.

Not here.

The cabin's quiet pressed in. A faint clock ticked somewhere. The fire made a low, dying sound. And then she heard him move—soft, deliberate, as if he wanted her to feel every second he chose not to rush.

"Eden," Daniel said again.

The name left his mouth like a correction.

Eliza went still.

He stepped into the lamplight, and she hated how normal he looked. Even without a suit, he carried himself like a headline. His hair was neat. His collar straight. His watch caught the light when he lifted his hand—just enough glitter to remind her he lived surrounded by expensive things and unquestioned access.

But his eyes—

His eyes were the same as they'd always been when the doors closed behind them.

He crouched in front of her slowly, like he was approaching something he owned and didn't want to startle. His gaze searched her face, waiting for defiance. Waiting for the version of her that fought.

She didn't give him that.

If he came, I will let him believe he has won.

Her heart wasn't calm. It wasn't safe.

It was anchored.

A steel rod through the center of her.

Daniel tilted his head, studying. "You made a spectacle of yourself," he murmured. "Do you know what you've done?"

Eliza let her eyes shine. Let her breath hitch. Let her shoulders soften the way he liked.

"I didn't mean to," she whispered.

It wasn't a lie. It just wasn't the whole truth.

He exhaled like a man burdened by love. Like a saint forced to carry someone else's weakness.

"You ran," he said, and the warmth dropped out of the word. "You disappeared. You humiliated me."

Eliza flinched on purpose.

The flinch pleased him—she saw it, a tiny flash of satisfaction he didn't bother to hide.

"And then," he continued, circling her slowly, "you show up in a nowhere town under a nowhere name, playing teacher to children like you're… normal." His voice sharpened. "Like you're allowed."

Eliza's stomach turned, but she kept her face soft.

"I was scared," she said.

Again—true, and not enough.

Daniel stopped behind the chair. She felt him there without seeing him, his presence pressing close like a hand around her throat. His palm settled on the backrest as if he were reminding her—she was a thing he had set down and could pick back up whenever he wanted.

"You're going to come home," he said.

Home. The Whitmore House. The cameras. The curated dinners. The smiling staff. The rooms where she learned to speak only when spoken to.

Eliza's pulse struck once, hard.

Daniel leaned in, mouth near her ear. "You're going to stop fighting me," he whispered, threat wrapped in silk. "You're going to be the wife you were meant to be."

A small sound escaped her throat—broken enough to satisfy him.

He mistook it for surrender.

Good.

"Publicist already has the story," he went on, almost conversational, like he was discussing a fundraiser menu. "Breakdown. Exhaustion. Treatment center. Privacy. Recovery." He paused, savoring it. "It plays well."

Eliza kept her eyes lowered so he wouldn't see what sparked behind them.

Daniel paced again, energized by his own performance. "And your reappearance couldn't have come at a better time," he said, smug. "Election season. People love a redemption narrative." His laugh was low, self-satisfied. "A faithful husband waiting for his fragile wife to return? It's practically a campaign ad."

A campaign ad.

He said it like she wasn't a person at all.

Eliza breathed slowly, the way Alice had taught her. Quiet through the nose. Deep to the belly. Steady enough to keep her mind sharp.

"Do you understand me?" Daniel asked.

There it was—the pivot. The test.

If she fought, he'd punish.

If she submitted, he'd preen.

Eliza lifted her face and made her eyes empty enough to pass for broken.

"Yes," she whispered.

Daniel's smile widened, private and cruel. "Good girl."

His fingers caught her hair at the base—not yanking hard, not yet. Just enough to remind her he could. He tilted her head back until her throat was exposed, until she had no choice but to feel the power in the position.

"You're going to stay here until I'm sure," he said. "Until you remember how to behave."

Eliza's breath stuttered.

Daniel watched it like it was a gift.

Then he let her go and stood, smoothing his cuff as if he hadn't just said something monstrous.

"When we leave," he added, "you'll be Eden again. You'll stand beside me. You'll smile. You'll do exactly what I tell you."

He glanced toward the window as if the woods outside were his audience too. "And you won't mention Black Hollow," he said lightly. "Because the TikTok nonsense is just that— nonsense."

Eliza swallowed. Her wrists burned. Her mouth tasted metallic.

"Okay," she whispered.

Daniel stared a long moment, satisfied with what he saw. He moved closer again, slow as prayer.

"I missed you," he said, and it was the most obscene lie he'd ever spoken.

Eliza let her lashes lower. Let her head dip.

Let him think she was giving up.

Because if he believed he'd broken her, he'd stop paying attention.

And if he stopped paying attention, she could survive long enough to destroy him.

His voice softened, almost tender. "Sleep," he said. "Tomorrow, we start over."

He stepped out of the lamplight.

The cabin went quiet again.

Eliza kept her breathing even. Kept her face still. Kept her mind sharp.

She didn't pray.

She counted.

Minutes. Beats. Openings.

And somewhere inside her—where fear used to live alone—something steadier held its ground.

Not hope.

Intention.

Chapter Sixty-One

Micah woke before his alarm.

For a moment he lay still, staring at the ceiling, waiting for the small buzz that had become routine—her name lighting up his screen, the message that made his mornings feel less like a grind and more like a choice.

Still up for coffee before work?

Sometimes she added a smiley face, like she was embarrassed to want something simple. Sometimes it was only one word—*please*—and it hit him harder than anything poetic ever could.

His phone stayed dark.

He checked it anyway. Once. Then again, as if the second look could change reality through sheer stubbornness.

Nothing.

He told himself not to make it a thing. He sat up, swung his legs over the side of the bed, pulled on his jeans. He dragged his hands through his hair and forced his breathing into something steady, something normal.

She was probably tired. She was probably still asleep. She'd been carrying more than anyone should have to carry and he'd watched her do it with a spine that never stopped surprising him. There were a thousand reasons she hadn't texted.

That list worked—until it didn't.

He walked into town and bought two coffees anyway. Because he was stupid. Because he was hopeful. Because it was easier to spend five dollars than admit the hollow in his chest had teeth.

He waited outside the bookshop with both cups warming his hands, watching people pass, watching time keep moving like it didn't care who was unraveling. A couple walked by laughing. Someone unlocked the door to the bakery. A dog strained against its leash like the world was full of miracles.

She didn't come.

Micah drank his coffee too fast, bitterness and heat scraping the back of his throat. He threw the second cup away without tasting it. It felt like a jinx to keep it.

He headed to school.

He told himself he'd see her in the hallway. He'd see her pushing her hair back with that distracted little gesture she did when she was thinking. He'd see her at the copy machine muttering under her breath about toner like it was a personal enemy. He'd see her—*of course he would*—because Eliza showed up. That was who she was. Even when the world tried to swallow her, she showed up.

He cut through the English wing and tried to keep his pace normal. He tried not to feel like the hallway cameras were watching him panic, like the fluorescent lights could expose the way fear had started to creep into his bones.

When he reached her room, the door was shut.

The lights were off.

No movement inside.

He knocked once. Soft, like he didn't want to startle her.

Nothing.

He knocked again, harder. The sound echoed down the hall and died without answer.

A student passed behind him laughing, backpack slung loose, life continuing with the careless momentum of teenagers who had no idea someone's world had just tilted.

Micah checked the clock.

7:28.

Eliza never missed work.

Not once.

He went to the front office and forced calm into his voice like it was a language he could still speak.

"Hey—Ms. Moore call in?"

The secretary frowned, already half-turning toward her screen. "No. Why?"

Something cold settled in his gut, heavy and immediate. Not a thought. A certainty.

He didn't wait for permission. He stepped back out into the hall, pulled out his phone, and called the one person who always had an answer first—whether he liked the answer or not.

Alice picked up on the second ring.

"Talk."

"She didn't text," Micah said.

A pause. Just long enough to sharpen.

"Text?" Alice repeated, like the word didn't belong in the conversation he'd just dragged her into.

"She didn't show," he corrected, because his voice had started to shake and he refused to let it. "She's not at school."

Silence on the line—sharp, fast thinking.

"Where are you?" Alice asked.

"Hallway outside her room."

"Go to the cabin," Alice said. "Now."

Micah didn't argue. He didn't ask why. He didn't waste time making himself feel better with questions.

He was already moving.

He stopped at Luke's room on the way out, pushed his head in just far enough to catch his brother's attention. Luke looked up from whatever he'd been doing, saw Micah's face, and straightened immediately.

"There's a problem with Eliza," Micah said. His voice came out too flat, too controlled. "Meet me at her place. Now."

Luke didn't ask questions either. He just grabbed his keys and followed.

By the time Micah reached the cabin, Alice was already there with Tonya. Both of them stood on the porch like they'd been summoned by instinct, by dread, by a thousand hidden contingencies finally clicking into place.

The cabin door was unlocked and ajar.

Not wide open.

Just… not right.

Micah stopped short on the threshold, heart stuttering, eyes scanning too fast—the way you looked when you already knew the answer and were still hoping to be wrong.

The chair near the table lay on its side, one leg caught on the rug like it had been kicked and forgotten. A mug had shattered near the sink. Coffee had dried dark on the floor in a streak that looked like a spill and felt like a warning. The lamp by the table was still on, casting a soft, wrong circle of light across the room.

Nothing was broken in a dramatic way.

No blood.

Just absence.

Luke came in behind him and made a sound Micah had never heard from him before—raw and cracked, like his bravado had been ripped clean off.

"Tell me she's not gone."

Alice's eyes sharpened, scanning the room the way predators scanned tracks.

"She's been taken," Alice said.

Tonya made a strangled sound and sank onto the edge of the couch like her legs stopped working mid-command.

"Micah," Tonya whispered behind him—his name like an apology and a prayer at the same time.

Luke stood with his jaw clenched, hands already balling into fists like he could punch his way to a solution. Like violence might fix this if he hit hard enough.

Alice moved with purpose, not panic. She crossed the room slowly, eyes tracking details that mattered: scuff marks near the door. The overturned chair. The faint indentation on the table where something heavy had been pressed down and removed.

"She's been writing," Alice said, already kneeling. "Documenting. Everything she remembered." Her voice stayed steady, but something in it went colder. "We need to find it. It's going to matter—saving her, and ending Whitmore."

Alice pulled open the drawer beneath the table.

Inside, wrapped carefully in a folded dish towel, was the notebook.

Beneath it—four envelopes.

Neat. Deliberate. Each name written in Eliza's hand like she'd been writing them her whole life.

Alice.

Micah.

Luke.

Tonya.

Tonya let out a sound that barely qualified as breath.

Micah didn't reach for his envelope.

He couldn't.

His hands didn't want to touch it because touching it meant acknowledging what it was: not a possibility, not a contingency—an aftermath.

Luke reached first, fingers trembling despite his usual swagger. "Jesus," he muttered, dragging a hand through his hair. "She really thought of everything."

Alice picked up her own envelope but didn't open it. Her gaze stayed on Micah with a gentleness that felt almost foreign coming from her.

"You should read yours first," she said.

Micah nodded once.

His throat ached.

Micah stared at the envelope for a long beat. His hands didn't want to open it because if he opened it, it would become real.

But it was real anyway.

He tore it carefully along the edge, like gentleness might bring her back. Like if he treated the paper right, the world would soften.

Inside was a folded letter—thick paper, ink pressed deep, as if she'd written it with her whole body.

Micah unfolded it.

And the first line stole the air from his lungs.

Micah,

If you're reading this, it means I didn't get the chance to tell you something in person. I need you to hear me before you blame yourself: you didn't miss anything.

You didn't fail me. I hate that I didn't say it out loud when I had the chance—not because I was afraid, but because I wanted to say it when it was quiet and real and safe.

I want you to know that choosing you was never a question. You never asked me to be smaller. You never tried to own me. You stood next to me and let me be myself—even when I was still learning who that was.

You gave me a life that felt gentle. Honest. Free.

I don't know how this ends. But I need you to hear this clearly: loving you changed me. It reminded me that love doesn't come with conditions, or punishment, or fear. That it can be soft and steady and still strong.

If I don't come back, please don't think of me as someone who was taken. Think of me as someone who chose her life—and chose you—with her whole heart.

Thank you for seeing me when I didn't know how to be seen.

Don't come for me like a hero. Don't rush in blind. That's what he expects.

Use what I wrote. Use my notebook. Use the patterns. Use the names. If he thinks he's won, he'll stop watching. That's the only edge I have.

Tell Alice I understand now.

Tell Luke I'm grateful he never made me smaller.

Tell Tonya I'm still angry, and I still love her anyway.

And Micah…

If there is a life after this, I want it with you. Not the life people stage for cameras. A real one.

Ordinary.

Safe.

Ours.

— Love, Eliza

Micah didn't realize he was crying until the words blurred and the room tilted again, not from panic this time but from grief too big to hold. He pressed the letter to his chest and breathed like something inside him had finally split open.

Tonya's voice came soft through her own tears. "She loved you. Not loved—*loves.*" She swallowed hard, wiping her face with the heel of her hand like she hated herself for breaking. "We'll get her back. I promise you."

Micah nodded, voice gone. "I know."

Luke opened his envelope next. His jaw tightened as he read, eyes darkening—not with jealousy, not with resentment, but with grief and a rough kind of respect that left him exposed.

"She told me," Luke said hoarsely, "that I never tried to cage her. That I made her feel strong." He blinked hard. "That mattered to her."

Alice finally opened hers.

She read it standing, spine straight, but her eyes softened in a way Micah had never seen before—as if the letter reached a place in her that nothing else ever had.

"She thanked me," Alice said quietly. "For believing her. For giving her a place to land."

Then she set the letter down and reached for the notebook.

This time, when she opened it, there was no hesitation.

The pages were full.

Dates. Locations. Names. Patterns.

Basements. Cabins. Rooms without windows. Men with titles. Men with money. Everything Daniel had done in the confidence of believing no one would ever dare to name it.

Alice flipped toward the back.

One location was circled twice.

His father's cabin.

"She didn't let him win," Alice said, voice steady, edged with something dangerous. "She let him think he did."

Micah closed his eyes as fury and terror collided so hard it stole his breath.

"We get her back," he said.

Alice met his gaze—sharp, resolved, lethal.

"No," she said. "We end him."

Outside, the trees stood quiet, indifferent, pretending they'd seen nothing.

But inside the cabin, something had shifted.

Eliza hadn't vanished.

She'd left herself behind—deliberately, lovingly—and with absolute faith that they would finish what she started.

And they would.

Chapter Sixty-Two

They brought her back in the daylight.

Daniel insisted on it.

He drove the black SUV himself, one hand loose on the wheel, the other resting casually on the center console, as if he weren't transporting a woman he had kept bound and hidden for days. Eden sat in the back seat, wrists restrained in soft cuffs that still burned, her shoulders stiff from enforced stillness. The windows were tinted dark enough that the world outside felt unreal—trees blurring past, roads stretching toward something inevitable.

"You've been very good," Daniel said, glancing at her in the rearview mirror.

Eden lowered her eyes.

"Thank you," she said quietly.

The words pleased him. She heard it in the subtle hum of his voice, the ease returning now that he believed she'd learned her place again. Daniel liked to believe obedience was something you could beat back into a person—that once submission cracked loose, it stayed broken.

He didn't see the way her stillness had sharpened.

"We'll be home by evening," he continued. "My team's already moving. Publicist. Stylist. Hair. Makeup." His mouth curved slightly. "We'll clean this… situation up. It'll take some work. You've let yourself go."

Eden said nothing.

"You always did look best blonde," he went on, eyes flicking to her reflection. "Long. Soft. Familiar. This—" he gestured vaguely, dismissively, toward her dark hair and uneven ends, "this is what happens when you forget who you're meant to be."

She nodded once.

"I'll have the hairdresser fix it," Daniel said, satisfied. "You'll be presentable before anyone sees you again. A mayor's wife doesn't get to look… neglected."

The word landed with deliberate weight.

Eden absorbed it without reaction. Inside, she cataloged everything—the route they took, the time between turns, the cadence of his confidence. Daniel Whitmore always talked more when he believed he had won. Always explained himself so he could hear his own authority echo back.

By the time the iron gates of the estate opened, he was already rehearsing the story aloud.

"Exhaustion," he said. "A private treatment facility. Stress. You wanted privacy. I respected that." He smiled to himself. "The public loves a husband who waits."

The Whitmore house loomed exactly as she remembered— immaculate, sterile, designed to impress and erase all at once. The front door opened before they reached it, staff moving with quiet efficiency, eyes trained carefully away from her wrists.

No one asked questions.

They never did.

The mansion smelled like flowers when they arrived.

Fresh ones. Pale pink peonies. Neutral. Forgettable by design.

Eden was led upstairs, untied now, supervised but no longer dragged. Daniel didn't need force when compliance performed just as well.

The hairdresser and makeup artists arrived within the hour.

The woman assigned to her was in her forties, sharp-eyed, professional, hands steady as she unpacked her tools. Eden sat beneath the bright vanity lights, posture perfect, gaze fixed forward.

"Oh," the woman murmured softly, fingers moving through Eden's hair. "You've changed it."

Daniel stood behind them, adjusting his cufflinks. "She went through a phase."

The hairdresser's eyes met Eden's in the mirror.

Just for a second.

Something passed between them—not pity. Understanding.

"I can fix it," the woman said carefully. "But it'll take time."

"That's fine," Daniel replied. "We have appearances coming up. I want her looking like herself again."

Eden didn't flinch when the dye touched her scalp. Didn't react as dark washed away and pale returned. Her hair was lightened, lengthened with extensions, smoothed until it fell exactly the way Daniel preferred. Long. Soft. Feminine.

She didn't move as makeup covered the faint marks at her throat, the shadows beneath her eyes.

Then the stylist arrived, garment bags lined up along the wall like soldiers.

They worked around her as if she were an object being restored.

The stylist chose a dress Daniel approved immediately.

Soft. Elegant. Conservative. Blue.

"She always wore blue well," he said, pleased. "Calming."

Eden stepped into it without protest.

By the time they finished, she looked exactly the way the world remembered.

Eden Whitmore.

The wife who smiled beside power and never made anyone uncomfortable.

Daniel watched from the doorway.

"There," he said when they were finished. "That's better."

Eden studied her reflection.

She looked like a woman who had been forgiven.

She didn't look like a survivor.

She didn't look like a threat.

Perfect.

As the team packed up, one of the stylists hesitated—just for a second. Their eyes met Eden's in the mirror, curiosity flickering, then something closer to recognition.

Eden gave a small smile.

Grateful. Empty.

The kind that convinced.

The press event was small.

Deliberately so.

A controlled room. Friendly reporters. Carefully chosen questions. Daniel's hand rested at the small of her back, firm enough to remind her he was there.

She smiled when she was supposed to.

She nodded on cue.

When asked how she was feeling, she answered softly, "Better. Grateful for the privacy my husband gave me while I healed."

Daniel squeezed her waist.

The cameras loved it.

No one noticed the way her smile never reached her eyes.

Or the way she never once looked at him.

The statement went out within the hour.

A difficult period. Privacy requested. Healing ongoing. The Whitmores grateful for support.

Eden nodded when prompted. Touched Daniel's hand when appropriate. Played the part so well it almost hurt to watch.

Almost.

Because beneath the silk and the polish and the carefully managed narrative—

She was watching.

She was remembering.

She was already inside.

Micah stood in Alice's office, jaw set, hands fisted at his sides. Luke paced. Tonya sat very still, eyes burning.

Alice watched the footage on mute.

"Good," she said finally.

Micah turned sharply. "Good?"

Alice met his gaze. "He thinks he's won," she said. "That's when men like him get careless."

She closed the file.

"We move now," Alice continued. "Quietly. Precisely. We let him keep believing she's his."

Luke swallowed. "And her?"

Alice's mouth curved—not in a smile, but something harder.

"She's exactly where she planned to be."

Chapter Sixty-Three

The door closed with a sound too soft to be comforting.

Eden didn't move.

She stood where Daniel had left her, hands folded in front of her, posture perfect because she knew he was watching somewhere—through cameras he pretended weren't there, checking even when he claimed trust.

Only after enough time had passed did she breathe out.

The room was unchanged.

That was the worst part.

The same bed.

The same neutral palette chosen by designers who believed calm colors could erase violence.

The same mirror, tall and unforgiving, angled to make her look smaller than she was.

She walked to it slowly.

The woman staring back looked exactly the way Daniel wanted.

Her hair was blonde again—long, smooth, professionally styled, every strand forced into obedience. The stylist had tsked softly, fingers too gentle, murmuring about damage and maintenance while Daniel stood behind her, correcting her posture with a hand at the small of her back.

You let yourself go, he had said mildly.
We'll fix that.

Her makeup was flawless. Concealer layered over exhaustion. Powder set over memory. The dress he'd chosen draped her body like a promise she had never consented to make again.

She raised a hand and touched her throat.

Her pulse was steady.

That surprised her.

Eden sat on the edge of the bed.

There was no notebook here.

No phone.

No proof.

Daniel had made sure of that.

When she arrived, everything she'd been wearing had been taken. Bag emptied. Pockets checked. Her cabin clothes folded away like evidence of a crime.

This house didn't allow secrets.

So Eden kept hers where he couldn't reach them.

Inside.

She closed her eyes.

And she remembered.

The basement.

The glass.

The way the girls wouldn't look at her.

The way Daniel's hand rested on her back while men laughed like nothing in the world could touch them.

She remembered Tonya's voice the night she said *run.*

Alice's voice on the phone telling her to bring nothing.

Micah's hands—steady, reverent—like she was real.

Luke standing too close, daring the world to test him.

She remembered writing.

Not words on paper.

Decisions carved into herself.

If he finds me.
If he takes me.
I will not disappear.

Eden opened her eyes and looked at the room again.

Daniel believed he had won.

He believed obedience looked like silence.

That submission looked like stillness.

That breaking someone meant they stopped resisting.

He had never understood women who survived by waiting.

Eden rose and walked to the window.

The grounds below were immaculate—security lights glowing, guards posted discreetly, everything designed to keep danger out.

Everything designed to keep her in.

Tomorrow, she would smile.

She would let him hold her arm.

She would stand beside him while his publicist told the world she had been unwell, overwhelmed, seeking treatment. She would nod while cameras flashed and strangers pitied her in the way that protected men like Daniel from consequence.

She would play Eden Whitmore again.

Because Eliza Moore had already done her part.

The life she built.

The people she loved.

The truth she left behind.

They knew where to look.

They knew what mattered.

They knew who he was.

Eden lay down on the bed and turned onto her side, back to the door, breathing evenly.

When Daniel came in later and curled an arm around her waist, she did not stiffen.

She let herself go soft.

She let him believe she was broken.

And in the dark—unseen, unarmed, but unafraid—Eden finished the thought she had been carrying since the night she ran:

You didn't win.

You just brought me exactly where I needed to be.

Chapter Sixty-Four

The house ran on routine.

Daniel liked it that way.

Breakfast appeared at seven with the same quiet precision every morning—silver lids lifted, coffee poured, plates set down without a single unnecessary word. Briefing calls started at eight. Staff rotated through the halls like shadows trained to be invisible. Security changed shifts just often enough to look diligent, never often enough to become unpredictable.

Predictability was Daniel's favorite kind of control.

Eden moved through it like she had never left.

She slid back into the rhythms with a precision that made Daniel smug, and she let him have his smugness. She let him believe the ease meant surrender. Let him mistake familiarity for obedience.

That mistake would cost him.

She took her coffee on the terrace, hands wrapped around porcelain she had once been terrified to drop. She wore the robe he preferred—cream silk, cinched neatly at the waist—because he liked his women soft and his authority unquestioned. Her hair fell in obedient blonde waves again, freshly styled into the version of her he thought belonged to him.

She let him see all of it.

Daniel sat with his tablet angled toward the sun, skimming headlines like they were trophies. He didn't look at her until he wanted to.

"You look better," he said at last. "The public noticed."

"I'm glad," she replied.

It was the truth. Just not for the reason he thought.

He reached for her wrist the way some men reached for a pen—absent, entitled. His thumb pressed into the soft inside like he was checking for a pulse, like he needed the reminder that she existed where he'd left her.

"Tonight's event is small," he said, eyes already back on the screen. "Donors. Friends. People who know how to keep their mouths shut."

Eden kept her breathing even. She didn't pull away.

"Yes."

"You'll stay close," he added. "Smile. Let me do the talking."

"I always did," she said.

The words pleased him. She heard it in the satisfied exhale, the subtle shift of his posture like the world had righted itself.

Daniel never questioned what came easily.

Upstairs, Eden moved through the bedroom alone.

She didn't rush. She didn't waste movement. She moved the way she had learned to move in captivity—quietly, efficiently, leaving nothing behind that could be traced except the version of her he already believed.

She chose jewelry with care, not because she cared about beauty, but because she cared about sensation. She avoided anything new. Anything that might draw attention. Anything that could be used as a conversation piece.

She selected the thin gold bracelet he had given her years ago. The clasp caught if you pressed it wrong.

She pressed it once.

A sharp sting. A tiny, private pain that grounded her in her own body.

Then she checked the room the way she always did now—vents, corners, mirrors, the subtle angles where a lens could hide. She didn't look for cameras where there had never been cameras. She looked for change.

There were no new locks. No added hardware. No fresh paranoia in the architecture.

He was confident again.

Dangerous men always got careless after they thought they'd won.

Eden opened the drawer beneath the vanity.

At the bottom, beneath silk scarves and perfume bottles arranged like a curated life, there was nothing she could use. No paper. No pen. No phone. No evidence.

She hadn't expected any.

Her notebook was gone.

But the notebook had never been the only record.

She had rebuilt it in her head every night since the cabin— pages she could recite in the dark, entries she had written into muscle and memory. She didn't need paper here.

She was the document.

She memorized details. Names overheard in hallways. Voices behind doors. The timing of meal trays. The cadence of Daniel's moods. The way he drank more before meetings that mattered, the way his temper sharpened when he felt watched.

And most importantly—

She listened.

Daniel talked when he felt powerful. He narrated his own cruelty like it was proof of intelligence, like the world existed to applaud his strategy.

Eden let him.

That afternoon, the call came.

Eden sat on the velvet settee in the study, a book open in her lap. She hadn't turned the page in several minutes. Her eyes tracked lines of text without absorbing them, the way she had learned to perform calm while her mind did something else entirely.

Daniel paced near the windows with his phone pressed tight to his ear, his voice clipped and controlled.

"No," he said. "Not tonight. Too many variables."

Eden kept her gaze down.

A pause followed. Daniel stopped pacing, staring out through the glass as if the grounds themselves were listening.

"Next weekend," he continued. "Hudson. The house on the river. Same setup."

Eden's fingers tightened on the edge of the page, careful not to crumple it.

"Yes. Same crowd," Daniel said. "They know what they're coming for."

Her stomach turned, slow and sick, but she didn't let it show in her face.

Another pause. His tone shifted—lower, sharper, the voice he used when he was discussing something he didn't want recorded.

"I don't want anyone external this time," he said. "Security stays internal. No freelancers. No mistakes."

Silence stretched.

Daniel exhaled through his nose, satisfied by whoever agreed with him on the other end. "Good. Then make sure the… inventory arrives early. I want them settled. Presentable."

Eden swallowed hard.

Behind the glass, her reflection stared back at her—still, obedient, invisible.

"No surprises," Daniel finished.

The call ended with a quiet tap as he lowered the phone. He rolled his shoulders once, like a man shrugging off an inconvenience, and let out a satisfied breath.

Eden forced herself to turn the page, because that was what a compliant wife did. She kept her movements smooth, unhurried, believable.

"What was that?" she asked, keeping her voice soft, careful. Curious—but not too curious.

Daniel glanced at her, a smile tugging at his mouth, indulgent and patronizing. "Business."

Of course it was.

She nodded as if that explained everything.

And maybe, horrifyingly, it did.

Miles away, Alice stared at a screen filled with timestamps.

She didn't need names yet. She needed pattern. Confirmation. A place where the truth could stop being theory and become evidence.

Tonya sat beside her, jaw tight, hands curled into fists. Luke paced the length of the room like a caged animal, energy striking the walls and bouncing back sharper. Micah stood still—too still—his eyes locked on the information Alice pulled together as if looking away might change it.

"That's it," Alice said quietly at last. "That's the event."

Micah's voice came out controlled, razor-thin. "She'll be there."

"Yes," Alice replied.

Tonya blinked hard, wiping at her face like she hated herself for crying. "How do we get inside?"

Alice didn't look up. "We don't break in," she said. "Not to Hudson."

Tonya stared. "Then how—"

Alice finally turned the screen toward them.

"We get invited."

Chapter Sixty-Five

Eden learned the house by listening.

Not to what was said to her, but to what was said around her—when men assumed she was decorative, when women assumed she was compliant, when staff assumed she was furniture and spoke freely because they believed she was too gentle to understand what she was hearing.

She folded herself into the background and let the house talk.

It talked in schedules and side doors and whispered names. It talked in the clink of ice against glass at noon. It talked in the way security tightened and loosened depending on which phone call Daniel had taken that morning. It talked in the way certain staff avoided certain hallways, like even the building had places it refused to fully inhabit.

The invitations arrived three days later.

Heavy black envelopes. Thick paper. Names embossed instead of printed. No return address—because the people invited already knew where gratitude should be directed.

Daniel flipped through them at the dining table, pleased, relaxed in a way he hadn't been in months. He poured himself a drink even though it was barely noon.

"Hudson's confirmed," he said to someone on the phone, holding one envelope between his fingers like it was a credential. "Saturday. Smaller crowd this time. Cleaner." then he disconnected the call.

Eden set down her fork slowly. "Cleaner?"

Daniel glanced at her, amused at the question. "Fewer variables," he said. "The kind of guests who understand discretion."

She let her mouth curve faintly, the practiced expression of a woman who had learned to look supportive without asking too many questions.

"I'll wear the sheer," she said. "The one they like."

Daniel's mouth curved. "You remember everything."

I remembered enough, she thought.

That afternoon, she stood in the dressing room while the stylist worked around her like a ghost.

Curling. Pinning. Restoring the image Daniel wanted displayed.

The woman avoided Eden's eyes in the mirror. Her hands were efficient. Silent. Not unkind, exactly—just careful in the way people became when they wanted to survive their proximity to power.

Witness.

When they were finished, Eden barely recognized herself.

Perfect hair. Soft makeup. A version of her polished until no cracks showed.

Daniel stood behind her, hands settling on her shoulders. His grip tightened just enough to remind her that beauty, in his world, was always a leash.

"You look like yourself again," he said.

Eden met her own gaze in the mirror and let the lie sit there, glittering.

No, she thought.

I looked like your mistake.

Miles away, Alice made the calls.

Not to police. Not yet.

She spoke to people who didn't appear in directories. Men and women who owed favors that had never been written down. The kind of debts that didn't expire because they weren't money. They were secrets. Lives. Choices.

"I need a guest list," Alice said into one secure line.

"I need access," she said into another.

"I need timing," she said into a third.

Luke leaned against the counter, arms folded, eyes dark. "You're sure she can hold?"

Alice didn't hesitate. "She's already been holding," she said. "This entire time."

Micah hadn't spoken in ten minutes. He stood like a man made of restraint, hands at his sides as if clenching them would break something he couldn't afford to break.

When he finally spoke, his voice was steady—but only because rage had crystallized into focus.

"She's not bait," he said.

"No," Alice agreed. "She was the key."

Tonya slid a tablet across the table. "Security contractor changed," she said. "Private firm. Internal clearance only."

Alice's mouth curved, sharp. "Good," she said. "That made them vulnerable."

Saturday came too quickly.

The Hudson house sat on the river like a secret no one admitted knowing—glass walls, long sightlines, private docks, enough isolation to make screaming irrelevant. It gleamed with money and intention, the kind of place where people pretended the view was the reason they came.

Eden stepped out of the SUV on Daniel's arm, heels steady on the stone path. She let the river air fill her lungs.

Count doors. Count exits. Count cameras.

Daniel leaned in, voice low, for her alone. "Tonight matters."

"I know," she said.

Inside, the house was a polished throat full of noise—laughter too smooth, music too soft, conversation pitched wrong. Men in tailored suits. Women in dresses chosen to imply power without challenging it. Security posted casually—too casually—hands near earpieces, eyes skimming instead of seeing.

Eden stood at Daniel's side beneath chandeliers and soft applause.

She smiled.

She laughed at the right moments, the same gentle cadence she had once perfected for cameras and donors and men who called themselves decent while looking away from cruelty. She let Daniel's hand rest possessively against her back while people congratulated him—on his resilience, on his patience, on being such a devoted husband.

Eden met the eyes of every woman in the room.

She saw the fear behind some smiles.

The hunger behind others.

The way certain men watched the room like they were shopping, like the world owed them bodies for the price of influence.

There was glass everywhere—mirrored walls, glossy surfaces, reflections that multiplied lies and made them feel normal.

When Daniel leaned close and murmured, "You're doing beautifully," Eden inclined her head.

"Thank you," she said.

Inside, her heart stayed steady.

The trap had a shape now.

And she stood exactly where it needed her to be.

Eden felt it then.

The pull.

The gravity of what lived beneath places like this.

Her stomach clenched, but she didn't slow. She didn't let her face change. She kept moving like she belonged to the evening, like she was exactly what Daniel had promised them.

Daniel greeted donors. Laughed. Shook hands. Played the role flawlessly.

Eden moved too.

She excused herself once. Then again. She drifted past rooms with glass walls and soft lighting, past hallways that looked decorative but weren't. Nobody stopped her.

Nobody ever stopped her.

She followed the sound—the hum beneath the elegance, the low current of something hidden, the way laughter shifted when a door opened and closed again.

At the top of a staircase, she paused.

A guard glanced her way.

Eden smiled like it was nothing. Like she was only a wife searching for a restroom in a house too large to be human.

"Bathroom," she said lightly, gesturing behind her.

He nodded and looked away.

Behind the glass—

Girls stood in soft, controlled lighting, too still, too quiet, their faces arranged the way fear arranged them when fear had learned there was no point in pleading.

Eden didn't flinch.

She memorized faces.

She memorized details.

She let the images burn into the part of her mind that had become a ledger.

Then she turned away slowly, calmly—because panic would make her suspicious—and walked straight into the arms of a man she didn't recognize.

"Lost?" he asked, voice too pleasant.

Eden looked up at him, eyes wide just enough to read as harmless. Confused. Grateful for direction.

"I think so," she said softly.

Behind him, the room shifted.

Earpieces crackled.

A door opened somewhere it shouldn't have.

And far away, in a van parked two blocks down, Alice watched the feed blink from amber to green.

"Now," she said.

The storm didn't announce itself.

It never did.

Chapter Sixty-Seven

The music never stopped.

That was the strangest part—the way the house kept pretending. Even when the first scream ripped through the lower level, raw and animal and uncontained, the speakers continued to pulse out something elegant and slow. Low strings. Polite tempo. A song selected by someone who believed taste could make anything palatable.

As if sound itself could enforce order.

As if beauty could anesthetize brutality.

Eden went so still she could feel her heartbeat in her teeth.

The corridor around her gleamed with that curated kind of wealth—glass, brushed metal, recessed lighting designed to flatter faces and hide shadows. The air smelled faintly of perfume and champagne, and underneath it, something else: disinfectant, cold and clinical, like a hospital trying to pretend it wasn't a place where people died.

The glass wall in front of her glowed faintly in the dim, seamless and polished, not a barrier so much as a feature—an architectural flex. She'd stood in front of mirrors like it before. Smiled beside them. Learned how to arrange herself so reflections only ever showed what was permitted.

Now it showed everything.

Behind the glass, the girls pressed together, bodies pulled tight into a terrified cluster as if the shape of them—shoulder to shoulder, hip to hip—might make them harder to take. Bare feet on cold tile. Fingers digging into each other's arms. Bruises blooming in colors that never quite healed, yellow fading into green, purple into gray, like their bodies couldn't keep up with the pace of cruelty.

Their eyes lifted when they saw Eden.

Not pleading. Not hopeful.

Wary.

As if help was just another lie men liked to tell before they hurt you.

Eden's throat tightened so fast it felt like a hand had closed around it. Something inside her split open—clean and silent and violent. The part of her that had learned to numb, to float, to survive by leaving her body behind suddenly slammed back into place.

This was real.

They were real.

They were not a headline. Not a rumor. Not something she could write about later with shaking hands and a locked drawer.

They were *right there*.

And they were looking at her like she was either the last door to daylight—or just another person who would turn away.

A presence shifted behind her.

Too close.

Too fast.

Breath warmed her shoulder.

"Hey," a man said, sharp but not yet panicked. "You're not supposed to be back here."

Eden didn't startle. She couldn't afford to. She forced her face into the shape Daniel preferred—soft, apologetic, harmless. The mask slid into place the way it always had, muscle memory built from years of learning what kept her alive.

She turned slowly.

"I got lost," she said.

Her voice came out exactly right. Small enough to be believable. Polite enough to be forgiven. Eden-perfect.

The man frowned, eyes scanning her dress, the blonde hair, the familiar shape of her face. The recognition didn't hit all at once—it flickered, uncertainty sparking into certainty.

The mayor's wife.

His hesitation was a single breath, a fraction of a second.

It was all the opening the world needed.

The lights cut.

Not entirely. Not dramatic like a movie. Just enough to disrupt—enough to make people blink, to make shadows swallow corners, to make the body realize something was wrong before the mind could name it. Emergency red pulsed along the floor in thin lines, glowing like veins.

And then the house exploded.

A door somewhere downstairs slammed open so hard it shook the walls. Shouts collided—real shouts, not laughter or polite conversation. The music kept playing anyway, obscene in its refusal to stop, as if the speakers were determined to maintain the illusion even as it died.

Men in suits scrambled. Women stumbled backward in heels, clutching drinks like shields. Security moved in a pattern that was suddenly useless—trained for discretion, not war.

Eden's body reacted before thought did.

She dropped.

She hit the floor the instant the first gunshot cracked through the air—a sound that didn't belong in a house like this. It wasn't loud like fireworks. It was sharp, final, a punctuation mark that turned every heartbeat into a countdown.

Glass shattered.

The sound was a scream all its own.

Shards rained down, glittering and vicious. Eden covered her head, curled instinctively, breath gone, the world narrowed to impact and terror and the sick certainty that this was exactly how people died—on floors, anonymous, while music played in the background.

Then arms wrapped around her.

Solid.

Real.

A body shielding hers.

A voice at her ear—ragged, furious, shaking with the effort of not breaking.

"Eliza."

The name hit her like a hand pressed to her spine, grounding her so hard her vision sharpened. It wasn't just a name. It was the life she had built. The quiet mornings. The classroom. The cabin. The pie on the table. The feeling of being chosen without being owned.

Micah.

He was there, breathing hard like he'd sprinted through hell to get to her. Blood streaked along his sleeve—someone else's, she registered distantly, because her brain couldn't hold anything that wasn't essential. His eyes locked onto hers with a ferocity that wasn't performance.

It was terror.

It was love.

It was rage.

"I've got you," he said.

Not a promise.

A fact.

Eden clutched him once—hard, desperate, the way you grabbed onto something solid in a flood. For half a second she let herself feel it: the relief of being found, the unbearable gratitude of *not being alone*.

Then she forced herself upright.

Because she couldn't afford to be only rescued. Not now. Not when she was the reason they were here.

"The girls," she gasped, voice shaking but clear. She pointed with a trembling hand. "Behind the glass."

Micah's face changed. His jaw clenched like something inside him had shattered and hardened into steel.

"I know," he said, already scanning, already moving. "They're getting them out."

A second gunshot snapped through the air. Someone screamed—a woman this time, high and keening, the kind of sound that didn't stop even when breath ran out.

And then she heard it.

Luke's name.

Not shouted casually.

Screamed like a prayer and a warning at the same time.

Eden's head turned.

At the far end of the corridor, Luke stood between chaos and intent, body angled like instinct itself had taken over. His shoulders were squared, his stance braced, his focus narrowed to one target.

Daniel.

Daniel Whitmore stood rigid and immaculate, a gun in his hand like it belonged there.

Like it always had.

Even now, even with alarms and shattering glass and bodies rushing in, Daniel carried himself like the room should still obey him. Like the laws of consequence were for other people.

Their eyes met across the distance.

For a heartbeat, the world slowed.

Luke didn't look at Eden.

He looked at Micah.

Just once.

A crooked half-smile ghosted across his mouth—familiar, almost gentle, as if he could soften the horror with one last piece of himself.

"Get her out of here, I've got this."

Micah's face tightened, terror and understanding colliding so violently it looked like pain.

"No," Micah started, but it didn't make it out as a real word. It came out as breath.

The shot came fast.

Too fast.

Daniel fired.

Luke moved.

He didn't think. He didn't hesitate. He stepped into the line of fire the way some people stepped into traffic without checking—pure instinct, pure choice, pure brother.

The sound was wrong.

Wet.

Heavy.

Final.

Luke's body jerked hard, and for a split second it looked like he might stay upright through sheer stubbornness. Like his body might refuse to accept what had happened.

Then he folded.

Blood bloomed across his chest, dark and awful, spreading like a secret finally exposed. He hit the floor hard enough that Eden felt it through the soles of her feet.

Micah's sound wasn't human.

It tore out of him, raw and ruptured.

"NO!"

Eden's scream followed, ripping through her throat like it had been waiting years for permission. It wasn't elegant. It wasn't controlled.

It was grief arriving early, before her mind could catch up.

The corridor surged with movement. Officers flooded in, shouting commands, weapons raised, bodies colliding. Daniel stumbled backward, the gun slipping from his hand as if even he didn't believe he had fired it.

He tried to speak.

Of course he did.

He always spoke.

His voice rose above the chaos, indignant even now, still trying to command the room with the story he thought would save him.

"You don't understand—this is a misunderstanding—she's my wife—"

Eden stood.

Her body felt distant, unreal, like she was moving underwater, but her feet carried her forward anyway. The noise dulled at the edges, as if her brain had decided there was only one thing worth hearing.

Daniel.

He was pinned to the floor, expensive suit wrinkling under the hands of men who did not care who he was. His face twisted with fury, not fear—fury that anyone dared touch him. Fury that the world had stopped agreeing with him.

Eden stopped just out of his reach.

Close enough to make him feel it.

He looked up at her, and in his eyes she saw the old reflex— the belief that if he just spoke the right words, if he pressed the right button, she would collapse back into obedience.

"You don't own me," she said.

Her voice didn't shake.

It surprised her, how steady it was, like something in her had finally set.

Daniel barked a laugh that sounded cracked, disbelieving. "Eden, listen—"

"My name," she cut in, voice sharp as steel, "is Eliza."

It wasn't just a correction.

It was a death.

The death of the version of her he had built.

For the first time, fear flickered across his face.

Not fear of prison.

Fear of *her*.

Because he finally understood something he had never understood before.

She wasn't trying to survive him anymore.

She was done.

Eden turned away.

Not because she didn't want the satisfaction of watching him break.

Because Luke was on the floor.

Because some losses demanded your whole body.

Luke died before the ambulance could arrive.

They didn't tell her right away.

They didn't have to.

Eden knew the moment she saw Micah's face when he came back into the room—ash-pale, eyes wrecked, hands shaking like he'd forgotten how to use them. He looked like a man who had been carrying a dam inside his chest and had just felt it split.

Alice stood behind him, rigid and silent, the way she only got when there was nothing left to plan. No angles left. No moves left.

Luke wasn't coming back.

The world narrowed to a thin, ringing quiet.

Not panic.

Not disbelief.

Just absence—sudden and complete, like a light had been switched off somewhere she hadn't realized she was relying on.

Micah crossed the room without speaking and pulled her into him so firmly it bordered on desperation. His chin rested against her hair like he was anchoring her to something solid. Like if he let go, everything would fall apart.

"I'm so sorry," he said against her temple.

The words broke on the last one.

Eden didn't cry.

Not yet.

Grief didn't arrive as tears at first. It arrived as numbness, as the inability to understand how the room could still contain air when Luke's lungs had stopped.

She stared at a spot over Micah's shoulder and tried to make sense of the fact that Luke had been alive an hour ago— smiling, moving, looking at her like she was worth the risk.

Now he was gone.

And Daniel Whitmore was still breathing.

Later—after the sirens, after the shouting, after the reporters tried to claw their way into the story—Alice pressed something into Eden's hands.

Her fingers were steady, but her eyes weren't.

"We found this in his jacket," Alice said quietly. "He wrote it before."

The envelope was folded once.

No name on the front.

Just paper softened by sweat and time, the kind of paper that had been carried close to a beating heart.

Eden sat alone at the kitchen table to read it.

The house around her had gone quiet in that stunned, hollow way places went quiet after tragedy—as if even the walls were listening.

Her hands trembled anyway.

Not because she couldn't read.

Because once she opened it, she would have to accept something she still wasn't ready to name.

That Luke had known.

That Luke had chosen.

That Luke had loved her in the only way he knew how—by giving his life to make sure she got to keep hers.

She slid her finger under the flap.

And let the paper open like a wound.

Eliza,

I don't know how to start this without sounding like I'm trying to be brave.

I'm not. I'm just being honest.

If you're reading this, then things went the way I knew they might. And I need you to know something first—before the guilt has a chance to take root.

You don't owe me anything.

Not your choice. Not your love. Not your grief.

I knew who you loved. I knew it early. Watching you with Micah wasn't painful the way people think it should be—it was clarifying. You weren't smaller with him. You weren't quieter. You didn't disappear.

That mattered to me.

What we had mattered too. Don't ever let anyone convince you otherwise. You reminded me of parts of myself I'd forgotten were still alive—laughter without an agenda, courage that didn't ask permission, tenderness that didn't demand ownership.

If this ends the way it might, I want you to live forward—not carrying me like a debt.

If I die doing this, it's not a tragedy. It's a decision. And it's one I would make again.

Protect him. Protect yourself. Finish what you started.

And Eliza—

Being loved by you was never a consolation prize. It was a gift.

— Luke

Eliza pressed the letter to her chest and finally broke.

The sound that came out of her wasn't loud. It wasn't theatrical.

It was raw and small and human—grief with nowhere to go.

Micah didn't interrupt. He didn't rush her. He stayed nearby, silent and present, letting her take the space Luke had left behind.

After the house had finally gone quiet again, Alice found her on the back steps.

Eliza sat with her arms wrapped around herself, staring out into the dark like she was still listening for something that might come back. She didn't look up when Alice approached. She didn't need to.

Alice didn't speak right away.

She sat beside her and held out another envelope.

Eliza's breath caught.

The edges were worn soft with handling.

"The coroner found this on him," Alice said quietly. "He had it in his wallet."

Eliza's hands shook as she took it.

"I didn't know if you'd want it back," Alice added. "But I thought you should have it."

Eliza swallowed hard.

It was her letter.

The one she had written before Daniel took her.

Luke,

I don't know how to explain what you gave me without sounding like I'm apologizing for something I shouldn't have to apologize for.

You saw me when I didn't know how to be seen anymore.

You reminded me that joy doesn't have to be careful. That laughter can exist alongside fear. That not every connection asks for surrender.

I love Micah. I need you to know that. Not in a way that diminishes what we shared—just in a way that's honest. He is where my heart settles.

But you changed my life.

You showed me the version of myself who still knows how to want things—how to take up space without asking permission.

I will carry you with me, always. Not as regret. As gratitude.

— Eliza

She folded the letter carefully and placed it back in the envelope.

Luke had known.

He had walked into the storm knowing exactly who he was and what it might cost.

And he had done it anyway.

Eliza lifted her face toward the night sky.

She wasn't broken.

She was grieving—and grief didn't undo the choices that had brought her here.

Outside, the night held still.

Inside, something resolved.

Luke had given her the freedom to live without guilt.

She intended to honor that—not by retreating, but by finishing what they had all begun.

And when it was over—when Daniel Whitmore was nothing but a cautionary tale and a prison number—Luke's name wouldn't be spoken with sorrow alone.

It would be spoken with love.

And it would last.

By morning, the story broke everywhere.

MAYOR'S WIFE RESURFACES AMID TRAFFICKING RING BUST.
PRIVATE DONOR EVENT EXPOSED AS FRONT FOR ILLEGAL DETAINMENT.
DANIEL WHITMORE ARRESTED ON FEDERAL CHARGES.

Photos flooded the internet.

Daniel in cuffs.

The shattered glass.

The girls wrapped in blankets, blinking into daylight like they'd forgotten what sunlight felt like.

And one photo—just one—of Eden Whitmore standing barefoot on stone, blood on her hands, face lifted toward the sky like someone who had survived the impossible.

She didn't correct them.

Not yet.

Later—much later—Eliza sat at the cabin again.

Micah sat beside her, silent, wrecked, breathing like each breath hurt. His hand covered hers on the table, not gripping, just there—proof.

Between them lay her notebook.

Open.

Finished.

Luke's name was written on the first page.

Not last.

First.

Eliza closed the book and rested her hand over Micah's.

"He saved us," she said.

Micah nodded once, throat working. "He knew."

She leaned into him, grief and love tangled together until she couldn't tell where one ended and the other began.

Outside, the trees stood quiet again.

But this time, the storm had passed.

And nothing Daniel Whitmore had built would ever stand the same way again.

Chapter Sixty-Eight

The courtroom was nothing like the rooms he used to control.

There were no chandeliers to soften shadows. No velvet drapes to swallow sound. No music murmuring in the background to blur the edges of what was being done. Just polished wood, hard benches, and the flat, fluorescent honesty of a place designed for one thing—witness.

Eliza sat at the plaintiff's table with her hands folded in front of her.

Not shaking.

Not hidden.

She wore navy—clean lines, modest sleeves, a hem that didn't invite comment. A dress chosen for comfort and conviction, not for anyone's approval. Her hair fell the way it wanted to fall now, natural in its color, loose in its shape. No stylist's hands. No dye. No careful obedience.

She looked like what she was.

A woman who had lived.

Micah sat behind her, close enough that she could feel his warmth without turning. It wasn't possession. It wasn't protection in the old sense—the kind that demanded payment.

It was presence.

A steady, quiet weight in a world that had tried to tip her over.

Two rows back, Alice sat with her spine straight and her face like stone. She didn't fidget. She didn't scan the room. She didn't perform worry. She looked like someone who had already fought this war in her head a thousand times and had come here to finish it.

Tonya sat beside her, eyes rimmed red but chin lifted, hands clasped so tightly her knuckles had gone pale. She looked like grief and guilt had tried to flatten her and failed.

And there—right behind Eliza's shoulder, like the outline of a missing limb—was the absence that hurt most.

Luke's chair sat empty.

No shifting. No restless knee. No crooked grin. No voice in her ear making a joke at the worst possible moment because he didn't know how to sit still with fear.

The empty space carried its own sound.

When the side door opened, a hush rippled through the room.

Daniel Whitmore entered in cuffs.

The murmur that followed was automatic, human—people leaning into the reality of it even as the judge warned them into silence. The man who had once commanded rooms with a smile and a hand at the small of Eliza's back now looked… smaller. Not frail. Not humbled. Just reduced. His suit still fit perfectly. His hair was still neat. His posture still carried the arrogance of someone accustomed to being believed.

But the inevitability was gone.

For the first time, he didn't control the narrative.

He was simply a man in chains.

The prosecutor stood.

"Call Eden Whitmore."

The name hit the room like a ghost.

Eliza rose.

She felt it—the echo of her old self in that name, the version of her that had smiled on cue and swallowed words whole— but she didn't flinch. She didn't shrink. She didn't look toward Daniel to see how he reacted.

She walked to the stand with measured steps, the click of her shoes loud in the hush. She raised her right hand and took the oath with a voice that didn't waver.

When she sat, Daniel finally looked at her.

Not with love.

Not with rage.

With calculation.

He was still trying to win.

"Ms. Whitmore," the prosecutor began, careful and steady, "can you tell the court why you disappeared last year?"

Eliza inhaled once.

Not to brace.

To anchor.

Then she told the truth.

She spoke of bruises hidden under silk. Of rules that changed daily—the kind designed to keep you off-balance, always guessing, always apologizing. She spoke of the way he could ruin a day with a look and call it concern. She spoke of doors locked from the outside and smiles practiced for cameras. She spoke of parties that weren't parties at all—of basements, glass walls, women who learned not to scream because screaming only made it worse.

She described what she saw with clarity, not drama.

Not to be believed.

Because she finally didn't care if they believed her.

The truth didn't require permission anymore.

She talked about the night she ran—how her body had moved before her mind caught up, how leaving didn't feel triumphant. It felt like surviving a fire by stepping into the cold.

She talked about Black Hollow.

About the cabin that had held her when she couldn't hold herself.

About walking into a school hallway with fear still clinging to her skin and choosing to be useful anyway.

About teaching teenagers how money could trap you, how debt could steal years, how power could be disguised as generosity. About giving them tools she hadn't been given, because if she couldn't undo what had happened to her, she could at least make sure someone else had language for it.

And then she talked about the notebook.

The dates.

The rooms.

The patterns.

The names he thought no one noticed.

She spoke of evidence—quiet and brutal in its existence— because Daniel had never understood that the most dangerous woman was the one who stopped reacting and started recording.

When she finished, the courtroom stayed silent.

Not performative silence.

Real silence—the kind that happened when people realized something had been happening in their world all along and they'd been looking away.

Daniel's attorney rose.

He was smooth in the way men were smooth when they thought tone could change reality.

"Mrs. Whitmore," he said, "isn't it true that you suffered a mental breakdown?"

Eliza turned her head and looked at him directly.

"No."

A beat.

"Isn't it true you were treated for—"

"No," she repeated, voice even. "What I suffered was abuse. What I sought was safety."

A murmur stirred, quickly suppressed by the judge's gavel.

Daniel shifted in his chair. His jaw tightened. The muscles in his face twitched like he'd swallowed something sour.

He didn't like being denied.

When it was his turn to speak, he stood with the same practiced confidence he'd used on cameras for years. He wore the expression he'd worn at fundraisers, at debates, at charity dinners: wounded virtue.

He spoke of love.

Of concern.

Of a wife who had been "unwell."

He spoke of enemies, of smear campaigns, of political vendettas.

He described her disappearance like it was a tragedy that had happened *to him*.

He described her return like it was his victory.

And for a moment, Eliza saw it—the old trick of him. The way his voice could fill a room and make people forget to ask why they were listening.

Then the prosecutor turned toward the screen.

"Your Honor, permission to play Exhibit 47."

The judge nodded once.

The footage began.

The party.

The hush behind the laughter.

The staircase.

The door.

The glass.

The room tilted—not in Eliza's body this time, but in the room itself. People shifted, hands flying to mouths. A woman sobbed openly. A man gagged and stumbled for the trash can. The judge banged the gavel again and again, face gone gray, voice raised to restore order that didn't exist anymore.

Daniel's expression cracked.

Not into remorse.

Into panic.

For the first time, he couldn't talk his way out of what they were seeing.

His shoulders sagged as if the weight of consequence had finally landed where it belonged.

When the footage ended, the courtroom was still.

Not silent.

Stunned.

And in that stunned space, Eliza felt something settle deep in her bones.

It was over.

Not the pain.

Not the grief.

But the reign.

The verdict came three days later.

Guilty.

On all counts.

Human trafficking. Conspiracy. Abuse. Obstruction.

The words landed one by one like nails sealing a coffin.

Daniel Whitmore was sentenced to decades in federal prison.

When they led him away, he turned once, twisting against the grip of the officers as if he could still create a moment where he mattered most.

His eyes found Eliza.

He tried to pull her into that last look—the old spell of him, the old demand.

She didn't give him the satisfaction.

She kept her gaze forward.

He could leave thinking she was cold, if he needed that to survive.

He could leave thinking she was empty.

But she wasn't.

She was free.

The press didn't call her Eden anymore.

They called her Eliza.

They called her brave. They called her a survivor. They called her dangerous, like truth was a weapon instead of a mirror.

She gave one statement.

Just one.

She stood at a bank of microphones with sunlight in her eyes and Micah's presence at her back and a world hungry for a quote.

"I didn't destroy a powerful man," she said calmly. "The truth did. I just stopped protecting him from it."

Then she walked away.

The school held her job.

The community held her hand.

The girls behind the glass were rescued. They testified. They were placed somewhere with locks that kept danger out, not them in. Counselors and advocates formed a shield around them that wasn't perfect, but it was real.

Names were named.

Money trails were followed.

Men who had spent years buying silence were dragged into light they couldn't afford.

New laws were written.

And when the noise finally faded—when the cameras moved on, when the pundits found a new horror to monetize—Eliza sat at her table with Micah beside her, Luke's letters tucked safely in a drawer that was never locked because she refused to live that way again.

She opened her manuscript.

The title stared back at her, finally right.

Married to a Monster

She wrote the last line slowly, deliberately, as if she were carving it into the page.

I survived. And then I lived.

Micah leaned in and kissed her temple.

Outside, the world kept turning.

This time, she was ready for it.

Epilogue

The nursery smelled like fresh paint and clean linen and something softer beneath it—hope, maybe. Or the kind of quiet that only came after a long storm finally broke.

Eliza stood in the doorway with one hand resting on the curve of her stomach, watching Micah crouch beside the crib. He adjusted the mobile for the third time as if precision could somehow prepare him for what was coming.

"You already fixed it," she said gently.

Micah looked up, caught, then laughed under his breath like he'd been found out. "I know. I just—" He shook his head, eyes shining in that way they did when he tried to pretend he wasn't scared. "I want everything to be right."

Eliza crossed the room slowly and pressed a kiss into his hair. "It already is."

Above the crib, a name had been carved into pale wood—simple, unadorned, steady.

LUCAS ANDREW

Micah followed her gaze. His throat worked once before he nodded, eyes going distant for a heartbeat.

"He would've liked this," he said quietly.

"He would've loved it," Eliza corrected. "He loved things that lasted."

They stood there with their hands intertwined, the past present but no longer sharp enough to cut. It lived with them now in the way real things lived—quietly, insistently, without disappearing.

The wedding had been small.

No press. No speeches meant for cameras. Just the people who knew them in the ways that mattered. Alice sat in the front row with her arms crossed and her eyes shining despite herself, as if emotion was something she tolerated like bad weather. Tonya cried openly, unapologetically, grief and relief tangled together in a way she no longer tried to hide.

Colleagues from the school came—people who'd first known Eliza as *Ms. Moore* and had never demanded more than her presence. A few neighbors from Black Hollow showed up too, the kind of people who brought casseroles and didn't ask questions, who had quietly decided she belonged long before the world knew her name.

And her mother—thrilled, fierce, exhausted from years of fearing the worst—held Eliza's hands before the ceremony and kissed her cheeks like she was making sure she was real.

Eliza didn't wear white.

She wore a soft canary yellow—something that let her breathe. Something that didn't feel like a costume or a proclamation. Just a dress. Just her.

When Micah said his vows, his voice only shook once—when he promised to choose her even if the world tried to rename her again. Even if it tried to turn her into a headline. Even if it tried to reduce her to what had been done to her.

When Eliza spoke, she didn't talk about survival.

She talked about love without conditions.

About being seen and not owned.

About choosing each other every day, not as a rescue, not as redemption, but as a life—ordinary and real and stubbornly theirs.

When they kissed, the applause didn't feel like performance.

It felt like release.

Later—much later—Eliza sat alone in her study with the baby monitor humming softly beside her. The sound was steady, rhythmic, alive. It threaded through the room like a promise.

Her manuscript rested on the desk in front of her.

Married to a Monster had gone to print six months earlier.

It had been banned in three states. Assigned in two college courses. Quoted in courtrooms. Passed hand-to-hand in quiet places where women still needed language for what they lived through. Whispered about in rooms where men like Daniel Whitmore still believed themselves untouchable.

Eliza hadn't written it to be brave.

She'd written it to be true.

Her phone buzzed.

Alice: He lost his appeal.

Eliza closed her eyes and exhaled—slowly, fully, like she was finally letting something leave her body that had lived there too long.

Then she stood and walked down the hall.

In the nursery, her son slept with his small chest rising and falling, safe.

Eliza rested her hand against the crib, fingers curling around the rail, grounding herself in the simple, staggering reality of it.

The world wasn't fixed.

It never would be.

But it was better.

And for the first time in her life, Eliza wasn't waiting for the other shoe to drop.

She had a home.

A family.

A future that belonged to her.

She turned off the light, leaving the door cracked open, and let herself rest inside the life she had fought for—

one she intended to keep.

A Note to the Reader

This story explores themes of control, manipulation, and abuse. While the characters and events are fictional, the experiences are very real for many people.

If you are in an abusive relationship—or if someone you love is—you are **not weak**, **not broken**, and **not alone**. Abuse thrives in silence, and help is available even when it feels impossible to ask for it.

You deserve safety.
You deserve autonomy.
You deserve a life that does not require you to disappear to survive.

If this book stirred something painful or familiar in you, please consider reaching out. Support is confidential, free, and available 24/7.

Resources for Help

United States

- **National Domestic Violence Hotline**
  1-800-799-SAFE (7233)
  Text **START** to **88788**
  thehotline.org

If you are in immediate danger, call 911.

International

- If you are outside the U.S., you can find local resources at:

  hotpeachpages.net

  (An international directory of domestic violence support services.)

If you're reading this and wondering whether what you're experiencing "counts," it does.
If you're reading this and thinking, *but it's not that bad*, you still matter.
If you're reading this and not ready to leave, that's okay too.

Help is there when—and if—you choose to reach for it.

You are worthy of safety.
You are worthy of love without fear.